WHO WAS RAFFLES?

To the immensely powerful Lord Lochmaben, he was the ghostlike invader who had penetrated the most jealously guarded country manor in England—to steal its most precious treasure.

To the redoubtable Inspector Mackenzie of Scotland Yard, he was a quarry to be hunted to the ~~~~~~~~~ e earth, or to the highest reach~~~

To the Amer~~~~~~~~~~~~~~~~~~~~~~~~~~~~~~~~~~~ vas a foe to be put down~~~~~~~~~~~~~~~~~~~~~~~~~~ o British sportsman wou~~~~~~~

To the ravishin~~~~~~~~~~~~~~ an Der Berg, he was the first target e~~~~~~~~~ ake her pistol's dead aim suddenly tremble.

To Queen Victoria herself, he was the donor of the most remarkable gift that she had ever received.

Who was Raffles? You'll love finding out. . . .

RAFFLES

a novel by
David Fletcher

POPULAR LIBRARY • NEW YORK

Based on the Yorkshire television series written by Philip Mackie and on characters created by E. W. Hornung.

RAFFLES

Published by Popular Library, a unit of CBS Publications, the Consumer Publishing Division of CBS Inc., by arrangement with G. P. Putnam's Sons

ISBN: 0-445-04311-3

Printed in the United States of America

10   9   8   7   6   5   4   3   2   1

One

THE FIRST STEP

•••—➤◈◄—•••

IN WHICH A REUNION BECOMES A UNION WHICH IS CROWNED WITH A GLITTERING PRIZE

THE LOYALTIES AND AFFECTIONS forged in boyhood, though frequently allowed to slacken with time and the demands of the adult world, are never broken. To this truth many former pupils of our better schools can testify and count themselves proud so to do. Nor is it uncommon for such precious links to be sought anew in times of distress, when the hapless man recalls the halcyon days of his upright youth and wonders bitterly how he came to stray from the path which then had seemed so straight and clear. Without honor in the present, we should not be amazed that a man might seek it in his beginnings.

Such feelings had recently occupied Bunny Manders and they had prompted him to pen a note to his schoolboy mentor and hero, A. J. Raffles. Time and the pursuit of different pleasures had severed these two, so that Bunny, in writing to the man who had become with almost insolent ease the glory of the M.C.C. (Marylebone Cricket Club), felt himself still the fag he had been in earlier days. How grand those school days had been when as an underclassman he'd been able to do even the most menial task for his upperclassman friend and consider it an honor. The days as Raffles's fag had been indeed some of the best of his life. Acting as he did on the promptings of feeling rather than of reasoned thought, Bunny was himself not quite clear about what he intended or expected from Raffles by way of reply. That missive, when it arrived at his Mount Street flat, proved to be civil enough and issued a general invitation to call upon Raffles at his rooms in the Albany. Since reason told Bunny that he could expect no more from the great man after such a passage of time, he had put the letter away, impatient with his own unspecified disappointment.

And there the matter might have rested were it not for a continued worsening of Bunny's fortunes which led him to contemplate a desperate act. Three years previously, Bunny Manders had come into a considerable fortune, an event which was contingent upon the deaths of most of his relatives. This loss he now counted as his sole piece of good luck, for as he contemplated ruin he could at least take comfort in the knowledge that his impending disgrace would not touch those whom he had loved. The fortune, needless to say, had disappeared and Bunny least of all knew where. Those pieces of jewelry and silver which had formed a part of his inheritance had now been sold and, as a daily reminder of calamity, he could not look around his flat without recalling that a bill of sale had been placed upon every stick of furniture it housed. In short, Bunny now possessed nothing more which might convert into cash, and the manager of his bank had coldly refused to extend his long-standing overdraft privilege.

In the light of such adversity can it be wondered

that Bunny felt desperate? It should rather be wondered that, in spite of all, a spark of hope, unformulated and unreasoned, still glowed in his breast. And that spark had become focused upon, even embodied in, the person of A. J. Raffles. At school he had more than once assisted Raffles out of some scrape or other and, in the roseate memory of those happy times, he conceived a stubborn impulse to turn to one whose resourcefulness had even outstripped his own.

So it was that, in the depths of despair, Bunny knocked upon Raffles's door one evening and awaited the response with some agitation. The unrecognizing expression on the handsome cricketer's face when he opened the door did nothing to put Bunny at ease. His visit suddenly appeared presumptuous, but that hope persisted and drove him on. Awkwardly he said:

"I wrote to you. Do you remember me? Bunny."

"Bunny," said Raffles reflectively, the name evidently striking no chord in his memory.

"You wrote back saying I could come and see you whenever I pleased," Bunny reminded him. "I was your fag at school."

At this, Raffles's face broke into a pleased and affable smile.

"Of course," he exclaimed, clasping Bunny's hand and drawing him into the hall. "Bunny! My dear chap!"

"You do remember," Bunny said with relief, surveying his friend with affection and open admiration.

"Well, well, well. Bunny! How are you? You haven't changed. Still the same innocent look."

"You haven't changed either," Bunny promptly replied.

"Still the same devilish . . ." Raffles laughed. "How long is it?"

"Must be ten years."

"Must be," Raffles agreed. "And what have you been doing with yourself?"

"Nothing much," Bunny confessed. "I don't need to ask what you've been doing."

"Don't you?" Raffles queried with amusement. "Why not?"

"I've read about you in the newspapers every day," Bunny said, removing his hat and cloak. "Famous cricketer!"

"Yes," Raffles agreed. "I do get my name in the papers as a cricketer."

"I should think you do. The things you've done for the M.C.C. and for England!" Bunny enthused. "I can recite your scores and your bowling analyses!"

"You always were keen on cricket," Raffles remembered, still smiling fondly at his enthusiastic visitor. "Come and meet two of my friends," he said, taking Bunny's arm and leading him toward a door.

At this Bunny fell back, partly out of embarrassment at intruding at a time when Raffles was entertaining, and partly because the presence of others dashed his hopes, so strongly fortified by Raffles's welcome, of seeking his help. Raffles, however, brushed aside Bunny's objections with an air of imperious authority that testified how little he had changed in the last ten years.

A cloud of cigar smoke hung in the spacious room into which Bunny was ushered. He had no opportunity then to examine it, but quickly took in two young male figures slumped in armchairs on either side of a card table, the setting up of which had obviously involved a considerable rearrangement of the furniture.

"Bunny, have you met Tremayne of the Life Guards?" Raffles asked, indicating a rather languid young man who sported a heavy cavalry moustache. "My old schoolfriend Bunny Manders," Raffles completed the introduction, and turned to his second guest. "And Alick Carruthers."

"Yes," Bunny said quickly and not without trepidation. "We know each other."

"Do we, by Jove?" queried Carruthers, leaning forward slightly and subjecting Bunny to a long appraisal. "Oh, yes," he said at last. "You're the chap who used to hang around dancing attendance on my cousin Maud."

The recollection of his affections for Maud was still painful for Bunny, and this slighting reference to them served only to reinforce that dislike of Carruthers which he had conceived previously. Politely, however, Bunny inquired after Maud, only to receive a noncommittal reply.

"Bunny was my fag at Uppingham," Raffles said, coming to his visitor's rescue. "Have a glass of Scotch, Bunny."

"Yes, thanks."

"And a Sullivan," Raffles added, indicating a smart cigarette box.

"Thanks."

"Only things I ever smoke," Raffles informed him.

Bunny could not help commenting that Sullivans were extremely expensive.

"That shouldn't worry you," Raffles said.

"Why?"

"I heard you'd come into money," Raffles explained, handing over a drink.

"Yes, I did," Bunny admitted, regretting that he could not then say more on that subject.

"Perhaps you'd like to speculate some of it on a

game of chance," Tremayne suggested, suddenly enlivened by this talk of money.

"Oh, you don't want to play baccarat, Bunny," Raffles said in a tone which, to Bunny's ears, instantly recalled their former relations.

"If you don't want me to," Bunny replied quietly, slipping quite naturally into the role he had so gratefully and successfully filled at Uppingham.

This, however, would not suffice for Carruthers. Quite rudely, he said:

"You don't want to play."

"Not if Raffles says not," Bunny declared.

"Scared?" sneered Carruthers.

"No."

This honest denial had no effect upon Carruthers, who then addressed himself to Tremayne as though Bunny were deaf or not actually present.

"He always was a bit of a softy. I remember him when he was courting Maud. . . ."

This insult was too much for Bunny, who little realized as his temper flared that he was playing directly into Carruthers's hands.

"I'll play baccarat with you," he announced.

"D'you know how to?" asked Carruthers.

"Yes."

"All you have to do is count up to nine," Tremayne supplied, enjoying himself hugely.

"Think you can do that?" sneered Carruthers again.

"Yes," Bunny said, taking a seat at the table and preparing for the game.

"Don't do it, Bunny. They're experts," Raffles cautioned, but Bunny was now beyond the reasoned counsel of his friend. The calculated insults of Carruthers and Tremayne had done their work. Fearing the worst, Raffles resignedly took his place at the table. His fears were soon justified. Bunny lost, and lost consistently, though whether as a result of a devilish run of bad luck or because of certain unsporting practices on the part of his tormentors, even Raffles could not be certain. Twice, at opportune moments, Raffles attempted to extricate his friend from what with each deal seemed more certainly a calculated fleecing, but Bunny angrily swept aside all suggestions that he should withdraw. Out of his depth he might be, but he steadfastly refused to lose further face by allowing Raffles to guide him into safer waters. But after some hours, when the pile of chips in front of Bunny had dwindled to almost nothing, Raffles could bear it on longer.

"Don't be an ass, Bunny," he said, standing up. "If Carruthers is on a winning streak . . ."

"What's the matter, Raffles?" Carruthers asked, trying to give an impression of injured innocence. "Don't you like to see me winning?"

"I don't like to see you taking money off a young fool," Raffles responded angrily.

"Who takes the same chance that I take," Carruthers pointed out.

"Oh?" Raffles said, letting his suspicions show for the first time. "What chance do you take?"

"Are you accusing me of cheating?" demanded Carruthers, half rising in affronted anger from his chair.

"Not unless you want me to." Raffles laughed. "Do you?"

"I've never heard of a fellow being insulted. . . ." Carruthers blustered.

"I haven't caught you cheating—yet," Raffles cut in coolly. "But you've had the most extraordinary run of luck I've ever seen, supposing you aren't cheating."

"By God, Raffles, you'll take that back!" Carruthers shouted, his face coloring.

"A bit strong, Raffles, I must say," Tremayne said in languid support of his friend.

"I'll put it another way," offered Raffles. "You're in my rooms. I didn't invite you here for the pleasure of seeing you rob a green youngster. The game is over. Will you please go?"

"No need to be unpleasant about it," grumbled Carruthers.

"Pleasantly, then. Will you please go? Or I'll throw you out."

"As soon as we've settled up," Carruthers agreed through gritted teeth.

The next moments, taken up by Carruthers's calculations with paper and pencil, were agonizing for Bunny. He did not trust himself to look up from the table while Tremayne and then Raffles silently checked the figures. At last Raffles laid the sheet in front of him. The sums he owed were greater and therefore worse than he had imagined.

"Afraid I haven't any cash on me," he apologized.

"I'll take a check," Carruthers said in a tone that made the offer sound like an order.

"I'll write each of you a check if I may," Bunny said, rising and reaching into his pocket.

"Mine is hardly large enough to deserve a check," Raffles said.

"But I have no cash . . ." Bunny repeated.

"Owe it me. You really didn't come here to gamble," Raffles answered sympathetically.

"No," Bunny said sadly. "To see you."

As he made out the checks for Tremayne and Carruthers, checks he knew could not possibly be met, his bleak awareness of impending dishonor was aggravated by the sense of a lost opportunity. If only he had been able to confide in Raffles! If only he had heeded

12

him! That, at least, would have afforded him a little self-respect. Bunny remained silent as the other guests happily pocketed their hollow winnings and loudly discussed plans for supper at Verrey's. Raffles soberly invited Bunny to remain for coffee, but he could not bring himself to accept. The enormity of his foolishness that evening, on top of all his other troubles, hung like a weight about his neck.

"Well," Raffles said as they stood in the hall. "That was a shame."

"Yes," Bunny agreed.

"Lucky you can afford it."

"Yes."

"Come again, when I'm by myself."

"Yes, please."

His tone, contrite, brimming with mixed emotions, touched Raffles who seized him, in an excess of friendship by the hand.

"Dear old Bunny!" he exclaimed. "Come any time."

"Thank you, Raffles. Good night."

And so saying, Bunny hurried away, his head down, not trusting himself to withstand the kindness and affection of the man he admired above all others.

Alone, Raffles exchanged his evening dress coat for an elegant silk dressing gown and pondered young Bunny's behavior. He recognized with a smile the stubbornness when baited that had always been a strength of Bunny's character. And he recognized that same innocence which, to his admitted surprise, the last ten years had neither dulled nor corrupted. But as he prepared for himself a pot of coffee and lit a Sullivan, Raffles could not help but remark a strangeness in Bunny's manner that evening; a strangeness which, he felt certain, could not be entirely explained by the unmannerly reception accorded him by Carruthers and

13

Tremayne, nor by the considerable sum he had lost. After all, Raffles thought, he jolly well paid up.

At that moment a loud rapping at the door broke in on Raffles's thoughts and perhaps because of their subject he was not greatly surprised, on opening the door, to find Bunny standing there. He did not stand there for long, however, but pushed almost rudely past Raffles and into the sitting room. In monosyllables he refused Raffles's offer of both coffee and a cigarette. Planting himself squarely behind the card table, and with transparent effort, he demanded:

"Raffles, will you listen to me for two minutes?"

"Certainly, my dear fellow. As many minutes as you like," Raffles agreed cheerfully. "Do sit down."

"No, I won't sit down," Bunny replied steadfastly. "And you won't ask me to, either, when you've heard what I have to say."

"Oh? How do you know that?" Raffles inquired politely.

"You'll show me the door and you'll be justified in doing it."

"And why will I show you the door?"

"Because neither of those checks was worth the paper they were written on. I'm overdrawn already at my bank."

Raffles digested this news without apparent concern.

"Most of us are in that state. Surely it's only for a moment?"

"No. Dishonored checks, Raffles! I'll be up in court! I'll be dishonored, too," Bunny burst out.

Patiently, but with an air of detachment that enabled his agile mind to leap ahead, Raffles questioned Bunny and was soon apprised of the true and terrible state of his affairs. The relief to Bunny of having at last unburdened himself was somewhat dissipated, however, by

14

the calm with which Raffles received his story. At its end, he said:

"You are in a really bad state, Bunny."

"Yes. I'm ruined," Bunny agreed bitterly, and having brought out the words at last, he moved swiftly and with determination toward the door. Raffles, however, was quicker and neatly interposed himself between his distraught friend and the exit.

"Where are you going?" he asked cautiously.

"None of your business. I won't trouble you any more."

"Then how can I help you?" Raffles asked reasonably.

"I didn't ask for your help," Bunny retorted.

"Why did you come to me?"

"Why indeed," Bunny sighed. "Now, will you let me pass?"

Gravely Raffles shook his head.

"Not until you tell me where you are going and what you mean to do."

"Can't you guess?" Bunny said, his tone revealing the stress of emotions under which he labored.

Raffles met his eyes and held them. Slowly, his own handsome features assumed that peculiar cast that had caused more than one of his acquaintances to describe him as "devilish."

"Yes, I can guess," he said quietly. "But have you got the courage?"

Bunny drew a sharp breath, much as though he had been slapped in the face. Then his innocent countenance became transformed by anger.

"You'll see!" he cried, tugging a pistol from the pocket of his cape and showing it to Raffles. "*Now* will you let me pass, or shall I do it here?"

So saying, he placed the cold muzzle of the pistol

against his unflinching temple and curled his finger around the trigger. Raffles, however, to Bunny's increasing dismay and hurt, made no move and spoke no word to deter him. Instead his face registered wonder and, fleetingly, admiration which gradually changed to an expression of pleased expectancy. Appalled and shaken, Bunny lowered the pistol.

"You cold-blooded devil," he hissed. "I believe you wanted me to do it."

"Not quite," Raffles said. "But I half thought you might and I was never more fascinated in my life. I never dreamed you had such strength in you, Bunny! I'll be damned if I let you go now. You're too good to waste. I'd no idea you were a chap of that sort." Raffles beamed, clapping his confused friend on the shoulder.

"Of what sort?" he asked.

"Such a determined little devil. But you'd better not try it again," he advised. "You may not have the same luck a second time. I'll take the gun before it goes off. We must think of some other way out of this mess," Raffles said reflectively, placing the pistol on a table.

"God bless you, Raffles," Bunny exclaimed, seizing his friend's hand emotionally. "I hoped you might help me. For the sake of the old school, if for nothing else. If you wouldn't, I was going to blow my brains out and I will still if you change your mind!" he concluded wildly.

"What a chap you are for jumping to conclusions!" Raffles said, somewhat offended. "I have my vices, Bunny, but changing my mind is not one of them. It'd be easy if I had the money to lend you," he went on, "but at this moment I'm as hard up as you are yourself."

This Bunny found extremely difficult to believe, which fact he communicated to his friend.

"Do you think because a fellow has rooms in this place," Raffles asked, waving a hand at his Albany suite, "and belongs to a club or two and plays a little cricket, he must necessarily have money in the bank?"

Evidently Bunny did think so and he supported his view by reminding Raffles that he played cricket throughout the season and did nothing during the remainder of the year. Ergo, he must have money.

"I have nothing but my wits to live on," Raffles insisted, without concealing that he regarded his wits as capital indeed. "We're in the same boat, Bunny. We'd better pull together."

Was this not precisely what Bunny had wished to hear, the very realization of that stubborn spark of hope that had, he now owned, quite saved him?

"I'll do anything in the world," he proclaimed. "I don't care what I do if only I can get out of this without a scandal."

Raffles contemplated his animated friend for a long and careful moment. No doubt Bunny meant it in his present mood, but in the morning, the day after? Against this doubt, Raffles weighed the faithful assistance that he had received from Bunny during many awkward moments at Uppingham. He had never flinched and he had never blabbed.

"I wonder if you're like that now?" Raffles mused.

"I don't know," answered Bunny promptly. "But I've never in my life gone back on a friend."

"That's what I remember of you," Raffles confirmed. "And I'll bet it's as true now as it was ten years ago. You would stop at nothing for a pal—what?"

"At nothing in this world," Bunny asserted.

17

"Not even a crime?" Raffles asked sharply, his face a veritable portrait of cunning watchfulness.

"Name the crime and I'm your man!"

Still entertaining certain mental reservations based on cautious consideration for the mood of euphoria which presently gripped his friend, Raffles applied his mind to the immediate problem. Five hundred pounds—the sum that Bunny had that very evening lost—must be secured by Monday. It was then Friday evening, and Raffles quickly deduced that since Carruthers and Tremayne each banked with different houses and, by good fortune, both of these were different from Bunny's, there was no possible fear of discovery before Monday morning. Having imparted this information to Bunny, Raffles changed tack.

"I'm playing at Lord's tomorrow. M.C.C. against the Australians. You come and find me in the pavilion at the end of play; and have a bag ready for a country weekend."

"Where?" Bunny asked, delighted at the prospect of a day's cricket, of watching the great Raffles in action.

"Buckinghamshire somewhere. Anywhere, evening dress and the rest. Then we'll trot off to Marylebone Station and buy our tickets."

"But where is it we're going?" persisted Bunny.

"I think I know where to raise that five hundred, Bunny," Raffles confided, his eyes lighting with enthusiasm at the prospect of a challenge.

"Where?" wailed Bunny.

"From Alick Carruthers. The man who took it off you."

If he were in any doubt as to the intact innocence of Bunny's mind, his friend's next, crestfallen remarks provided Raffles with proof positive that nothing had changed.

18

"Carruthers detests me. He'd never lend it me!"

"I'm not suggesting we should borrow it, Bunny," Raffles said with deadly seriousness.

"What, then?"

"I'm suggesting we should take it."

"Steal it?"

" 'Name the crime and I'm your man.' That's what you said, Bunny. Well, now I've named it."

Bunny was quite stupefied.

"Steal?" he questioned weakly.

"Take it back from Carruthers as he stole it from you. I tell you, Bunny, I'd have caught him cheating if I'd watched him more carefully. I've always suspected him of being a cardsharp. I tell you, any money you can take off Alick Carruthers, you're fully entitled to."

Raffles's voice and his air of animated determination fired Bunny to the task more than his logic. This Raffles saw and was quick to press home the advantage he had won.

"And if it saves you from disgrace, that's as good a cause as can be."

"Right," Bunny agreed.

"It's just like the old days, what?"

"Me helping you to climb back into the dorm," Bunny reminisced happily.

"Partners," Raffles said, extending his hand. "In crime."

Bunny grasped his hand warmly.

"Partners," he agreed. "In crime!"

So great was Bunny's relief at this most unexpected way out of his difficulties that he slept that night like the proverbial log. Nor did he falter in the light of day. Any doubts about the propriety of Raffles's scheme were allayed by a dogged belief in that man's utter reliability. If Raffles said, as he most certainly and persuasively had, that it was all right to take money dishonestly won by Alick Carruthers, then that was sufficient for Bunny. It was, to his simple, honest mind, inconceivable that a man who could bowl with such grace and precision as Raffles did that afternoon could be anything other than an out-and-out hero. Consequently, the plan outlined by Raffles went smoothly. Bunny collected his friend with pride from the pavilion at the match's end and accompanied him to Marylebone Station where, in no time at all, they were installed in a first-class carriage enroute for rural Buckinghamshire.

It was during the course of this journey that Raffles revealed more of their destination and his plan to save his friend. Their host was to be Lord Lochmaben, father of the scurrilous Alick Carruthers, who had lately been elevated to the peerage. No doubt this event would lend spice to their annual weekend for the local peasantry, a social occasion centered upon a cricket match against the village, but which also traditionally included a fancy dress ball. Bunny was relieved to hear that he and Raffles would arrive too late to take part in the ball, but he expressed further doubts about his own welcome at the festivities.

"I sent them a telegram," Raffles drawled. "I'm a catch because I'm an England player. I told them, if they want me they've got to have you."

"Oh," said Bunny uncertainly.

"You've no idea how rude you can be," Raffles explained, "when you're famous and wanted."

But even this did not mollify Bunny. Something else troubled him and it soon sprang to his lips.

"I wondered," he said, attempting an unconcerned tone. "Will Maud be there?"

"Who?" asked Raffles.

20

"Maud. Carruthers's cousin."

"Ah. No. No, Maud isn't there. She's gone home to her people."

"In Devonshire?"

"In Devonshire," Raffles confirmed.

Somewhat unconvincingly, Bunny said: "Good."

This disposed of, Raffles returned to the recently acquired Lochmaben peerage, the receipt of which Lady Lochmaben had instantly celebrated by the purchase of a tiara. A tiara, moreover, which Raffles had twice seen and which he pronounced to be positively bulging with diamonds.

"I just hope she doesn't guard her treasure too closely," he said.

"But . . ." expostulated Bunny, "are we proposing to steal from Alick's parents? I thought it was from Alick himself."

"Alick lives on his parents. Doesn't work for a living. It's the same thing," Raffles explained, contemplating his fingernails.

"But surely one doesn't steal from people one knows," Bunny ventured.

"No. One doesn't normally."

"It seems rather vulgar," Bunny said, avoiding Raffles's fixed gaze.

"Almost as vulgar as cheating at cards or passing a bad check," he agreed in a cold, steely voice.

This, as Raffles had calculated, was sufficient to squash any further objections Bunny might entertain. The latter, harshly reminded of his own foolishness and plight, stared miserably out of the window.

"By heavens!" Raffles exclaimed suddenly, slapping his knee. "I will have that tiara. My mind has been running on it ever since I first saw it."

"When do you propose to get it?" Bunny asked neutrally, not wishing to reveal his curiosity.

"After the ball is over. About four in the morning," came the prompt reply.

"I shall be sleeping soundly," Bunny said with relief.

"No you won't. You'll be giving me your able assistance," Raffles corrected him.

Bunny knew that it must be so and looked at Raffles, prepared to confirm his promise of the night before, but the light, steely and not inappropriately gemlike look, which he saw in Raffles's eyes, started a new thought in his mind. A new and rather disturbing thought.

"Raffles?" he asked carefully. "Have you done this kind of thing before?"

"Why, yes. Once or twice," Raffles said with a shrug, turning toward the window and becoming, as far as Bunny could tell, quite absorbed in the late sun-mellowed countryside through which the train was then passing.

It would not be accurate to say that this offhand admission surprised Bunny. He had read it in Raffles's eyes even before he framed the question and, indeed, it made better sense of a certain enigmatic quality Bunny had fleetingly noticed in his old friend the night before. Surprising, then, the admission was not, but still it proved hard for Bunny to digest. It occupied him for the remainder of the journey and throughout the carriage drive from the rural station to Lochmaben Hall. Raffles seemed content to leave Bunny to his own thoughts. interrupting them once only to predict that they would be greeted by a cold supper, laid in the library.

And so it proved to be. The house, handsome and ablaze with lights, murmurous with the sound of distant music and gaiety, swallowed them up unnoticed, save by the butler who conducted them to the library, while permitting himself a few congratulatory remarks on Raffles's performance against the Australians that afternoon. The meal, however, proved to be excellent, especially the lobster which the wine perfectly complemented. Replete and satisfied, Raffles fell to musing on the prospect of tomorrow's match and his own status as guest of honor when they were interrupted by a gentleman who appeared to be no less a personage than Charles the First of England! At sight of him, Bunny rose to his feet.

"Raffles!" the man exclaimed, advancing toward the cricketer. "Delighted you could come. Have they given you enough to eat and drink?" With a sigh of relief, the gentleman divested himself of a long, Carolinian wig, and added: "I wish my political convictions had allowed me to be Oliver Cromwell."

Simultaneously, Bunny recognized Lord Lochmaben and recalled the fancy dress ball. Raffles responded in similar hearty style to this singular greeting and begged leave to introduce his friend.

"Haven't I seen you before?" Lord Lochmaben asked.

"Yes . . ." Bunny began, but was instantly cut short.

"Don't matter. Any friend of Raffles's is a friend of mine. Suppose you're not a cricketer? Never mind. You can help the scorer with those little tin plates. Excuse me while I just put something in the safe. My wife's worried about burglars."

At this—to Bunny—alarming remark, he noticed an object, immediately recognizable as a tiara, wrapped in a soft cloth, in Lord Lochmaben's hand. His lordship bustled across the room and pressed a switch which caused one section of the bookcase to swing outward into the room. Bunny, aware that his mouth was open, shut it promptly.

"Don't know why she should worry," Lord Lochmaben said, his fingers deftly turning the dial to find the safe's combination. "Hasn't been a burglary round here for twenty years or more. Anyway, what could they do with a tiara if they got it?"

Raffles had resumed his seat and maintained an air of total disinterest in the safe, the combination and her ladyship's fear of burglars. Nervously, Bunny tried to follow his example while Lord Lochmaben applied a key and opened the safe.

"There," he said, placing the tiara in the safe and closing the door with a solid click.

"Safe as houses," chuckled Raffles.

"Funny you should say that," said the peer. "I made a speech in the House of Lords the other day about crime and sending people to prison. Burglars should get twenty years in jail. It was reported in the *Morning Post*," he finished blithely and would, no doubt, have expanded upon his theme had not a young woman, charmingly attired as Columbine, entered the room at that precise moment.

"Uncle, I've been sent to find you," said Columbine. "You've got to come and dance the waltz with Aunt. She says she can't do it with anyone but you."

"She's right at that," agreed the peer.

Columbine, however, had espied and recognized Raffles. Smiling, she advanced toward him.

"How do you do, Mr. Raffles? I recognize you from your caricatures in the sporting papers. You're very like."

"How do you do?" said Raffles, bowing.

"And your friend . . ." She turned to Bunny and instantly felt a thrill of recognition. "Bunny!" she cried. "What are you doing here?"

"I came with Raffles," he said, mortified to be thus brought face-to-face with Maud, a young woman who still possessed the ability to rouse in him strong and disconcerting feelings. "I didn't think I'd see you here," he said, casting Raffles a deeply reproachful look. "In fact, I'd been told I wouldn't. Or I wouldn't have come."

"You didn't want to see me?" she queried, with a flash of that coquetry which Bunny remembered so keenly.

"Well, no, under the circumstances . . ."

"Must go and dance, I suppose," Lord Lochmaben interposed. "You young people do as you like. Suppose you will in any case. Maud here stands up for women's rights, heaven help us."

"I am a Socialist, Uncle," the young lady said firmly.

"Well, I must go and dance," said Lord Lochmaben, shaking his head at such folly and walking toward the door.

"I mean," said Bunny, seizing his opportunity, "I didn't want to see you . . . when . . ."

"If you didn't want to see me, you don't want to see me," Maud rejoined.

"I don't . . . want . . . to . . . I . . ."

"Mr. Raffles, will you ask me to dance?" she said, turning her back on Bunny.

"Will you do me the honor of dancing with me?" said Raffles, smiling graciously.

"On condition that you will ask me again," she said, melting into his arms and allowing him to waltz her toward the door through which they instantly vanished, as though absorbed by the music which drifted pleasantly into the library.

"What I mean is . . ." Bunny began, but there was no one to hear. And indeed, even had Maud been standing before him, Bunny doubted that he could have expressed either the nature of his feelings for her or his conviction that they were doomed. It was true that Bunny had paid court to Maud Carruthers and that he would never forget the tender signs of warmth with which she had received him. But his own disastrous affairs, coupled with the unconcealed dislike of her cousin, who let it be known that Maud was intended to make a dazzling match, had deterred his spirit, if not his affections. There had been nothing to do but withdraw and so save himself the torture of looking upon that which he knew he would never possess. Anxious to avoid a further meeting with Maud, Bunny inquired as to the whereabouts of his room and went miserably up to bed.

Although there was much to occupy his mind, sleep soon overcame him. It is very likely that he would have slept untroubled until the breakfast gong had not Raffles shaken him awake at four o'clock. When at last Bunny was able to comprehend what was happening, he sleepily followed Raffles's instructions to "get your trousers on and a pair of rubber shoes." When Bunny had done so, Raffles insisted that they wait for a few moments, his keen ear cocked for the slightest noise. This prudent delay only increased Bunny's mounting nervousness, a fact which he shiveringly communicated to Raffles.

"Yes," the latter said in a tone of nonchalant excitement. "It's rather like sitting with one's pads on before going in the game."

"Very like," Bunny whispered.

"An ordeal," mused his friend, "which engenders a

general quaking of the inner man. But you'll be all right when you're at the wicket."

To this Bunny could only smile. At last Raffles motioned him forward and together they stole silently down the stairs. To Raffles's surprise, the hall was dimly lit. He paused, considering this unexpected occurrence and, in a low tone, advised Bunny that the lights had probably been left on for the return of Alick Carruthers.

"Or perhaps the lights are for us, to see our way," Bunny joked, not at all liking the prospect of encountering the son of the house again.

Raffles had crept a few steps down the stairs before the import of what Bunny had said impressed itself upon him.

"By God, I think you've hit it, Bunny," he said, seizing his friend and hurrying him into the library.

With the swiftness of a racing carriage whose driver has been promised double fare, Raffles saw it all. The whole thing was a trap. Supper laid in the library where the tiara was kept when not adorning her ladyship's head. And quite by chance, Lord Lochmaben's showing them the whereabouts of the concealed safe, while giving the impression that he neither feared nor expected burglars. Such chances, Raffles knew, were to be trusted at peril. Such chances were a trap, and a devilishly cunning one at that.

"The whole things smacks of Inspector Mackenzie, Bunny. Just mark my words," cried Raffles.

"Who's he?" inquired Bunny, shivering.

There was no time for Raffles to give more than the briefest facts about Inspector Mackenzie of Scotland Yard, an indefatigable Scotsman who had been hot on Raffles's trail more than once and who had, it flattered

Raffles to know, conceived something resembling a personal vendetta against him.

Bunny, of course, was all for giving up, though not, it should be understood, out of fright. His good, loyal but limited brain simply saw the task as impossible, while his inexperience of crime made him accept defeat with an eagerness which Raffles quickly countered with sound arguments.

"Give up? And Monday morning, Alick Carruthers with your check? Dishonored?"

"Never mind," Bunny said sadly, resigned once more to his fate.

"That's the whole thing, Bunny. I do mind. Alick took your money and he's going to pay for it tonight. Or his family is going to pay for him," he corrected himself.

Something glinted in Bunny's wide blue eyes, something which a lesser man than A. J. Raffles might have taken for sentimental tears.

"You're doing this for my sake, Raffles?" he asked in a hesitant voice.

Raffles's face remained an unmoving mask of determination.

"No one likes being beaten by Alick Carruthers," he said. "Come on. Best be quick."

With one graceful bound the amateur cracksman had crossed the room and pressed the switch which caused a section of the bookcase to swing out, revealing the safe. Raffles surveyed that object with a smile of pleasure before stepping up to it and applying his sensitive fingers to the combination dial. As he did so he felt regret that Lord Lochmaben had made his task so easy. This was a safe worthy of Raffles the artist, and he would have enjoyed cracking it without aid. Swiftly the combination was achieved and Raffles

28

delved into his pocket for a bunch of skeleton keys—the burglar's friend, as he confided to Bunny. The second key on the ring fitted and with a well-tempered click the safe door opened, revealing the glittering tiara within.

At the very moment when Raffles drew forth the prize, the unmistakable sound of wheels crunching on gravel penetrated the library, causing the celebrated cricketer to freeze, and his friend to start with apprehension.

"Alick!" hissed Raffles.

Instantly Bunny bolted for the door, but a sharp word from Raffles stopped him midstride. Almost simultaneously, it appeared to Bunny, Raffles had lowered the light to an obscuring dimness and crossed the room to set his ear against the paneled door. However, this device soon proved superfluous since Alick Carruthers entered the hall with such a raucous shouting, both for attendance and to his giggling and evidently tipsy companion, that all could be heard clearly through the closed door of the library.

It quickly transpired that Carruthers was much the worse for drink, which perhaps explained why he had brought with him a Miss Polly Perkins of the Royal Holborn Theatre of Varieties. This creature burst frequently into vulgar song, much to the delight of her protector. But not, it soon became apparent, to that of Lord Lochmaben whose gruff, disturbed voice soon cut across the noise of the revelers. Bunny, hearing Lord Lochmaben order his son curtly to bed, heaved a sigh of relief. Footsteps receded. Silence reigned.

"Phew!" said Raffles. "Better wait a minute in case they come back."

Bunny nodded, glancing about the dim room. The safe, he noticed, was not only exposed but open. He drew Raffles's attention to this and, on receiving the latter's assent, hurried across to close it and so conceal their handiwork. Bunny had no sooner reached the safe than Raffles heard a sharp click and saw the handle of the library door turn. The sound, he saw at a glance, had not reached Bunny. There was nothing for it but to step smartly behind the long velvet curtains, which offered concealment both for himself and for the tiara which he still held.

The door opened and a voice, shocked and hurt, cried:

"Bunny!"

That young man, his face the very personification of guilt, turned, his hand resting on the open door of the safe, to meet Maud's eyes.

"You—a thief?" she said, her tone incredulous. "Alick woke me," she explained, stepping into the room. "I came down for a book."

However, what she had discovered had quite removed her desire for the soothing qualities of literature. She turned upon her heel and placed a quivering hand upon the door handle.

"Put it back," she said firmly. "Whatever it is you've taken. Put it back and I'll see you tomorrow."

With these words, the young woman glided silently out of the library. As she did so, Raffles stepped from his hiding place, a sympathetic smile on his face.

The task of piloting Bunny back to his room was, Raffles was later to reflect, every bit as difficult as his most ingenious burglaries. Yet he succeeded, as he had triumphed in those other feats, and moments later the two friends were seated side by side on Bunny's bed. The latter could say nothing except miserably repeat that Maud took him for a thief.

"Ah," agreed Raffles, after considering the situation. "But why are you a thief?"

"Because I was helping you, because you're my old friend, because I'm broke," Bunny said, making it sound like a catechism of despair.

"Bunny," Raffles said, with thinly stretched patience, "that is the truth and you will have to learn the truth is something nobody believes at the right moment, when it matters. You have to tell them what they will believe."

"What?" Bunny asked morosely.

"Don't bother your head with philosophical abstractions," Raffles said, clapping his friend on the shoulder. "Just tell me, if you can, does Maud sleep with her window open?"

"I have absolutely no idea," Bunny replied, drawing himself up in resentment of what such a question implied.

"Never mind. You go to sleep and dream of her," Raffles advised, moving to the door.

"Where are you going?" Bunny said, about to follow him.

"I have to do a little more burgling," was all that Raffles would say before he slipped through the door of Bunny's room, leaving his friend confused and speechless.

After her unexpected encounter with Bunny, Maud had returned directly to her room. She, too, had entertained some sincere affections for Bunny and his withdrawal from her society had disturbed her. Now she felt nothing but confusion. How was it possible that she could have held such tender thoughts of a man who . . . It was unbearable. She drove all memories of Bunny from her mind, but lay sleepless and anxious in her bed. Her anxiety was soon increased by a sound, a sound which, had she not known better, she would have attributed to her window being raised. With a start, Maud sat up. It was her window, and worse, a dark figure was entering, was stealing toward her.

"Come any nearer and I shall scream!" Maud announced bravely, clutching the sheets to her bosom.

"In that case, I shall not come any nearer," replied a familiar, charming voice.

"Mr. Raffles, is it?"

"You recognize me. . . ."

"From your voice."

"You have a sharp ear."

"You may have forgotten that you danced with me half the night. And you talked to me," Maud said.

"May I talk to you again?" begged Raffles in a wheedling tone.

"On condition I put the light on."

"Oh, why?"

"I can't see if you are telling the truth in the dark," she replied, turning away to light her bedside lamp.

"But do you know what the truth is?" Raffles asked, smiling down at her.

"The truth is that you have done something very silly in climbing through my bedroom window and now, no doubt, you are going to say something very silly. That is enough silliness for one night. You had better go."

Maud, whose heart was racing, but no longer with fear, felt quite proud of this speech, but Raffles, his face still tenderly smiling, refused to heed it.

"You don't want to know the real truth?" he questioned her.

"No. When people say that, it is generally a preamble to something unpleasant. Nor do I wish to hear compliments. Go," she ordered.

"And leave them unsaid?" Raffles's tone indicated that to do so would be tantamount to committing a crime against nature.

"You will have time to pay them at the cricket match tomorrow," Maud said.

"I'm delighted to accept the implied invitation." Raffles bowed gracefully. "But I don't think," he added, fixing her with his most appealing stare, "what I have to say can wait till tomorrow. By the time of the cricket match, you may have taken an irrevocable step."

"I am not likely," retorted Maud, blushing, "to die so soon, nor to marry."

"But it is possible that you will go to the police," Raffles said, coming to the point and noting the involuntary start his words produced from her. "I am not here on my own behalf—would that I were—but on behalf of Bunny."

This news caused the young woman to lower her eyes, though whether it was his reference to Bunny that caused her to do so or disappointment that he was not primarily concerned to press his own case, Raffles gallantly refused to consider.

"You know what he has done?" she said at last, and in a small voice.

"He has told me all," Raffles told her. "He came to my room and confessed."

"And sent you to plead for him," Maud said scornfully.

Raffles shook his head slowly.

"I come not to plead but to explain."

"I am a very simpleminded person, Mr. Raffles," said Maud. "When I see a man with his hand in an open safe, I jump to the conclusion that the explanation is that he is stealing whatever lies inside."

"Certainly," Raffles agreed. "But why?"

"Because he wants to have it and he feels no qualms about depriving the owner of it."

"Miss Carruthers," Raffles said reproachfully. "And you a Socialist!"

"Are you going to tell me that the thief merely seeks a more equal distribution of property?" she demanded with some heat.

"That is the effect of what he does," reasoned Raffles. "But I do not claim it as a justification. No, the disappointment which you must have noticed in my voice was due to your automatic assumption that the motive for theft was mere greed—lust for possession, was necessarily selfish."

With a disparaging shrug, Maud said:

"And you will argue that Bunny's motive was entirely altruistic?"

"It was," Raffles assured her.

"For whom was he thieving then?" Maud challenged, her disbelief quite unconcealed.

"For me."

"You, Mr. Raffles! You, the rich, the famous, the successful, the handsome! . . ." Maud stopped, her cheeks coloring at her indiscreet words. There was nothing for it, she perceived, but to hurry on in the hope that it might pass unnoticed. "The great cricketer? Why should poor little Bunny, nothing little Bunny, steal for you?"

"Because," said Raffles, turning his face from her, "I may be famous, but I'm not rich. I'm broke, and worse than broke. I'm in debt. Unless I can pay it by Monday, I shall be disgraced, ruined, thrown out of society and into prison. The England team will have to look for another all-rounder," he concluded sadly.

Maud could scarcely believe this confession, so at

variance with the facts was the impression created by her nocturnal visitor.

"You mean to tell me Bunny took . . ."

"Your aunt's tiara . . ." Raffles supplied.

". . . to save you from ruin?"

"Greater love hath no man than this: that he commits burglary for his friend," Raffles intoned solemnly.

"I didn't think Bunny had it in him," Maud said wonderingly.

"He's solid worth, Bunny—through and through. He's an admirable chap."

"And you want me to forgive him, and forget I saw him at the safe, because he acted like a hero?"

"No. I simply want you to know the truth of what has happened. The rest I must leave to your conscience."

Throughout this exchange Raffles had kept his hands behind him. Now he brought them forward and held toward Maud a small leather traveling bag.

"I give you this," he said.

"What is it?" Maud cried.

"Your aunt's tiara. Now I must go."

He placed the bag on the foot of Maud's bed.

"But you can't," Maud protested as he moved toward the window.

"Bunny gave it to me out of love. I give it to you . . ." Raffles paused, allowed his words to hang unspoken, but seeing Maud's young and eager face, he added: "for much the same reason. Goodbye."

"But Mr. Raffles! You'll be disgraced, ruined. . . ."

"There are other countries in the world . . ." Raffles said quietly.

"But the England team!"

"England will have to learn to do without me."

35

"But if I give it back to Aunt. . . ."

"The rights of ownership are sacred," Raffles reminded her. "The rich are entitled to the fruits of their exploitation."

"I dare say it's insured," Maud said, following her own thoughts.

"The insurance companies will not have to disgorge any of their multiple millions."

Beseechingly, in a tiny voice, Maud said:

"What do you want me to do?"

"To remember why the theft was committed," Raffles said, "and to greet me tomorrow with a smile on your lips."

"I will," promised Maud, greatly moved.

Swiftly, Raffles snatched up her small hand and kissed it. Before the touch of his lips on her soft skin had faded, he stood already at the window.

"Do be careful," implored Maud.

"My death or my ruin. What's the odds?" Raffles called, swinging his leg over the sill and commencing the climb down.

The next morning, Raffles's handsome countenance betrayed no sign of his disturbed and taxing night. He strode onto the cricket field every inch the conquering hero and applied himself to the task of getting out the rustic eleven with dispatch and style. Maud had greeted him, according to her promise, with a warm smile and, during the opening overs, contrived to draw an embarrassed Bunny aside. Fearing justified recriminations, that young man was quite taken aback when Maud informed him, her eyes fixed on Raffles as he prepared his slow run up, that she was extremely proud of him. By the time he had absorbed this pleasant information and found the courage to inquire why, Maud had drifted away into the elegant crowd, while the scorer was impatiently signaling for Bunny's aid.

During the next hour or so, Bunny was kept busily at work and so did not notice the appearance at the edge of the field of two unmistakable policemen in plain clothes. Needless to say, their arrival did not escape Raffles, who jokingly asked Lord Lochmaben what their presence portended. The latter, however, hurried away without giving an explanation. Raffles calmly assumed captaincy of the gentlemen and applied himself to the game once more.

At lunchtime Raffles's personal analysis was eight for thirteen, an achievement which drew spontaneous applause from Bunny as he hurried forward to greet his friend.

"More to the point," Raffles said, brushing aside his congratulations, "what have those two coppers been up to?"

"No idea," replied Bunny, for whom such considerations were meaningless when he was immersed in a game of cricket.

"Hope they've been going through our bags," said Raffles casually.

"Why?" asked Bunny, feeling alarmed.

"Because there's nothing there," he said coolly, turning away to accept the congratulations and apologies of Lord Lochmaben, who remained bluffly vague about the presence of the police and his own long absence from the game.

In fact, their bags had been searched and thoroughly, with exactly the result Raffles had anticipated. Particular attention had been paid to the luggage of A. J. Raffles, for all was as Raffles had divined the previous night. The cunning hand of Inspector

Mackenzie was indeed at work in this affair, and suspicion was not yet entirely allayed.

With a confident smile, Raffles greeted Maud and courteously agreed to take her in to lunch. As they strolled together, an elegant and charming couple, across the lawn of Lochmaben Hall, Maud gently reminded her escort that he had promised her compliments last night.

"And you shall have them," Raffles promised.

"And you shall have a reward," she countered. "For your bowling, if for nothing else."

"How splendid to have a reward from you," Raffles said.

"I shall give you back your bag."

"My bag?"

"The little bag you gave me. I would rather you had it than me."

"You are very kind," Raffles said, inclining his head.

As he did so his sharp eyes glimpsed a plain clothes policeman watching their progress from a distance, and saw Bunny dragging along behind with a hurt look on his face.

"Shall I get it for you now?" Maud asked.

"Not now," Raffles said quickly, turning her away from the vigilant policeman. "I suppose there is no possibility of your bringing it to me in town?"

"Alas, no. I shall not be coming to London for weeks," Maud said with true disappointment.

"Then would it be possible," Raffles inquired, "to let me have my reward this evening, just before I go back to London? In private, say on the terrace, where no one can see us?"

With a pretty inclination of her head, Maud silently indicated that it would be possible and that it would please her to concur.

When the match was resumed after lunch Raffles, almost single-handed, completed the rout of the village eleven, a fact which put Lord Lochmaben into the very best of moods. Something of this goodwill benefited his chastened son who, with the unsuitable Miss Perkins clinging to his arm, prepared to return to town with the rest of the company. His father had not, as Alick had feared in the sober light of day, cut off his allowance, but had strongly advised him to drop his racy companion forthwith.

During this exchange, Raffles was involved in one of a more tender nature in the shadows of the secluded terrace. There Maud tremblingly pressed the small leather bag into Raffles's hand and accepted his grateful speech of thanks with downcast eyes.

"And you will turn it into money to pay your debt?" she shyly inquired.

"I have a dubious acquaintance who will turn it into money," Raffles told her honestly.

"Which will save you from ruin and disgrace? Will it? Will it really?"

"After tomorrow," Raffles reassured her, "I shall owe a debt to no one but Bunny—and you."

"Bunny will be your friend," Maud said. "And I, shall I be your friend, too?"

This was said with such melting, tremulous charm that Raffles could find no answer better than to enfold the young woman in his arms and tenderly kiss her.

"My friend for always," he vowed, releasing her and so taking his leave.

Without more ado, Raffles joined the assembled company, thanked his host for a most enjoyable weekend and followed the others into the carriage which was to convey them to the railway station. Once there, Bunny and Raffles were obliged by politeness to travel with Alick Carruthers, the painted Miss Perkins and others. Squashed so together with that not very congenial company, Bunny had no opportunity to question his friend, but gave himself up to brooding thoughts of Maud. She would not, he knew, be proud of him once she heard of his disgrace.

Raffles, too, had lapsed into a silence which continued throughout the drive to his rooms at the Albany. There, leaving Bunny to unload the bags, Raffles went to speak to the porter. It was without surprise that he learned from this man that a gentleman was awaiting him above.

"A gentleman?" Raffles queried.

"Well, no, not actually, sir," the porter confided. "He's the police."

"Scots by any chance?"

"Yes, he had a Scotch accent now you mention it, sir."

It was exactly as Raffles had expected, and he set about at once to deal with the situation.

"Bunny," he called to his friend. "Do you mind waiting down here for a minute? There's someone up there to see me. Beckett here will help with my bags, won't you, Beckett?"

Both Bunny and the porter readily agreed. Raffles and the latter collected together his luggage, including the small leather bag, and set off up the stairs. There, outside Raffles's front door, stood the tall frame of Inspector Mackenzie, his bearded, granite face expressing an eager suspicion but no true pleasure at seeing Raffles.

"Inspector Mackenzie," Raffles greeted the man cheerfully. "I'm sorry to have kept you waiting. I came just as fast as I could. Come along in and have a glass of Scotch."

So saying, Raffles opened his front door and nodded to the porter that he could go. Obligingly, Inspector Mackenzie gathered up those items of Raffles's luggage which the athlete could not manage and followed him into the sitting room.

"Scotch?" repeated Raffles, lifting the fine cut-glass decanter from the small table on which it habitually stood.

"No thank you, sir. I'm on duty," replied the inspector.

"Then what can I do for you?" Raffles wanted to know, pouring himself a tot.

"You can permit me to search your bags, sir," said Mackenzie with something that might pass in such a man for glee.

Raffles raised his eyebrows in surprise and annoyance.

"I have reason to believe," he said, "my bags have been searched by the police already today."

"Aye," confirmed Mackenzie. "At Lord Lochmaben's. We have been in communication with the Buckinghamshire constabulary, but I doubt the efficacy of their method of searching. And maybe there's something in the nature of an additional bag?" he suggested, his gimlet eyes moving suspiciously to the small bag which Raffles had carried himself into the room.

"Of course you have a warrant?" Raffles challenged.

"Of course, sir."

"Then I can't stop you. Proceed," he added sulkily.

Raffles drained his glass and refilled it while Inspector Mackenzie commenced a detailed and thorough search of his bags. This was conducted in silence, Raffles leaning nonchalantly against the marble mantel while maintaining the air of one who is unfairly suspected and wrongfully treated. At last Mackenzie straightened up, his face contorted by a thunderous frown.

"Ah," he said softly, moving toward the little leather bag. "Last but not least, eh?"

"Last *and* least I should have thought," Raffles said carelessly.

Ignoring him, the inspector placed the bag on a table and opened it with something akin to reverence. Then he plunged his hand inside. At once an expression of dismay, turning to outraged anger, crossed his face. Quite forgetting himself, he snatched up the bag, inverted it and shook it with more force than was strictly necessary.

"Why is this bag empty?" he demanded, turning to Raffles.

"I expect it's because I didn't put anything in it," replied the other insolently.

It is impossible to convey in words alone the noise which escaped the inspector's lips at that moment. His face became diffused with an angry red which quite made Raffles fear for his health. Flinging the bag from him, Inspector Mackenzie of Scotland Yard strode from the room, his coat swirling behind him. In the hall he collided with a similarly hurrying Bunny, who fell back in awe to allow this stern personage to sweep by him and down the stairs. Catching his breath, Bunny hurried into the sitting room, fearing some calamity.

"Who was that storming out of there like a tropical typhoon?" he asked of Raffles.

"Inspector Mackenzie. Have a drink to celebrate his Scotchness," replied Raffles. "He didn't find it," he added, pouring a drink for Bunny.

"Find what?"

"The tiara."

"But . . ."

Bunny's mouth dropped open. His honest blue eyes widened. He looked to Raffles the very picture of astounded innocence and the sight gladdened his heart.

"He looked," Raffles explained, gesturing toward the open bags and their displaced contents. "He looked everywhere but in the right place."

"Wh . . . where?" stammered Bunny.

"Where would you say is the right place for a tiara?" Raffles asked solemnly, but Bunny was so amazed that he could not force his brain to work.

Raffles, taking pity on him, perched on the arm of a comfortable chair and, with a bravura gesture, doffed his glossy top hat. There, perched at a rakish angle on his brow, was the gleaming tiara of Lady Lochmaben. Bunny, seeing this, opened his eyes and his mouth even wider as Raffles permitted himself a slow smile of satisfaction.

Thus it was that on the following Monday morning, Bunny was able to pay into his account a sufficient sum not only to meet the checks presented by Carruthers and Tremayne, but to pay off his overdraft and leave him funds to spare. For the first time in many weary months, Bunny was free from worries. The gladness this reversal in his fortunes inspired in him was, however, nothing compared with the warm gratitude he felt toward Raffles, whose partner and boon companion he was, from that time forth, always proud to be.

Two

A COSTUME PIECE

••••———◆———••••

IN WHICH RAFFLES RESPONDS TO A UNIVERSAL CHALLENGE AND BUNNY IS PLACED AT MORTAL RISK

FEW THINGS SADDENED the heart of Raffles more than the decline of a good club, especially one in which he had spent many happy hours. Yet such was the dreary fate of the Old Bohemian in the autumn of 1896. It was therefore with some jubilation that Raffles, after an excellent lunch consumed on those very premises, drew his friend's attention to a notice prominently displayed in the hallway of the club.

CLUB DINNER IN HONOR OF REUBEN ROSENTHALL

8 October 1896

Raffles forthwith declared his intention to attend the dinner and to take Bunny with him.

"To do honor to Mr. Rosenthall?" expostulated Bunny.

"Yes, exactly," Raffles confirmed, sweeping his friend along en route for the Albany.

"But why?" demanded Bunny with some truculence, which was quite unlike him.

"Haven't you read about him in the evening newspapers?" inquired Raffles with surprise. "He's rich as Croesus. A multimillionaire!"

So much Bunny had already gleaned but saw in this no cause to honor a man he also believed to be a notorious ruffian, a bully and a bad character. Indeed he gave it as his considered opinion, as the pair gained access to Raffles's rooms, that the club's inexplicable willingness to entertain such a man was indisputable evidence of the evil days on which it had fallen.

Having wrung from him at last the cause of his objections to Mr. Rosenthall, Raffles inquired of Bunny:

"How do you know him to be a ruffian and a bully and the rest of it?"

"By reading about him."

"Ah!" breathed Raffles, as thoug illumination had at last appeared and made all clear. He lifted his chin, a gesture which lent his handsome face a somewhat arrogant cast, and drawled: "You believe what you read in newspapers. I myself don't believe they can be trusted to get anything right, except perhaps the cricket scores. I think Rosenthall deserves to be given the benefit of the doubt."

But Bunny, who had evidently made up his mind irrevocably, was not to be so easily persuaded.

"What doubt?" he asked, with a hint of scorn in his voice.

"I myself was on the club committee that decided to invite him. I might say that I persuaded the committee."

Having made this revelation Raffles paused, covertly studying the confused and astonished expression on his friend's countenance, before continuing in harsher vein.

"And I find it a bit hard," said he, "that my own childhood friend refuses to back me up."

The barb struck home. The war between his feelings

45

about the rascally Rosenthall, as he supposed him, and his much deeper loyalty to Raffles, to whom he owed so much more than his present solvency, showed clearly on Bunny's transparent face.

"Honestly, Raffles, I didn't realize . . . I wouldn't have dreamed . . . If I'd known that it was *your* idea . . ." he stammered.

"You know now," Raffles coolly reminded him.

"Yes. I'm sorry."

"So you'll come to the dinner?"

"Well . . . I . . ."

"For my sake?" wheedled Raffles, displaying a sudden flash of that charm against which Bunny could muster neither defense nor argument.

In this way it was decided that Bunny should accompany his dear comrade and leader to the dinner. It proved, despite apprehensions to the contrary, a pleasant enough affair for the most part. Raffles could have wished that more than the twenty or so members who sat at table could have seen fit to attend, but he confided to Bunny that he deemed the number sufficient to impress the colonial gentleman.

For his part, Bunny stared in awe at the guest of honor and his companion. Reuben Rosenthall was a big, burly, brute of a man whose very appearance seemed to give ocular proof of the opinion Bunny had earlier formed of him. His florid face was fringed with a vast red beard, while both his wealth and his innate vulgarity were ostentatiously displayed by two gigantic diamonds worn respectively on his swelling shirtfront and his little finger. They gleamed with a purple glow, every bit as dazzling as the sharp glint in Raffles's eyes on beholding them. Beside the guest of honor sat his constant companion and, some said, bodyguard. He was an ugly, powerful man, once famed for his prowess in the ring. His name was Billy Purvis.

At last the glasses were charged with port and Digby, then president of the Old Bohemian, rose to propose the loyal toast. The gentlemen sprang to their feet with military precision and drank to Her Majesty. All, that is, save Rosenthall and Purvis, whose slovenly stance and careless mumbling of the toast did nothing to ameliorate Bunny's poor opinion of them. On completion of the toast permission was given to smoke, much to Raffles's relief. He immediately produced his silver cigarette case and offered Bunny a Sullivan, gratefully lighting one for himself.

"Now for the fun," he whispered.

"Fun?" demanded Bunny, who could not envisage any such likelihood in that company.

"The speeches," Raffles elucidated. "I fancy they will be amusing."

Not so that of the president, whom Raffles *sotto voce* dubbed an ass in Bunny's ear. Fumbling, halting and displaying not a little embarrassment, Digby attempted to extol the virtues of Mr. Rosenthall, the self-made Diamond King of South Africa, whom he accurately and to general laughter likened to one of his own rough diamonds.

Happily, Raffles was not to be altogether disappointed of his fun. Rosenthall lumbered to his feet on being invited to reply to the toast of welcome and forthwith demanded more brandy, retaining the timorous waiter and uncivilly requesting a double measure. Then, in an accent unmistakably Cockney in origin, but overlaid with that of South Africa, he commenced his singular speech.

"Gentlemen. I call you 'gentlemen' because that's what *you* called *me* and because 'gentlemen' means you ain't poor. You ain't poor like I used to be. But you ain't rich like I am now. Nobody ain't rich like I am now. I could buy up the whole lot of you and never know the difference."

Bunny shot Raffles an alarmed yet knowing look, but the latter refused to meet his eye. He stared instead at the speaker with amused fascination.

"You asked my money here," Rosenthall went bluntly on, "in the hope that some of it would stay here. But I ain't such a mug as all that. No, if you want to rob me, you come and rob me fair and square. And if you do you'll find three Kaffirs on the premises who worked down the mines with me when I started. And Billy Purvis, my mate."

"Right," agreed the pugilist, frowning monstrously at the assembled company.

"And me. Now Billy, he knows how to handle his fist and so do I."

"Right again," asserted Purvis.

"And we'll be pleased to take on any of you gentlemen, if you cares to call."

Rosenthall downed his brandy at a gulp, calling at once for more and bidding the trembling waiter to replenish Purvis's glass at the same time.

"To prove," resumed the Diamond King, "I'm as good a man as any of you, and better, which of you goes round with a diamond like this in his shirt front? And another like this on his finger? I wouldn't take fifty thousand pounds for the two of 'em. Now you show me the man who wears twenty-five thousand pounds on his chest, and another twenty-five thousand on his finger. You can't," he sneered, " 'cos there isn't one, except me. He doesn't exist. And if he did he wouldn't have the guts to wear 'em. But I have. And here's why."

To the astonishment and alarm of the gentlemen, Rosenthall drew an ugly-looking revolver from his pocket and brandished it wildly at them. Purvis whispered to him uneasily.

"Billy," came the reply. "Go over there and let me shoot a sovereign out of your hand."

"No," declined Purvis. "Don't be a fool, Rube."

Rosenthall ignored his friend's counsel.

"See that wall over there?" he shouted. "I'll write my initials on it. R. for Reuben and for Rosenthall. Same as I'll write my initials on anyone I catch trying to take away what's mine."

The nervous protestations of Digby, who rose at that moment, were lost in the sharp and repeated retorts of the revolver as Rosenthall emptied its chamber into the wall. When, in the ensuing silence, those gentlemen who had sought sanctuary under the dining table cautiously raised their heads, it was to see a rough R. inscribed on the designated wall. Alone among the company, Raffles was clearly impressed.

"There!" said Rosenthall, with unconcealed pride. "Now does anyone want to try to get the better of me?"

The instinct born of intimate friendship enabled Bunny to divine the impulse which seized Raffles. For one moment he feared his friend would leap up there and then and accept the insolent challenge. Quietly, in a warning voice, Bunny spoke Raffles's name.

Rosenthall meanwhile pocketed his weapon and drained his glass. At a sign from him, Purvis stood up.

"Don't fret," Rosenthall said condescendingly, "I'll pay for a new wall."

And with this promise, the two extraordinary guests hurried from the room and from the club.

Later that evening a rather morose Bunny slumped

in a comfortable chair before Raffles's Albany hearth, while his host, who had been silent for some time, poured them whisky nightcaps.

"The devil of it is, Bunny," Raffles mused, "I have set my heart on having those diamonds. I was only sorry I couldn't get on my hind legs and say so."

"You very nearly did," Bunny reminded him.

"Lucky for me I managed to restrain myself," he retorted dismissively, quite having overlooked Bunny's timely, steadying word. "I have had those diamonds on my conscience for some time. One couldn't hear so much about them without longing to have a go for them, but when it's a question of Rosenthall practically challenging the world, the thing becomes inevitable."

"Of course," Bunny said, accepting his nightcap, "I'm your man. But I don't actually see the necessity. We've got enough to live on for months."

"Necessity, my dear Bunny?" Raffles said, his eyebrows arched in amused condescension. "Does the writer write only when the wolf is at the door? Does the painter paint for bread alone? Must you and I be driven to crime like 'Arry of Bethnal Green and Dick of Whitechapel?' "

On this lofty, interrogatory note Raffles paused, settling his foot comfortably on the fender and contemplating his whisky nightcap. Bunny, sensing that Raffles was in philosophical mood, kept silence.

"You pain me, my dear chap. Art for art's sake is a vile catch phrase, but I confess it appeals to me. And I am an artist," he asserted.

"An artistic thief?" suggested Bunny.

"In this case my motives are absolutely pure. I thieve for the sake of thieving. If I don't have a try for those diamonds, by heavens, Bunny, I shall never be able to hold my head up again!" he cried with sudden resolution.

In the months that had passed since his happy reunion with Raffles, Bunny had learned much, and chief among his lessons was the fruitlessness of seeking to dissuade the great man once he had set his mind upon a course of action. In fact, Bunny could muster only two arguments against this present determination and they were, firstly, that they did not need the money since the Lochmaben tiara had proved a prize indeed, and secondly, that going for Rosenthall's diamonds would be exceedingly dangerous. Not that Bunny was the sort to flinch at danger, as Raffles well knew. It was rather a lethargic caution, endemic in the man, that saw no point in running unnecessary risks. Raffles, of course, was of an entirely different sort and, in the event, Bunny advanced neither of his objections. Privately he wondered if the inevitable close of the cricket season was responsible for this restlessness in his friend. For, truth to tell, Bunny had feared some such renewal of criminal activities for some weeks. Yet there was nothing for it but to go along. As cheerfully as he could manage, Bunny asked:

"What do we do?"

"I must plan the operation," Raffles replied abstractedly. "That will mean my watching the house. It will mean a week's work at least; it may mean lots of other things that will take longer."

"But why shouldn't we both watch the house?" queried Bunny.

"Because two eyes are as good as four, and they take up less room," Raffles said wisely. "There'll be plenty for you to do when the time comes—that is, if you're really in?"

"Of course I am!" Bunny said. "You can't leave me out of it."

"You shall have your share of the fun, that I promise you, and a purple diamond all to yourself," Raffles promised enthusiastically. "Come back in a week, there's a good chap."

That week—for Raffles's tone had been unmistakably one of dismissal—proved a salutary experience for Bunny. He was determined to play the game and to obey Raffles to the letter, even though it irked him to be cooling his heels while his friend was busily plotting and scheming. Yet these annoyances were nothing compared to the loss of Raffles's company. Bunny had cash and acquaintances in plenty. He might go about as he pleased and lead the only life for which he was suited, that of a leisured gentleman, but without Raffles as companion all that he did seemed to lack savor. By the middle of the week Bunny was reduced to staying in all day at Mount Street, anxious for some word from Raffles, and staring longingly at the calendar from which he crossed the slow days with impatience. But no word came even when the week had passed. Having fulfilled his part of the bargain, Bunny went boldly to the Albany and inquired of the porter if Mr. Raffles was at home. He was not, and to that interminable week another interminable day was added. Early the next morning, Bunny again presented himself at the Albany, this time certain of encountering his friend before he could set about his business. But again Bunny was disappointed. Two alarming prospects now began to tease at Bunny's mind. Either Raffles had decided to exclude him altogether from the plan, or something had occurred to prevent him from contacting Bunny. All day Bunny pondered these possibilities. If the first hypothesis were true then Bunny meant to have it out with him. If the latter were the case, then Bunny's duty was quite clear. Whatever proved to be the explanation, Bunny felt justified in seeking Raffles out and demanding an explanation.

It was late afternoon when Bunny reached this resolve and dusk when he arrived in St. John's Wood. He felt better now that he had determined on action and quite proud of himself for thinking to look for Raffles at the scene of the intended crime. The house which Reuben Rosenthall had rented stood on the corner of a pleasantly leafy suburban road. It was a large, square house, fronted by a semicircular drive which bordered plots of grass and shrubs. The gates at either end of the drive stood open when Bunny arrived and the house, in spite of dim lights burning within, had an unoccupied appearance. In the thickening twilight, Bunny stood and looked at the house with considerable curiosity. It would be jolly, he thought, to stroll up the drive and take just a peep inside. Raffles momentarily forgotten, and gripped by the excitement of the moment, Bunny stepped forward and would have continued openly to the house had he not heard a shuffling step behind him.

Nervously, Bunny swung around and found himself contemplating a hideous scrap of humanity. The gnarled and dirty face of a tramp peered up at him from beneath the brim of a battered billycock. This headgear was the only recognizable article of human clothing about the figure. The rest was, at least at first glance, a mere random heap of shredded rags. Yet the voice which issued from this bent and shambling creature, who hissed: "You fool! You utter idiot!" struck in Bunny a chord of instant and happy recognition.

"Raffles!" he cried with surprised pleasure.

"That's right," grumbled Raffles. "Give me away. Tell all the neighborhood."

With this, the tramp turned away from him and began a slow, limping exodus down the road, muttering loudly about the meanness of supposed gentlemen. Bunny stared after the figure for a moment, and then slowly began to follow him. At last the figure found a pool of deep shadows into which it disappeared. Bunny increased his pace, fearing to lose his friend, but the sudden flaring of a match told him that Raffles now deemed it safe to speak to him. That signaling match was, when Bunny hurried up to him, being applied to a foul-smelling pipe on which Raffles puffed with every appearance of enjoyment.

"You must forgive my heat, Bunny," he said as the young man drew close, "but it really was very foolish of you."

"Why?" asked Bunny innocently.

"Why?" Standing and staring at the house! And you were going to walk up to it and look in the windows."

Bunny could not deny it, although he still could not see anything so very wrong in it.

"Here I am," complained Raffles, "trying all kinds of dodges—begging at the door, hiding in the shrubbery. . . . This is a costume piece, Bunny, and you rush in in your ordinary clothes! I tell you, they're on the lookout for us night and day."

"Well, if you'd told me so before, I shouldn't have come," Bunny defended himself sulkily. "It's only because you didn't tell me."

Raffles puffed contemplatively on his evil pipe for a moment or two.

"Perhaps you're right," he said. "I've been too quiet."

"And you said, 'Come in a week,' and I went to

your rooms and you were out and. . . ." Bunny said, pressing home his advantage.

"I'm going to walk to the Finchley Road," Raffles interrupted him, glancing up and down the deserted thoroughfare. "I want you to follow me, but for heaven's sake keep your distance and don't speak to me again until I speak to you. That won't be," he added, as he began to shamble off, "until I've gone home. And I don't mean the Albany either, all right?"

Thus began a journey that Bunny was never to forget. Recalling it later, it most resembled those journeys we sometimes make in our nightmares, journeys as tortuous and unfathomable as the nature of man himself. It began, as Raffles had promised, in the Finchley Road where Bunny was subjected to the novel experience of riding in an omnibus. Any pleasure he might have taken in the event was, however, nullified by the choking reek of Raffles's pipe and his anxiety as to their destination. For a moment, as Raffles dismounted at Piccadilly, Bunny thought that he must have misheard and that the Albany was, after all, to be their goal. How, he wondered, would a tramp, and such an unsavory tramp at that, gain entrance to that august establishment? But Bunny had not misheard and was soon conveyed to Sloane Street, by courtesy of a second omnibus which Raffles once again exchanged for a third, alighting finally in the King's Road Chelsea.

From the way Raffles set off, shuffling and swaying, down that thoroughfare, Bunny deduced that their flirtation with the omnibus was at an end. And oh, how his feet longed for a carriage! But tramps did not hail hansom cabs and, besides, Raffles soon led him where no carriage could possibly penetrate. This was a maze of unlit, twisting alleys which lay to the south of the King's Road. Dank and dark alleys, the like of which

Bunny had never before seen. Nor would he have done so now were it not for the glimpsed figure of Raffles ahead, turning and burrowing yet more deeply into this sinister hinterland, which presently became eerily misted by wisps of river fog. The necessity to keep his costumed friend in sight, a task aggravated by the fog, left Bunny scant time for reflection or apprehension. At last Raffles turned into a flagged passage which, Bunny was almost certain, contained no exit. He slowed his steps with instinctive caution. Ahead of him, no more than a darker shadow in the darkness, he saw Raffles approach and enter a building which blocked the end of the alleyway. When he reached the point Bunny found himself, his heart beating fast and loudly, facing a closed door. He found and turned the handle and the door opened at once. Holding his breath, Bunny stepped into the total darkness within.

That darkness, however, was total only for a moment. At the far end of the room a gas mantle glowed, sputtered, gained strength and at last revealed Raffles, now upright in the stance of the athlete and gentleman he was. Relieved, Bunny turned to survey the strange room they had entered. It was lofty, with a large skylight against which the October night pressed ominously. It was barely furnished. A cheap bed, a washbasin in one corner and, as though to provide a focus and an explanation, an easel on which was set up an unpainted canvas. A row of pegs held Raffles's evening dress suit, his cloak and topcoat.

"Do you like it, Bunny?" Raffles inquired, divesting himself of some of his rags and moving to the basin where he commenced to remove the grime which adorned his features.

"Is it yours?" asked Bunny, who was still experiencing some difficulty in fitting Raffles into this place.

56

"I am its lawful tenant. Though I need hardly tell you that my name is not Raffles here. The landlord only lets to artists but, as you know, I'm an artist in my way. That's the canvas," he said, nodding toward the easel. "I'm always going to make a start on, just as soon as I've found my ideal model."

"And you use it as a dressing room?" Bunny guessed as Raffles changed swiftly into his more familiar garb.

"It's useful for that," he agreed, "and there's no saying how useful it might be for something else at a pinch."

"You never told me about this place," Bunny reproached him. "As your friend, I think you might have," he added.

"Circumstances are conceivable in which it would have suited us both for you to be in genuine ignorance of my whereabouts. We can't always have the luck on our side, Bunny. The day may come when I have to run for my life to escape the long arm of the law. One might bolt farther and fare a good deal worse than this place. And I'd like to have you with that splendidly honest bewilderment on your face, swearing perfectly truthfully that you've no idea where I've gone. D'you see?" he concluded, taking a Sullivan from his cigarette case and lighting it with evident pleasure.

"Yes, I see," Bunny conceded. "But I don't so much like your valuing me for my honest bewilderment."

"And for many other things too!" Raffles assured him. "Have a Sullivan? You've no idea how good they are after that filthy shag."

Bunny accepted the cigarette and listened while Raffles explained the virtues of his studio and revealed that a large cupboard against one wall contained a variety of disguises, ostensibly intended for models when he finally set about his painting, but which had frequently helped him in his criminal career.

"I only hope I've got something that'll fit you," he broke off suddenly, looking at Bunny with a tailor's eye.

"Me? Why?"

"You'll want a costume for when we have a go at Rosenthall's place."

"Oh," said Bunny brightly. "When will that be?"

"I don't know yet," replied Raffles offhand.

"I take it rather badly of you, Raffles, that you still won't trust me enough to tell me your plans," Bunny said testily.

"My dear Bunny! I apologize profusely." Raffles smiled. "I had intended to write to you as soon as it was the right moment to go for the diamonds. I was going to ask you to look me up at the Albany and I was going to unfold my plan and take you straight into action, then and there. There's nothing like putting the nervous players in straightaway," he added cheerfully.

"Do you think I'm a nervous player?" Bunny asked, a trifle hurt.

"You must try to forgive me," Raffles said. "I was thinking of how well you played on our last trip, when you hadn't any time to weaken beforehand. Believe me, you've got to be even cooler and smarter on this job," he cautioned, his face suddenly growing serious. "Rosenthall and Purvis are a lot tougher opposition than Lord Lochmaben and Alick Carruthers."

"I thought you would find them so," Bunny said in a tone which might have been mistaken for crowing.

"All the more credit to us for lifting the diamonds!" Raffles beamed. "And the first move in the game is to have a jolly good dinner, with a bottle of wine, while I tell you my adventures in St. John's Wood."

58

This was a most pleasant prospect, but one for which, Bunny was constrained to point out, he was not suitably dressed. Raffles soothed him by promising that they would call in at Bunny's flat on their way to dine.

"Where shall it be? The club? I can think of no better place to plot Rosenthall's downfall," Raffles cried happily, leading the way.

And so it was to the Old Bohemian that, with the benefit of a cab, which obligingly waited in Mount Street while Bunny changed, they repaired within the hour. Raffles, after his long sojourn away from the benefits of such institutions, could think of no greater pleasures than those which awaited him as he ordered dinner. However, the scarred wall, sole memento of Rosenthall's visit to the club, was sufficient to boost his resolve to have those diamonds.

While they waited for the meal, Raffles told Bunny about the irregular hours kept by Rosenthall and Purvis, hours which threatened to make their task even more difficult. Yet to offset this difficulty Raffles confessed that he had gleaned one potentially useful piece of information. After a night's heavy drinking, Raffles had overheard a quarrel between the boxer and the Diamond King during which Purvis had openly taunted Rosenthall with the fact that he was wanted in South Africa for illicit diamond buying. Judging from the response this brought forth from Rosenthall, Raffles had no doubts that the charge was true.

At that moment the wine waiter approached and Raffles, after a moment's consideration, ordered the Chambertin, remarking pleasantly that the wine was reputed to have been Napoleon's favorite tipple.

"And Mr. Rosenthall's, too," said the waiter dourly.

"Oh, really?" said Raffles.

"He downed three bottles that night we had him as a

guest. Not to speak of the brandy afterwards. But it was the Chambertin that started him off," the waiter related. " 'Don't have stuff like this in South Africa,' he kept saying. Wanted to know where we got it."

"Did you tell him?" Raffles inquired curiously.

"I was going to, but by then he'd started shooting," replied the waiter with a shudder. "I'll fetch your Chambertin, sir."

"Interesting," said Raffles as the waiter moved out of hearing.

"Mm," said Bunny, who did not think it so particularly. "So, what do you mean to do?"

"Get in when Rosenthall and Purvis have gone out, and get out before they come back," Raffles replied with every appearance of believing that the matter truly was that simple.

"But," said Bunny with some pride, "Rosenthall always wears those diamonds in his evening dress when he goes out in the evening."

"Then we must make sure this is one evening when he is not in evening dress," smiled Raffles pleasantly, turning his attention to the hors d'oeuvres.

Of course, Bunny could appreciate this, but he did not see how it might be done, nor did Raffles then feel disposed to enlighten him. And Bunny, for his part, was content to leave the matter there, having had sufficient adventure for one day and being concerned now simply to enjoy the company of his old and much-missed friend.

The very next morning Raffles, in his capacity as a member of the Wine Committee of the Old Bohemian, visited the eminent establishment which supplied the club's cellar and, while discussing vintages with the knowledge and discrimination of a connoisseur, helped himself to two sheets of the firm's impressively headed notepaper. On this, with Bunny's aid, he later penned an invitation to Mr. Reuben Rosenthall. Couched in the most flattering terms, the invitation promised a selection of wines and a cold buffet, besought Mr. Rosenthall to bring as many guests as he liked, and casually added that dress would be informal.

"There!" said Raffles, waving the sheet in the air. "That should do the trick. I've given him a choice of dates, Bunny, in case he's otherwise engaged."

"But how will you know which date he's going to come?"

With a sigh of sorely tried patience, Raffles fixed his friend with a grave eye.

"By reading his answer, of course."

To obtain which, Raffles had to acquire and don the uniform of a post-office employee. Thus garbed he began to loiter around the mailbox closest to the Rosenthall mansion, from which, at last, he retrieved the letter of reply to his invitation. To Raffles's delight, Rosenthall had accepted, and while he was out on this carefully contrived wild-goose chase, Raffles and Bunny would pay him a visit.

"*En travesti!*" Raffles announced happily.

"What?" said Bunny.

"My dear Bunny, if we are to play the part of burglars, we must dress the part. I told you this was a costume piece."

And so, the following Friday night, Bunny found himself once again in Raffles's Chelsea studio. There he put on trousers of a rough material and a striped jersey.

"All I need is a mask," he said, surveying himself in the glass.

Raffles, who was similarly attired, threw him one.

"And a sack labeled SWAG in large letters. . . ." Bunny added, slipping the mask into his pocket.

"Sorry, haven't got one," Raffles said.

"Then I'd be the spitting image of a comic burglar in *Alley Sloper's Half Holiday*."

"That is the whole virtue of your getup," Raffles explained. "The last thing you want to do is to announce your identity. Like that you'll pass for Whitechapel if the worst comes to the worst, and you don't forget to talk the lingo."

"I'm not very good at Cockney," Bunny said doubtfully.

"If you're not sure of it, better sulk like a mule, and leave the dialogue to me."

"Right."

"Mask in your pocket?"

"Yes."

"Shooter in your other pocket?"

"Yes."

"Don't use it unless you have to."

"I won't," Bunny promised.

"Come on then, I'd treat you to a cab, but an omnibus is more our style, don't you think?"

The friends made the long journey by omnibus from Chelsea to St. John's Wood. Raffles seemed perfectly at home, peering out into the dim and largely deserted gas-lit streets and addressing Bunny occasionally in a ripe Cockney accent. Once again Bunny had cause to admire the skill and ingenuity of his friend, a true gentleman who could yet alter himself to fit even this unsalubrious background.

By good fortune, the rowdy and nocturnal habits of Reuben Rosenthall and his prizefighter friend had driven the occupants of the house next door to theirs to seek the peace of the countryside. This fact Raffles had ascertained during his long surveillance of the premises, and so it was with confidence that he led Bunny to a secluded spot in the shrubbery adjacent to the low stone wall which bounded Rosenthall's property. There they lay in wait, their spirits lifting when a coach and pair drove up to the house. The driver stepped down smartly and knocked on the front door. This was opened by a dusky Kaffir, one of several who made up the entire and bizarre domestic staff of the establishment.

After a while, Rosenthall and Purvis emerged, arguing and calling to each other in loud voices. Their departure, however, was delayed by the desire for brandy, two large glasses of which were brought to them in the coach by a second Kaffir. At last, fortified by that fiery beverage and shouting vulgar epithets at one another, the pair set out on their journey.

"Give it another minute," Raffles whispered. "The state they're in they may have forgotten something and decide to come back for it."

They waited, but there was no sign of any return. The silence was complete. Bunny stared toward the house which was now mostly in darkness, dim lights in the back rooms and only the hall indicating the presence of the Kaffirs. Quietly, Raffles told him to put his mask on and slipped his own over his handsome features.

"What about the Kaffirs?" Bunny asked nervously.

"I'll lay long odds that the sight of you in that mask will scare any Kaffir ever born," Raffles said.

"Really?" said Bunny, rather pleased at the prospect.

"You may have to tickle them up a bit with your shooter, too," Raffles conceded.

"You don't mean kill them?" Bunny said in alarm and too loud.

"Good Lord, no! Killing's not in our game," Raffles said, shocked. "Ready?"

"Ready."

"Follow me."

Lithely, Raffles slid silently over the garden wall. Bunny followed as quietly as he could. It was Raffles's belief that the Kaffirs would be in the kitchen cooking up a supper of mealies and that their dread of their master would make them extremely reluctant to enter any of the main rooms. Like a shadow, treading lightly on rubber-soled shoes, Raffles glided across the gravel and up to the facade of the house. There, as his earlier surveillance had shown him, was a most convenient pair of french windows, and to them, closely followed by Bunny, he went. Swiftly he ran his hands over the windows and, with a gasp of surprise, found that they yielded at the lightest touch. Motioning to Bunny, Raffles led the way into the house.

"Close the curtains," he hissed, producing a pocket torch.

When Bunny had done so, Raffles switched on the torch, directing its discreet beam around a large and well-appointed room. It came to rest upon the top of an ornate mahogany desk, in the very center of which lay a bunch of keys.

"Luck again," exclaimed Raffles, darting to the desk. "Now where does he keep those diamonds?"

Quickly he tried one of the keys in the lock of the central drawer. It fitted, turned, and when he slid the drawer open, the beam of his torch struck purple fire from the diamonds. A soft whistle of amazement escaped Raffles.

"What incredible luck!" he said. "Take them, Bunny, and put them in your pocket."

Bunny, his eyes fascinated by the gleaming jewels, stretched out his hand to take them when, with a suddenness that completely numbed him, the room was flooded with bright electric light. For a moment, neither he nor Raffles could see against the unaccustomed glare, but as their eyes slowly adjusted, they found themselves face to face with Reuben Rosenthall and Billy Purvis, both holding a revolver in each hand. At the sight of them, Rosenthall roared with laughter. Bunny could not speak, and Raffles thought it wisest not to.

"Good evening, boys," roared Rosenthall. "Glad to meet you at last. Shift foot or finger though and you're dead men. I know you," he said, brandishing a revolver at Raffles. "I've been watching you all week. Plucky smart you thought yourself, didn't you, with your clever disguises? But you weren't as clever as all that. You left the same tracks every day, and every night, all round the blessed premises. And your invitation was a bit suspicious, too, so we dismissed the carriage down the road and came in the back way, specially to make your acquaintance."

Again Rosenthall laughed, hugely enjoying the incompetence of this burglar who had displayed such unexpected ingenuity in casing the job.

"All right, Guv'nor," Raffles said in a Cockney drawl, "it's a fair cop."

"By God it is!" agreed Purvis. "And I've a good mind to plug you for a couple of stinkin' thieves."

"Oh, yes. We know all abaht that," responded Raffles cockily.

"What d'you mean?" growled Rosenthall, a frown furrowing his bull-like forehead.

"Set a thief to catch a thief," Raffles answered enigmatically, but with confidence.

"Spit it out," ordered Rosenthall, "or by Christmas I'll drill you!"

To lend force to his threat, he leveled both pistols at Raffles's chest.

"What price the breakwater then? At Cape Town, you old I.D.B., you."

For a moment Rosenthall stared at this chirpy burglar in amazement. Then a chortle of mirth escaped him.

"Where the hell did you get hold of that?" he demanded.

"It's all over the place where I come from," Raffles assured him.

"Is it? And who started it going all over the place?"

"I dunno. Ask the gen'leman on your left. P'raps he knows."

At this Rosenthall turned toward Purvis who was plainly discomfited.

"Did you, Billy?" Rosenthall asked in a menacing tone.

Being a pugilist, Purvis preferred fists to guns, and believed that attack was the best form of defense. He therefore pocketed his pistols, bunched his hamlike fists and with an incoherent growl advanced upon Raffles. In order to do so he had no choice but to interpose himself between the yet armed Rosenthall and his prey. For a split second, then, Raffles was obscured as the ogrelike shadow of Purvis fell across his slighter but more athletic figure. Seizing his moment, Raffles threw himself toward the french windows just as Rosenthall, seeing the trick, shouted for Purvis to get out of the way. Too late. Raffles was already speeding away from the house. And it was also too late for

Bunny. That young man, released as from a spell by Raffles's swift movements, turned a fraction more slowly toward the windows and received a felling blow from Purvis for his pains. He collapsed unconscious on the floor as Rosenthall burst out of the room in pursuit of Raffles. But there was no sign of him. Furiously Rosenthall fired two useless shots into the air. Reason, however, insisted that the escapee could not have gone far and he ordered Purvis out into the garden where they conducted a thorough search. Throughout, Rosenthall cross-questioned his now doubted friend about Raffles's charge, but Purvis remained steadfast in his denials.

During the moments of this search, Bunny slowly regained his senses. Cautiously he opened one eye and found himself staring into the wild faces of three Kaffirs who were stooping over him with upraised clubs. However, he also saw that his masked visage struck them with at least as much terror as they induced in him. Once again, he had time to reflect, Raffles had proved to be correct in his surmise. And thought of Raffles reminded him not only of his plight but of the pistol in his pocket. Feigning more dizziness than he actually felt, Bunny struggled up and surreptitiously snatched the revolver from his pocket. Holding it at arm's length, he rounded on the petrified natives.

"All right," he said in a shaky voice. "Put those clubs down and put your hands up, or I'll shoot you full of holes. I will," he assured them, waggling the gun.

Muttering in some foreign tongue, the three Kaffirs dropped their rude weapons and backed against the wall.

"And stay there until I'm gone," Bunny ordered

boldly, taking a cautious step backward toward the windows.

At the same moment there was a deafening report and the gun spun from Bunny's hand as though ripped away by some terrible mysterious force. Smiling, Rosenthall stepped through the french windows, his smoking pistol proudly displayed.

"Some shooting, eh?" he said with cruel geniality. "I used to be Buffalo Bill in a traveling circus 'fore I made my pile," he added by way of explanation. Then he rounded on the Kaffirs, abusing them and dismissing them with ugly promises of punishments to come.

"And you," he sneered, turning back to Bunny. "You thought you were going to get away, did you? Not bloody likely! Right, let's have a look at you."

So saying he reached out a massive hand and roughly tore the mask from Bunny's face.

"You're a baby-face, ain't you?" he mocked, on seeing Bunny's innocent, boyish physiognomy. "Where's your big brother, then? Run off and left you all alone?"

Bunny would not deign to reply to these sneering taunts. Besides, he minded Raffles's advice concerning his lack of expertise in the Cockney lingo.

"So you tried to take my diamonds, did you? I said, did you? Answer me, blast you!"

"No," Bunny said, blushing.

"Don't want to answer me, eh?" Rosenthall said, his face becoming sly behind his fiery beard. "Why? 'Cos you're afraid your voice might give you away? Is that it? Are you a gentleman in disguise, eh?" he guessed with alarming accuracy.

"No!" Bunny exclaimed quickly, but even to his own ears, the single syllable sounded in the undeniable accents of Uppingham.

68

It was evident from Rosenthall's pleased expression that he, too, had noticed that, whatever he was, Bunny was no common burglar.

"How did you get mixed up with that pal of yours, then?" Rosenthall wanted to know. "He's a proper Cockney and no mistake." Reaching out he grabbed Bunny by the front of his striped jersey and pulled him horribly close. "Where did he go to? Where's he hiding? I'd like to find out where he got that tale of me being an illicit diamond buyer, 'cos the man who told him that tale is going to suffer for it."

"Quite right, too," interjected Purvis, who now advanced upon the quaking Bunny. " 'Cos whoever it was, it wasn't me."

"Where's he gone then, your pal? Tell us and we'll let you go free," Rosenthall promised.

"You can go to hell," Bunny said loudly and fearlessly.

"You going to let him talk to you like that?" demanded Purvis in a shocked tone.

"You go and get me a length of whipcord from that storeroom under the stairs," Rosenthall snarled, still obviously suspicious of his bodyguard.

Cowed, the prizefighter did as he was bid. Rosenthall looked from Bunny to the open drawer where the diamonds lay, shining and tempting.

"Now, you come for those diamonds, didn't you?" he asked. "You want only an arm's length away from you. Why not take 'em? Reach out your hand and take 'em, go on. Try and see what happens."

"No thank you," said Bunny politely.

"You afraid of my gun? There's nothing to be afraid of. I'd just shoot your fingers off, one by one, that's all."

Just then Purvis reappeared, carrying a length of

whipcord. At a sign from Rosenthall, he commenced to tie Bunny's thumbs painfully together, then his wrists. When these were quite secure, Purvis stooped to bind his ankles.

"Now fasten the rope onto that water pipe, just for fun," Rosenthall ordered, gesturing toward the designated pipe.

When this was done, Rosenthall advanced on Bunny who was quite helpless.

"How you feelin' now? All right, are you?" he asked, giving Bunny such a blow in the chest that he could not prevent him falling to the floor. "Forgive us for the moment, will you?" Rosenthall bent over him, speaking with mock politeness. "We'll be back as soon as we've had our supper," he promised, aiming a kick at Bunny before leading Purvis out of the room.

Bunny struggled as hard as he could against the bonds which rendered him helpless, but his struggles only succeeded in making the cords cut more painfully into his flesh. From another part of the house he heard the unmistakable sounds of carousing. A shudder passed through him, for he knew that Rosenthall inebriated would present an ever greater threat to his safety than Rosenthall sober. Oh, where was Raffles! At that moment he would have given anything in the world for sight of his friend's face, the sound of his voice. He was torn between hope that Raffles had got far away and the devout wish that he would return while Rosenthall was otherwise occupied to slice through his bonds with a keen blade. This thought made him renew his struggles with desperation.

The voices which reached Bunny were indeed fortified by alcohol. Rosenthall was a worried man. Raffles's jibe about his nefarious activities in his adopted country worked like a thorn in his flesh. Veering between suspicions of Purvis and the need for his consolation, he drank more than his usual excessive amount. Purvis, aware of his friend's uncertain temper, did his best to placate and reassure him, but Rosenthall refused to listen. At Purvis's suggestion that they should send for the police, hand Bunny over and have done with it, he flew into a rage and staggered out of the dining room and down the passage to where Bunny lay still bound.

The sight of him, fresh-faced and unmistakably a gentleman even in that undignified posture, sparked something in Rosenthall's brain. As the thought took shape he pulled Bunny up and said:

"I've seen you before, haven't I?"

"No," said Bunny, alarmed and simultaneously offended by the reek of alcohol on his tormentor's breath.

"At that club." Rosenthall pursued his thought doggedly. "You an Old Bohemian?"

"No," Bunny said, glad that he could answer truthfully, for it was Raffles who was a member, not he.

"Anyway," said Rosenthall thickly. "Listen. You're going to tell me who told you that story about me in South Africa."

"What story?" asked Bunny at his most innocent.

"That damned lying story about me being I.D.B."

"I'm not going to tell you anything," Bunny retorted.

"Not to oblige me?"

"No."

"Right," said Rosenthall, releasing him and withdrawing several paces. As he did so he pulled a revolver from his pocket.

"You still sure you don't want to tell me?" he asked.

"I'm not going to tell you anything," Bunny repeated stoutly, trying not to look at the gun.

"P'raps you don't know," Rosenthall mused shrewdly. "P'raps only that Cockney pal of yours knows. Where do I find him, eh? Where is he?"

"You'll never find him," Bunny said, feeling suddenly glad and proud that Raffles had escaped and, in that particular at least, had succeeded in baffling this villain.

"Tell me," Rosenthall thundered, "or I'll blow you into the middle of next week."

"Steady on, Rube. It'll be murder," said Purvis from behind the swaying man.

"Just want to make him talk," Rosenthall said gruffly.

"I know. But if you hit him, you're in for it. It'll be murder."

"He's a burglar, ain't he?" declared Rosenthall.

"Yes, but he's unarmed and tied hand and foot. It's plain murder," Purvis insisted.

"Untie him then. Give him a chance. Then I can shoot him while attempting to escape." He grinned with sadistic pleasure.

"You're drunk," Purvis said. "Pull yourself together. You ain't a-going to do what you'll be sorry for."

"I said untie him!" bellowed Rosenthall. "I won't shoot at him. I'll only shoot round and round. I wouldn't hurt him. You untie him."

Reluctantly Purvis crossed the room and quickly unfastened Bunny's bonds. The latter, who had observed the state of things carefully, rubbed his chafed wrists and awaited developments expectantly.

"Now behave like a sensible man," Purvis advised Rosenthall, moving away from Bunny.

"Sensible man," agreed Rosenthall. "Just want to ask him. Do you know who told that wicked story about me?"

"Yes," Bunny said promptly.

A look of savage eagerness crept over Rosenthall's florid features. He leaned forward anxiously.

"Who?" he whispered.

"He did," Bunny said casually, nodding at Purvis.

"I never . . ." he shouted, moving toward Bunny with clenched and upraised fists.

Two shots rang out in quick succession. To Bunny's appalled amazement he saw the pugilist's hands unclench with the impact of the bullets, one in each hand. He turned his face away while Purvis stared at his mutilated fists in shocked bewilderment.

"Rube," he groaned. "What did you do?"

"You told him," he accused.

"I never, Rube. Honor bright."

"Then who did?"

"I don't know. But it wasn't me."

Something in Purvis's voice evidently reached Rosenthall's befuddled conscience. Menacingly he turned back to Bunny, the gun horribly raised.

"Is that the truth? Last chance, mind. Last chance, or I shoot," he vowed, taking aim at Bunny's heart.

"Now, then, what's going on in here, eh?"

Simultaneously, all three men turned toward the french windows through which a uniformed policeman had stepped. To Bunny this portly, heavily moustached personage appeared as a savior indeed. But it was Purvis, hastily concealing his bleeding hands, and thereby displaying a fortitude that did not fail to impress Bunny, who was first to respond.

"Nothing, officer. Nothing at all," he said through gritted teeth.

"I heard shots from outside," replied the policeman portentously. "What were those shots?"

"Shots?" repeated Purvis.

"Definitely shots," said the policeman, rocking back and forth on his heels.

"Oh, they were . . ."

"We caught a burglar," Rosenthall interrupted, indicating Bunny. "Trying to rob us."

"A burglar, eh?" said the policeman with interest, peering around the room until his eyes lit upon Bunny's gun where it had fallen. "And he was armed, was he?"

"Yes, he was," agreed Purvis quickly.

"So I see. Would you mind picking that up for me, sir?" asked the policeman of Purvis.

The latter, anxious not to reveal the destruction of his hands, glanced nervously at Rosenthall, who grasped the situation.

"Pick it up yourself, can't you?" he retorted rudely.

"Yes, I can, sir," admitted the policeman. "If you're not willing to help."

"Help!" scoffed Rosenthall as the policeman stopped to retrieve Bunny's gun. "A fine lot of help we get from you. Coming when it's all over. We might have been burgled and murdered in our beds."

Ignoring this, the policeman calmly and slowly examined the gun.

"Hasn't been fired," he announced at last. "So I take it the shots I heard were fired by you, sir?"

"Yes, they were," Rosenthall admitted. "To protect my household. I'm entitled to do that, aren't I?"

The policeman gave him a doubtful look and slowly unbuttoned his breast pocket, from which he drew a black notebook.

"Could I know your name, sir?"

Rosenthall gave it promptly and with braggartlike pride, adding unnecessarily that he was known as the Diamond King of South Africa.

74

"Diamonds," said the policeman reflectively. Then, as if he had remembered something that quite clarified the situation, he added: "Oh, yes, we know all about you."

"What d'mean by that?" Rosenthall blustered.

"I just mean they'll be very interested at headquarters to know what happened at your place."

"And why should they be interested?" demanded Rosenthall, openly suspicious.

"Could you show me exactly where those shots of yours went, sir?" asked the policeman coolly.

"What does it matter? They didn't kill anybody."

"No," put in Purvis quickly. "They didn't do no damage to nobody."

The policeman, somewhat grudgingly, made a note in his book and then asked if the gentlemen had actually witnessed the burglary.

"Yes, we did," Rosenthall promptly confirmed.

"And what did you see him taking?"

"He was after those two diamonds in that drawer."

"Ah," said the policeman, advancing toward the desk and peering with interest into the drawer. This maneuver brought him very close to Bunny, yet kept his back toward Purvis and Rosenthall. At first, Bunny was rather taken aback to receive a knowing wink from the policeman but then, more astounding even than his arrival, he made out under the helmet, the walrus moustache, the welcome features of Raffles! His mouth fell open in amazement.

"Very nice," said the policeman. "Total value what? Fifty quid?"

For a moment it seemed likely that Rosenthall would be an immediate victim of apoplexy. It was all Bunny could do not to laugh out loud with relief and delight.

"More like fifty thousand," spluttered Rosenthall at last.

"Yes, well . . ." said the policeman doubtfully. "It looks as though I shall have to take you along with me," he said turning back to Bunny. "Now, are you going to come quietly?"

"Yes," said Bunny brightly. "I'll come quietly."

"Good," said the policeman, producing a pair of handcuffs and snapping one about Bunny's eagerly extended wrist before fastening the other about his own. "Well, I'll be seeing you, sir, at Marylebone Police Station," he informed Rosenthall.

"Do I have to?" said the Diamond King, not at all relishing the prospect.

"We'd like to see you there, sir. I'll tell you when it's to be."

"All right," grumbled Rosenthall.

"Oh, and I'd better take these," he said, as though he might have forgotten, scooping up the diamonds and placing them carefully in his tunic pocket.

"Hey!" protested Rosenthall. "What you taking them for?"

"Material evidence," said the policeman gravely.

"Is that the law?" demanded Rosenthall.

"Have to be produced in court, sir. I'll write you a receipt if you like, but they're quite safe with me. Just remember my number—P.C.43, Marylebone Station."

"I'll remember," promised Rosenthall with a face like thunder.

"Any time after they've been produced in court, you can have 'em back," promised the policeman. "Providing you can produce evidence of ownership, of course."

"What d'you mean?" asked the astounded Rosenthall.

"How you got them, where they came from, things like that," explained the policeman with the air of one who is sorely tried by the legal ignorance of foreigners.

"Listen," threatened Rosenthall, "you blasted coppers . . ."

"You keep a civil tongue in your head," warned the policeman. "Or I'll take you in, too."

At that moment a groan escaped Purvis, who was swaying visibly on his feet.

"You'd better look after that pal of yours," the policeman advised. "He ain't feeling too good. Well, come on, Mr. Burglar, off we go to the station," he said with a sharp jerk on the handcuffs. "Good night, Mr. Rosenthall. We'll be seeing you down at the station, I've no doubt."

So saying, the policeman marched Bunny out of the room and down the corridor to the front door. He did not speak again until they reached the gate.

"All right now," Raffles whispered, turning along the dark street where the silhouette of a waiting carriage could be dimly seen.

Raffles hurried toward it and, with a nod to the driver, scrambled in after the handcuffed Bunny. Immediately he produced a key and unlocked their common fetters.

"How on earth did you manage it?" demanded Bunny, his face positively glowing with admiration.

"Purely by luck," said Raffles, scribbling a note in his book. "It was no trouble at all to get away, but it was a piece of luck I had these togs with the rest of the costumes at the studio. The helmet," he added informatively, "is one of a collection I made up at Oxford. You know it was all the rage then, pinching policemen's helmets. I always thought it might come in useful a second time."

Raffles had finished writing and now he folded the note and addressed it to Scotland Yard.

"What's that for?" inquired Bunny, flexing his sore wrists with relief.

"To allay suspicion and arouse some," Raffles replied enigmatically.

With this Bunny had to be content until the cab drew up at the familiar entrance to the Albany. There, Raffles gripped his arm tightly while instructing the driver to make all haste to Scotland Yard with the message, adding a handsome tip as encouragement.

"I told him we had to stop off here to pick up an accomplice of yours," Raffles explained, removing his helmet and moustache, "and have sent him for aid at once. Good evening," he boldly greeted the porter.

"Good evening, Mr. Raffles," the porter replied, smiling broadly. "Been to a fancy dress do, have you?"

"Yes," laughed Raffles. "A costume piece. Good night."

"Good night, sir."

"But you haven't really sent for the police, have you?" asked Bunny as soon as they were out of earshot of the porter.

"Not sent for, but to," he explained, opening the door to his rooms. "I had to allay our worthy driver's understandable suspicions. But the note he will deliver will send the whole of the detective department to visit Mr. Rosenthall within half an hour. And I like to think they will ask some embarrassing questions."

"I hope they give him as bad a time as he gave me," said Bunny warmly, sinking gratefully into the comfort of one of Raffles's chairs.

"I hope they'll give him a worse time," said Raffles. "Of course, the whole thing was a gamble, but a fair one. I felt he was the man to play with his mouse as long as possible."

"He was," agreed the mouse with a shudder.

"Well, it's been more of a costume piece than I intended, but we've come out of it all right. In fact," he added soberly, "we're very lucky to have come out of it at all. But, in addition . . ."

With that devilish smile that Bunny knew so well, Raffles drew the ring and the shirt stud from his pocket and tossed them like dice onto the table.

"One for you and one for me . . . ." he said gaily, pouring them both a generous measure of Scotch and passing Bunny the box of Sullivans.

Solemnly, the two friends toasted each other while contemplating the purple fire for which so much had been risked.

In due course, the illicit acquisition of those diamonds by Reuben Rosenthall was established by Scotland Yard, who lost no time in taking the appropriate steps. The worthy detectives, however, remained in ignorance of the good use to which they were subsequently put. Not only had their appropriation bound Bunny in eternal gratitude to A. J. Raffles, to whom he truly owed his life, but the cash they raised kept both young men in liquor and cigarettes for many months. If this should be thought a frivolous use of their gains, it should above all be remembered that this money made it possible for Raffles to play for England the following summer!

Three

THE CHEST OF SILVER

••••————◆————••••

IN WHICH BUNNY IS KEPT IN IGNORANCE WHILE RAFFLES TAKES UP CRAMPED QUARTERS AND INSPECTOR MACKENZIE IS GIVEN A SPORTING CHANCE

PART OF A. J. RAFFLES's great success in his unorthodox and unpublicized career may be attributed to his endeavors to keep himself well informed and so at least one step ahead of his enemies. Reason and his knowledge of the dour Scot told him that the mysterious disappearance of Reuben Rosenthall's gems could not fail to arouse the interest of Inspector Mackenzie. And since he knew full well that Mackenzie's interest, once aroused, invariably settled upon himself, it followed as the night the day that Raffles should take precautions. As it happened, a bare month after the nervewracking costume piece, Raffles had no more nefarious plans in mind than the redecoration of his Albany suite and the installation therein of electric light and a telephone receiver. The latter was an instrument which greatly delighted Bunny, who had recently become the proud owner of one on which, as he frequently said, he longed to be able to talk to

Raffles. For himself, Raffles had been much impressed by the dazzling electric lights at Rosenthall's mansion and had set his heart upon illuminating his rooms in this modern fashion. The advantages over gaslight were, to him, self-evident, save that the greater candlepower of electricity would reveal the rather dilapidated state of his decor. This, he knew, would not at all suit the management of the Albany who were justifiably keen on the good upkeep of the rooms. He had therefore repaired to the office to set their minds at rest about the painting and to inform them on the alterations he desired to effect. For his courtesy he received a hint, no more, that a certain party from Scotland Yard had intimated his intention to make a very thorough search of those self-same rooms at some not too distant date. Thus forewarned—a reward which Raffles averred invariably followed from a policy of civility toward managers, porters and others of that ilk—he was able to lay his plans.

He was, in fact, perfecting the last details of his scheme, while stowing a quantity of silver in a large, ironbound chest, when the doorbell interrupted him. He had taken the unusual precaution of locking his front door from the inside while thus engaged, a fact that aroused Bunny's curiosity when Raffles finally admitted him. And Bunny, who had a habit of gaining a deal of confidence when an adventure was behind him and none in prospect, jumped to a convenient conclusion. This conclusion concerned one Crawshay, a professional thief, or "professor" as the parlance of the underworld would have it, of some resource and daring whom Raffles had encountered in the past and with tales of whose exploits he had lately regaled Bunny. Now the locked door, the half-full chest of silver and his newly acquired knowledge of Crawshay all fitted together in Bunny's mind.

"You think Crawshay is in London," he said, eminently pleased with his powers of deduction.

Raffles looked at him with surprise, which he quickly concealed.

"I had imagined him comfortably in jail," he replied laconically.

"Never," denied Bunny. "He's far too good a man to be taken. From what you tell me, anyway," he added politely.

"You think so?" inquired Raffles, who did not much care for Bunny's admiration of that criminal.

"I should call him," said Bunny, "the very prince of professional cracksmen."

"Should you?" said Raffles, raising his eyebrows. "Then you had better prepare to repel princes when I'm gone."

"Gone? Where?" asked Bunny, startled.

"Scotland," replied Raffles, returning to his task of packing plate and ornaments into the chest.

"At this time of year?" said Bunny, baffled.

"I go there," explained Raffles patiently, "not as a sportsman or a tourist, but as a student, to learn the language."

"Gaelic?" said Bunny.

"No, you ass. But my Galloway Scots might be better, and I mean to spend a week making it so."

Bunny, who was not at all sure what Galloway Scots was and who could not think why Raffles should wish to better it, said so.

"Some of my accents have come in useful even in your time, Bunny," Raffles reminded him. "What price my Cockney in St. John's Wood, eh?"

The efficacy of that linguistic feat on Raffles's part could not be denied.

"All right," Bunny agreed, "but why are you taking this herd of white elephants with you?" he questioned, aiming a kick at the stout chest.

"A fine way of referring to family heirlooms, with a noble crest on them," Raffles reproved him. "Lord Mulgrave and others would be very upset to hear you talk like that."

"Well," conceded Bunny, "I can see the fun of pinching them, but I can't see why you've kept them."

"Love of beautiful things, Bunny. And because my fence wouldn't dream of handling them unless they were melted down. And who would be such a Philistine as to melt this?" he inquired, caressing an elegant silver jug.

"I would for one," said Bunny.

"And Crawshay would for another. You're all the same, you journeymen of crime. You've no souls," complained Raffles, placing the jug carefully within the chest.

"And you think Crawshay is after your silver?" said Bunny in a tone of triumph.

"I heard a little whisper in the underworld," Raffles admitted with a shrug. "And since I am going away, taking the opportunity to have these rooms freshened up, the electric light and the telephone put in . . ."

"Good," interrupted Bunny approvingly.

". . . leaving the Albany people to supervise things, I shall give them the run of the place and go away leaving everything unlocked."

"Except this," Bunny said, kicking the chest a second time.

"Except that. It's not going with me, nor is it remaining here."

"What are you proposing to do with it?"

"Ah," said Raffles, straightening up from the chest. "You have a bank and a bank account?"

"Yes," said Bunny, mystified.

"Then go to your bank and pay in this bundle of notes," Raffles told him, producing a wad of cash from his pocket. "Say you had a good week at Liverpool and at Lincoln. Then ask them if they can look after your silver for you."

"My silver!" squeaked Bunny in alarm.

"I should explain to them that it's a lot of old family stuff you've a good mind to leave with them till you marry and settle down."

"And I take that damned great chest down there?" Bunny queried, staring at the despised object.

"And they store it in their strong room," Raffles agreed.

"But it's full of stolen stuff!" said Bunny, much concerned. "Somebody might . . . well . . . be eager to look inside . . ." he said faintly.

"I don't think so, Bunny," Raffles reassured him. "I did wonder about your taking it to your place under cover of night, but that'd look so damned suspicious. No, it's better to do it openly, in broad daylight, like the honest citizens we are."

"I suppose so," Bunny reluctantly agreed.

"Then you must have a cab this minute if you're to get to your bank before it closes," Raffles said, pressing the bundle of bank notes into his hand. "And prepare the way for the chest to arrive there tomorrow. Then come round," he went on, leading Bunny into the hall, "at a quarter to ten in the morning, in a growler. The chest'll be ready for you."

"What train are you going on?" Bunny inquired as Raffles helped him into his overcoat.

"The eleven-fifty from Euston."

"I'd like to see you off," said Bunny shyly.

"Just as you like," Raffles demurred. "Count the notes before you hand them in. Racing men always know how much they've won," he advised, hurrying Bunny through the front door.

"Yes, I will," he promised. " 'Bye, Raffles. See you tomorrow."

Raffles closed the door with a fond smile, certain that Bunny could be relied upon to do exactly as he asked. And so Bunny did, without deviating in the slightest particular from his instructions.

The following morning, eschewing his usual constitutional to the Albany, Bunny equipped himself with a stout four-wheeled growler and arrived at the entrance prompt at a quarter to ten. His amazement and disappointment on hearing that Raffles had already gone can be imagined. He quickly realized that the eleven-fifty train which Raffles had planned to catch had been the eleven-fifty P.M. The porter confirmed that this was so, and told how Raffles had waited for his friend in vain. However, the porter had the chest in safekeeping and had thoughtfully retained the services of a friend to assist him in loading its great weight onto the roof of the conveyance. All this Bunny watched with mounting nervousness. Now that he had come to it, the prospect of driving through the streets of London with a small fortune in stolen silver openly in his possession was a daunting one. But he did it, leaning out of the cab's window, anxiously watching the swaying chest lashed to the roof. He did it because he had promised to do it, because he had promised Raffles, and the remembrance of his absent comrade did much to bolster his courage.

At the bank, which they reached safely, Bunny

found that he required all the courage he could muster. Not only was there the constant fear that the clumsiness of reluctant porters would cause the chest to drop, spilling its telltale contents all over the floor, but there was also, when they finally reached the barred strong room, the question of a receipt. The rather aloof clerk announced that such a document could not be issued without a full examination and itemization of the chest's contents. At this, Bunny quaked, turned pale and mumbled that he could not be bothered to unpack it all and would therefore do without a receipt.

It was with considerable relief, therefore, that Bunny finally issued from the bank, his deed done. It was a fine, cold morning, with bright sunlight turning the heavy frost to a crystalline brilliance. Tempted by the weather and mindful that he had not yet taken his constitutional, Bunny decided to stroll homeward through the pleasantly populated streets and to use the time to plan some diversion for himself. Having deposited the chest, he felt that he had earned some agreeable reward. But what? Once again the absence of Raffles took the zest out of any plan he might devise. In fact, he began to feel quite out of spirits until he found himself outside the doors of the Albany once again. Well, he thought, since he was there, he might as well pop in and see how the renovations and installations were progressing. For the second time that morning he greeted the affable porter.

"I think I'll run up to Mr. Raffles's rooms and see if everything's all right," he informed that good man.

"Yes. They're all up there, sir. The decorators, the electricians and the police."

"The police!" Bunny squawked, his voice cracking as it had not done since he was at Uppingham.

"Yes, sir," replied the porter cheerily. "They've been

up there since just after you left. You only just missed them."

Bunny thanked his stars that he had done so. Crawshay was one thing, but the police! He hurried through the charming court of the Albany and mounted the staircase to Raffles's rooms with bounding steps. Anxious as he was, he must know what this sinister visitation portended. His hurrying passage was, however, temporarily halted at the front door by a uniformed constable who demanded his name and business. Bunny answered that he had promised to keep an eye on the rooms during the occupant's absence. Apparently satisfied, the constable admitted him.

The hall was a maze of electric wiring and workmen through which Bunny picked a cautious way. Before he had reached the sitting room, scene of so many happy hours, he heard a voice, rich, deep and undoubtedly Scots. Inspector Mackenzie, he thought with alarm. And there, indeed, as he entered the room, was the man he had last seen swirling like a typhoon out of these very chambers, on his hands and knees, peering suspiciously under Raffles's carpet.

"Inspector Mackenzie," Bunny said.

Slowly, the granite-faced detective raised his head and fixed a glittering eye on Bunny, whom he but dimly remembered.

"Do I know you, sir?" he asked.

"Manders," said Bunny. "Bunny Manders. We sort of collided in the hall once. Friend of Raffles."

"Ah, yes," said the inspector, getting to his feet. "I remember very well."

"What are you doing here now?" Bunny asked as casually as possible, trying to sound as though a police search were an unremarkable occurrence.

"Searching," came the terse reply.

"Have you got a warrant?" Bunny asked firmly.

Mackenzie shot him a challenging look, but Bunny managed to stare him out without flinching.

"You are right to ask me, sir," Mackenzie said ponderously, producing the warrant from his pocket. He handed it to Bunny. "I thought I would take advantage of Mr. Raffles's absence, in order not to disturb him in any way. . . ."

"What are you looking for?" Bunny asked, handing back the warrant. "What do you think you'll find?"

"They are two very different things, Mr. Manders. If you ask what I *hope* to find, the answer would be 'some evidence,' " the inspector answered, savoring the last two words with ominous pleasure.

"Evidence of what?" persisted Bunny.

"Of my theory about Mr. Raffles," Mackenzie replied at once. "He has gone to Scotland, I understand?"

Bunny confirmed that he had.

"I do not deny," said the inspector, his eyes gravely traversing the room, "that the man has his good points."

"He is my friend," said Bunny stoutly, stung to defend Raffles. "And the greatest man on earth."

This claim drew Mackenzie's eyes back to Bunny.

"Is that so?" he asked wonderingly. "You mean as a cricketer, maybe?"

"Nothing to do with his cricket," replied Bunny. "He just is."

Mackenzie took a moment to digest this assertion which he obviously found bizarre to a degree, then turned his attention back to the room.

"It seems to me that your friend had a while back a greater collection of elegant ornaments to decorate his walls," he said slowly. "There was a deal of silver here. . . ."

"Yes, well, he got rid of all that quite a long time ago," Bunny said quickly.

"Did he now. Melted it and sold it, did he? Well, it's to be expected. In that case I must look in other directions for my evidence," he said.

"Yes, I think you must," said Bunny.

"Rest assured, sir, that the long arm of the law will pluck at his collar one of these days," vowed Mackenzie, advancing slowly toward Bunny. "And that the long legs of the law will keep pace with him till then."

"Is that your message to him?" asked Bunny, retreating across the room.

"It is."

"I will convey it to him on his return from Scotland," Bunny said, noting that this mention of the inspector's homeland seemed to work on him with a mellowing effect.

"I hope he'll return a better man, from contact with the Scots," murmured the inspector.

"Good God!" Bunny expostulated before he could trim his tongue. "A nation only fit to play golf and football!"

The cold expression with which Mackenzie faced him was terrible indeed, but Bunny was resolved to stand his ground, to defend his country as roundly as he had his friend.

"I confess," the inspector hissed, "I find that preferable to a nation that is fit only for cricket and crime!"

This remark struck too close to the truth for Bunny's comfort. He opened his mouth to speak, and then closed it.

"Mind," said the inspector, "I am accusing nobody. I merely think it within the bounds of possibility that he overlooked some small thing—a piece of silver maybe—which is identifiable as stolen goods. And now good day to you, sir," he added brusquely, dismissing Bunny with a wave of his arm and resuming his inspection of the floorboards beneath the carpet.

Bunny did not linger. With racing heart, he hurried to shake the dust of the Albany from his feet. Inspector Mackenzie was an awesome foe indeed, and one for whom, he felt, Raffles had insufficiently prepared him.

Later that evening, after an excellent dinner at the Old Bohemian, of which he now was, thanks to Raffles's generous sponsorship, a member in his own right, Bunny was handed a letter. He recognized the distinctive hand of his friend at once and eagerly inspected the postmark. This clearly informed him that the letter had been posted in Crewe, with the result that his hopes that Raffles had returned unexpectedly were immediately dashed. Glad of any news, however, he tore open the envelope and read the single sheet avidly.

My Dear Bunny,
    'Ware Prince of Professors! He was in the offing when I left. If slightest cause for uneasiness about bank, withdraw at once and keep in own rooms like a good chap. Enjoy yourself,
                                        A.J.R.

An enigmatic note indeed, and one which Bunny surmised from the noticeably shaky handwriting had been penned in haste on the railway train and posted during a brief stop at Crewe. So Crawshay was in the offing, but what could possibly cause uneasiness about the bank? It was altogether too much for Bunny and, he wryly reflected, quite sufficient to ensure that he did not enjoy himself at all!

The following morning, the letter not having proved so alarming as to prevent or disturb his slumbers, Bunny was roused by the imperious shrilling of his telephone. Yawning, he answered and at once became utterly awake. The guttural voice on the other end of the line was indisputably that of Inspector Mackenzie, who requested Bunny's immediate presence at Raffles's rooms. Before Bunny could form a request for any explanation, the inspector had cut short the conversation. There was nothing for it but to comply, which Bunny did with all haste and much foreboding.

He arrived at the Albany in record time and rather breathless. He had not even paused to purchase a morning newspaper. The same policeman was keeping watch at Raffles's front door and he admitted Bunny at once. To his surprise, he found the inspector in sole possession of the partially decorated and wired flat.

"Mr. Manders," said Mackenzie with a pretense of pleasure. "I'm sorry to rouse you from your bed."

"It's just that I was rather late last night," Bunny explained.

"I apologize indeed."

"Where are the workmen? Haven't they come?" he asked, glancing at the deserted room.

"I gave them half an hour off," said Mackenzie loftily.

"Oh. Why?"

"So that I might have the more privacy to speak with you," replied the inspector with all reasonableness.

"What about?" inquired Bunny, surreptitiously crossing his fingers.

"Have you any knowledge of Mr. Raffles's whereabouts?"

"He's in Scotland," Bunny informed him.

"Where in Scotland?"

"He didn't give me his address, but he said something about Galloway."

"Ah," said the inspector. "If he was going to the Rhinns of Galloway he would change at Carlisle, and maybe also at Dumfries."

"He wrote me a note from Crewe," Bunny offered. "I've still got the envelope with the postmark," he added, producing it from his pocket and, after withdrawing the note, handing the empty envelope to the inspector.

"Crewe," he said, inspecting the envelope minutely. "What was in the note?" he barked.

"Oh, just a reminder about things. The train must stop at Crewe for five minutes."

"Aye, it does," Mackenzie confirmed, returning the envelope to Bunny. "The Rhinns of Galloway," he intoned dreamily. "What would he be doing there?"

"He said he was going there to improve his accent," replied Bunny rather doubtfully.

"He's a sensible man," the inspector approved. "There is no purer form of English than that spoken by the Lowland Scots of Galloway."

"Yes," agreed Bunny happily. "That's what he said."

"And if he was on that train, which I admit I do not doubt, he could have been in London last night," the inspector mused, as though speaking to himself. "No matter. There are other criminals in the world, I suppose."

92

"You wouldn't dare say that to his face," Bunny protested.

"I daresay not. For the first time in my life I have unjustly suspected him," the inspector admitted with obvious regret. "Good day to you, Mr. Manders," he added abruptly, turning on his heel and dismissing Bunny.

The interview, such as it was, left Bunny feeling both uneasy and rather let down. It was a great thing, of course, that Inspector Mackenzie should be convinced of Raffles's innocence, but innocence of what? And how sincerely convinced was the inspector? Bunny carried these disturbing questions to the turkish baths in Northumberland Avenue, an establishment which had, in the past, proved conducive to thought and relaxation.

And so it proved again, at least until Bunny reached the rest room where, wrapped in a soft towel, he stretched out on a couch with a feeling of pleasant inertia. Next to him was a portly figure whose face, above the usually concealed rolls of flesh, he recognized as belonging to a regular at the Old Bohemian. This gentleman also recognized Bunny, though not for himself but as the constant companion of the great Raffles, whose skill with a cricket ball he soon fell to extolling. Bunny, who could neither recall the gentleman's name nor felt disposed to conversation even upon such a congenial topic, answered him in desultory fashion and was considerably relieved when he immersed himself in a daily newspaper.

"I say!" exclaimed the portly gentleman almost at once. "Did you see this? Bank robbers in Sloane Street! 'An audacious burglary,' he read aloud. 'has been committed on the premises of the City and Surburban Bank in Sloane Street!' "

Bunny leaped to his feet.

"That's my bank," he said, and immediately felt faint so that he had to sit down again. "What did they do?" he asked in a small voice.

The gentleman peered at the newspaper for a moment and then asked:

"You got anything in the strong room?"

"Yes!" Bunny gasped.

"Then you're probably unlucky. Someone broke into the strong room last night."

"What did he take?" demanded Bunny in a sweat of agitation.

"It doesn't say exactly. Chests of plate, apparently."

"What?" howled Bunny.

"And other valuables," the man added.

Disaster stared Bunny in the face. " 'Ware the Prince of Professors!" he recalled, feeling ill. It must be Crawshay. Only Crawshay would dare. And if he had acquired that ill-gotten, motley collection of silver, Raffles would be inexorably in his power! To the amazement of the portly gentleman and the masseur, who had just then come to attend Bunny, the young man fled to the changing room and out into Northumberland Avenue, where he hailed a passing cab. He had little idea what he was going to do, but he must discover the fate of that incriminating chest, be it never so dreadful!

On arriving at the bank Bunny found that he was not alone in his anxiety for his property. A formidable lady was in the process of haranguing the clerk about the loss of her jewel case. When at last her invective was exhausted and she swept out, loudly informing all and sundry that she would send her butler that afternoon to close her account, Bunny stepped up to the cage. The clerk recognized him at once, but his face showed no pleasure.

"Is my chest safe?" asked Bunny.

"Your chest was at the bottom of it all," retorted the clerk rudely. "You drove up with it on the roof of a cab," accused the man. "Any thief could see it a mile off."

"But did the thief get the silver?" insisted Bunny, coloring.

"I am sorry to say," replied the clerk bitterly, "the thief did not get your silver. The two thieves had just got to it when they were interrupted by the night watchman. They felled him to the ground," he added dramatically, "and made their getaway."

"Thank God!" said Bunny fervently, feeling quite weak with relief.

"Are you thanking God for the knocking out of the night watchman, or the fact that the thieves escaped?" inquired the clerk sarcastically.

"No," said Bunny, offended. "Just that my things are safe. They didn't even open the chest?" he asked.

"Life is so unfair," regretted the clerk, "that they did not even open the chest."

Overjoyed to hear this, Bunny decided it was time to stand on his dignity.

"My silver shall not embarrass you any longer," he said with hauteur. "I meant to leave it with you, but after what you have said, I certainly shall not." Then, suddenly inspired, he added: "I shall consider sending my butler round to close my account. Be so good as to fetch my chest at once."

Muttering under his breath, the clerk went away to do so. It was a long and suspenseful wait for Bunny while the heavy chest was carried up from the strong room and then laboriously loaded once more onto a growler. It also cost him a great deal in tips, but he was determined to follow Raffles's written instructions, marveling as he did so that his friend should have foreseen some such eventuality. At last Bunny and the chest were deposited at his Mount Street front door. The chest, however, would not fit into the hand-operated lift and once more Bunny had to dig deep into his pocket to persuade the porter to assist him in conveying it up four flights. Panting, aching and exhausted, the two men deposited the cumbersome chest in Bunny's sitting room whereupon Bunny immediately sat upon it to catch his breath. He felt that he could have stayed there forever, and certainly would have done so for some minutes at least had he not been summoned to the telephone.

"Hello?" he said grumpily into the mouthpiece.

"Hello, Mr. Manders," came the almost jovial voice of Inspector Mackenzie. "I'm speaking from Mr. Raffles's flat. The telephone has been installed."

Guiltily, his heart beating, Bunny turned to stare at the chest of silver.

"I was telephoning merely to say," continued Mackenzie, "will you be sure to let me know the moment Mr. Raffles arrives back in London?"

"Certainly. Yes, I will. The moment I see him," said Bunny. "Goodbye."

Never in his life had Bunny been in such desperate need of a drink. The exertion, the tension and the apparently inescapable attentions of Inspector Mackenzie had quite worn him out. He reached for the decanter of whisky and poured himself a good measure. With eager anticipation, he raised the glass to his lips when:

"Well, Bunny. I'm back."

Raffles's voice! Bunny was so startled that the glass dropped from his fingers to roll across the carpeted floor. He whirled around to face the door, but there was no one there. He looked at the window but that, too, was entirely innocent of any figure. Could it be, thought Bunny desperately, that recent events were causing him to hear voices?

"Here, Bunny."

The voice, still certainly that of Raffles, drew his eyes to the chest and, even as he stared at it, the central section of the domed lid was raised, was thrown open to reveal the smiling face of Raffles! Bunny's jaw dropped in amazement.

"Yes," said Raffles, sitting up stiffly, "I'll have a shot for once and be damned to the time of day. The beauty of all laws," he philosophized, "lies in the breaking, even of the kind we make unto ourselves. Not too much soda," he added, rising majestically to his full height from the cramped chest.

When Bunny had recovered himself sufficiently to furnish them both with stiff glasses of Scotch, Raffles showed him the carefully concealed ventilation holes in the cavernous chest which now contained nothing but a litter of costly looking jewel cases.

"So you were the burglar!" Bunny exclaimed at last. "Well, I'm just as glad I didn't know."

"You're a brick, Bunny," said Raffles, wringing his hand. "That's the thing I longed to hear you say."

"Why's that?" Bunny asked.

"How could you have behaved as you have done if you'd known?" queried Raffles rhetorically. "How could any living man? Irving himself couldn't have done it. But as your own natural self, Bunny, you were superb."

"I have never been so miserable in my life," Bunny complained.

"You were marvelous in your misery," Raffles assured him.

"I have never had so much trouble or spent so much money in tips," he continued.

"Yes, the lower classes were rebellious and rapacious," Raffles sympathized, "but it shall be returned to you, Bunny, a thousandfold," he promised.

"From what you stole?" Bunny inquired.

"Your bank, Bunny," said Raffles excitedly, "had in its not very safekeeping the richest pearls, the most dazzling diamonds imaginable. I dare swear there's enough to keep us both in ease and affluence for a year or so."

But these treasures did not serve to cheer Bunny, who still strongly resented what he took to be Raffles's lack of confidence in him.

"All the same, you might have trusted me! I know you don't credit me with much finesse, but I would undertake to keep your secret and do quite as well. The only difference would be in my own peace of mind, which, of course, doesn't count," he finished huffily.

"I know you would have done your damndest, Bunny. There's no limit to your heroism! But I remember the human element: the involuntary cry of surprise, the unconscious gesture that gives the game away. Your ignorance was bliss—for me at any rate. It meant I had nothing to worry about," Raffles said warmly.

"All right, you kept me in the dark. But there's one thing you didn't know," Bunny said petulantly, "and that I found out."

"What's that?" inquired Raffles eagerly.

"Inspector Mackenzie has been taking advantage of your absence to search your rooms very thoroughly," Bunny said proudly.

"Has he now?" Raffles smiled knowingly, and that smile made it quite clear that to him Bunny's news was old hat.

"You know!" he cried accusingly.

"Well," Raffles admitted, making light of it, "I knew he'd been talking to the Albany management, and I knew he'd got a warrant for the search. I decided to leave him a clear field." He shrugged.

"That's why you got rid of the silver," Bunny realized.

"So that Mackenzie should draw a blank, and the Albany management continue to think me pure as the driven snow," Raffles assented.

"But where did you stow the silver?" Bunny queried, for it was obviously not in the chest.

"In my luggage: a suitcase and my cricket bag."

"You mean you took them to Scotland?" said Bunny in surprise.

"I took them as far as the cloakroom at Euston," Raffles explained. "From whence someone will have to fetch them," he added.

"I can do that," Bunny offered.

"Thank you, Bunny," Raffles said graciously. "You do understand I didn't go to Scotland?" he asked carefully.

"But you went to Crewe," Bunny asserted.

"Simply to post you a letter!"

This revelation rather touched Bunny who only slowly grasped that the journey to Crewe and the letter posted there were actually designed to provide Raffles with an alibi. He had immediately returned to London and to the Albany where he had concealed himself in the chest. He had remained in those cramped and not very congenial quarters until the bank had grown silent and deserted. Then he had emerged from his hiding

99

place, helped himself to the choicest items of jewelry the strong room had to offer and then had set about forcing the grilled door to make it appear that someone had broken in. It was during this part of his plan that the unfortunate nightwatchman had appeared, leaving Raffles no choice but to hit him over the head with his crowbar.

"That wasn't like you, Raffles," Bunny said reproachfully.

"I know it wasn't, Bunny," Raffles concurred in a tone of regret. "But things like that are really inseparable from victories like mine."

This talk of the robbery reminded Bunny of the *Pall Mall Gazette* which had been delivered in his absence. He fetched it and handed it to Raffles, that he might read of his victory.

"I acknowledge the foul blow," Raffles said, scanning the report, "but here's evidence that it was mercifully struck. The victim has already told his tale, and added his own embellishments. There were *two* burglars—yes, of course! It took two men to overpower him," Raffles added with sarcasm. "Well, all I could do after knocking that chap out was retire to the chest and wait. Wait for twelve hours or so for you to come!"

"I was late because I didn't buy a paper. . . ." Bunny apologized.

"I've helped you out of more than one tight spot, Bunny, but by heavens you paid it all back by rescuing me from that strong room."

"Do you really mean that?" cried Bunny, elated.

"I do. Now, d'you mind if I use your bathroom?"

"No, of course not," Bunny said, crestfallen.

"And while I'm having a bath, could you run along to the Albany and get my dress clothes? I really can't go out to dinner in these," Raffles said, looking at his crumpled suit.

"Mackenzie may be there," protested Bunny. "He asked me specially to let him know the moment you came back to London."

"Did he now," said Raffles. "Then as a solid citizen you must certainly do so—tomorrow. I shall come back to London tomorrow," he announced resolutely.

"But if I go for your clothes . . ."

"The porter will know if he's still up there."

"All right, But if we go out to dinner the police may see you," Bunny pointed out.

"We shall dine at the club. And I am happy to say we have not yet allowed any member of the force to become a member. Mackenzie," he added darkly, "if he were such a fool as to try, would be blackballed unanimously."

So saying, Raffles hurried off to his bath while Bunny set out upon and accomplished his mission without difficulty or mishap. Then and only then did the ingenuity and brilliance of what Raffles had achieved strike him. This, despite the very real anxiety caused to himself must, he was certain, be numbered among the most daring of Raffles's exploits. Raffles, later that evening, tended to agree with him. Replete, bathed and comfortable, he confessed that he felt the satisfaction of a job well done.

"I was sitting in this very chair," Bunny said suddenly, "when they brought me your letter from Crewe. Where," he reminded his friend, "you brought up Crawshay again."

"Did I?" said Raffles without interest.

"Yes, you jolly well did," Bunny said somewhat pugnaciously.

"The whole point of that letter," Raffles declared,

101

"was to make you anxious about the fate of that silver. And make you rush to your bank next morning to take the chest out again—before I died of waiting," he added ruefully.

"But you needn't have written a downright lie about the fellow," Bunny reproached him.

"Nor did I, Bunny."

"No?" said Bunny, confused and doubtful.

"No," Raffles repeated sagely.

"Your letter said the Prince of Professors was in the offing," Bunny reminded him.

"So he was. Absolute truth."

"Crawshay?"

"No, Bunny," Raffles said, sitting upright in his chair, his eyes enlivened with that devilish glitter that had lowered the morale of the very finest batsmen the world had to offer. "Me! Time was when I was an amateur. After this job, I take leave to consider myself a professor of the professors," he concluded.

Bunny could think of nothing to say. He certainly could not deny the justice of Raffles's claim to the title, but he took it badly that it should have been won on the certainty of his being slow-witted. The thought hurt and, like many a man before him, he sought to assuage that hurt with alcohol. Even when the pair returned to Bunny's Mount Street flat, he continued to ply the whisky decanter with unwanted profligacy until Raffles felt constrained to inform him that he was drunk.

"Wouldn't you be drunk if you'd been through two days of absolute hell, not knowing what you were doing or why, or what the whole thing was about, just blindly obeying orders, a private soldier in an army where the general is hundreds of miles away and probably making fun of you?" he asked in a rush, returning to what was becoming, in Raffles's view, a rather tedious theme.

"I never make fun of you, Bunny," the "general" defended himself gravely.

"You do. You make fun of everyone," Bunny accused. "Like Inspector Mackenzie."

"I assure you I take Inspector Mackenzie very seriously," Raffles said.

"But you're making fun of him all the time. And of me, too. Like when you don't tell me he's going to search your rooms, and I have a terrible interview with him where he practically accuses us of stealing the silver, and I have to act indignant, and he doesn't know that I've just stored the silver in my bank . . ." he wailed. Then a new thought struck him. "Except that I hadn't. It's in your damned bags at Euston. And I don't know that, and neither does he. And you're laughing at us for a pair of fools!"

"Bunny, listen to me," said Raffles very seriously. "I make no excuses for the way I treat people. I treat them as I find them. I think Mackenzie is an ignoramus and an ass, so I treat him as one. But not you."

"Yes!" insisted Bunny. "A ventriloquist's dummy!"

"You are my friend," argued Raffles. "My right hand man, my partner. Do you think I would have an idiot as my partner?"

Even through the fog of alcohol which befuddled his brain Bunny could see the wisdom of this question. The conclusion he drew from it cheered him a little.

"I agree I don't always tell you everything," Raffles went on, "because I think it better for you not to know."

"That's just it," Bunny intervened, returning to the attack. "You're wrong. I'd be much happier knowing."

"Then by George, Bunny, you shall have the chance

103

to prove it," Raffles exclaimed, slapping his thigh. "Tomorrow, as ever was. And I'll kill two birds with one stone."

"What do you mean?" asked Bunny, blinking.

"I shall make it perfectly plain to you what I'm doing, and I shall treat Mackenzie as an intelligent human being. In fact, I shall give him a sporting chance," he cried gleefully.

"How?" said Bunny sleepily.

"You must study my words carefully, Bunny. I said a *sporting* chance. Good night."

Bunny managed to mumble a "good night" before stretching himself out on his bed.

"A sporting chance," he murmured as the room began to spin about him rather pleasantly. "A sporting *chance*."

The next morning Raffles dispatched a somewhat worn Bunny to Euston to collect his bags, while he returned to the Albany and his own rooms. He was delighted with the progress made and especially with the electric light which he switched on with excitement.

"How many candles is that, would you say?" he inquired of a workman, staring into the dazzling illumination.

" 'Bout a thousand."

"Mm," said Raffles. "I must invite only ladies with perfect complexions."

After having inspected the rest of the alterations, which he found most satisfactory, he picked up the unaccustomed telephone and asked to be connected with Inspector Mackenzie of Scotland Yard. The latter did not seem at all glad to hear from him, which may in part have been the result of the thick Galloway accent in which Raffles mischievously chose to address him, but he did confirm that he would call at the Albany forthwith.

Humming to himself, Raffles made another tour of inspection which was no sooner completed than Bunny arrived, laden with his bags.

"Give me those," said Raffles. "We'll have them up on the table here. Now," he went on, when the bags were placed to his satisfaction, "prepare your mind for a pleasant surprise."

Bunny looked suitably expectant.

"Inspector Mackenzie will be here within a quarter of an hour."

"What!" cried Bunny, appalled.

"Don't say I don't tell you everything," Raffles warned.

"But the silver . . . all that silver . . . in your bags!" Bunny moaned, almost beside himself with anxiety.

"Bunny," said Raffles sharply. "It's no good my telling you things if you're going to panic like this."

"Hide it," besought Bunny, looking wildly around the room for a suitable cache.

"Besides, I told you, I'm going to give Mackenzie a sporting chance."

"It means ten years in jail for you! And at least five years for me! I mean . . . all he's got to do is open those bags and that's the end of it for you and me."

Acknowledging the point, Raffles calmly opened a bag to display a harmless shirt and a pair of innocent cricket pads.

"Raffles," implored Bunny, "I beg you to somehow get rid of that silver before Mackenzie comes here."

"But I said I'd give him a sporting chance. And by heavens that's exactly what he shall get!" said Raffles with resolution.

Any further protests of Bunny's were silenced by the ringing of the doorbell. To Bunny's ears it sounded horribly like the knock of doom. Raffles, however, moved calmly to the front door to greet his visitor. Mackenzie stepped a trifle hesitantly into the hall and launched at once into an abject speech of apology.

"I am heartily ashamed of the suspicions I harbored about you," he said. "I could hardly wait for your return to tell you so, and to apologize. Since I have searched your flat and found nothing, and since you were away in Galloway at the time of the bank robbery—I confess I have nothing against you, not even the shadow of a suspicion."

"Of course you haven't, Inspector," Raffles cordially replied. "And I'm glad to hear you say so. But come in. Mr. Manders is here and he'll be glad to hear you say it, too."

Although Mackenzie did not appear too keen to repeat his apologies, he followed Raffles into the sitting room where Bunny was fussing about the luggage, arranging shirts and other items of clothing.

"Hello, Bunny," Raffles called. "You starting to unpack for me? Good man. I hate packing and unpacking. The inspector came here to apologize," he added as the two men nodded to each other.

"I'll take the bag in the bedroom," Bunny said, grabbing up the suitcase and staggering with it toward the door.

Raffles smiled at his clumsy departure, remarking to Mackenzie that Bunny was a good-hearted soul.

"Aye, if a man has a good heart. . . ." the inspector agreed. "Well, I'll not be troubling you any longer, Mr. Raffles."

"Goodbye then, Inspector," said Raffles, holding out his hand.

106

"By the way, did you have a good time in Galloway?" the inspector asked, staring at Raffles's luggage with some interest.

"I did indeed," Raffles informed him.

"And you took your cricket bag?"

"I take it with me wherever I go," Raffles asserted as the inspector peered suspiciously at it. "In the hope of a game."

"And did you get one?" Mackenzie asked sharply.

"Alas, the only game they seemed to have heard of was golf," he confessed.

This produced a dry but pleased laugh from the stern detective.

"A royal and ancient game, Mr. Raffles. Better by far than any of your cricket," he said, spitting out the last word with disdain.

"So they all told me," replied Raffles equably.

"Well, goodbye," the inspector repeated jovially. "If you hoped for cricket in Scotland," he called as he went to the door, "you were a fool. Goodbye."

Laughing himself, Raffles went to the open cricket bag and took from beneath the boldly displayed pads, two of the choicest items of silver in his illicit collection. He contemplated them with affection.

"Bunny," he called. "You can stop unpacking now."

Almost at once Bunny appeared, his face and pale gray suit liberally streaked with soot.

"I was trying to stuff the silver up the chimney," he explained in answer to Raffles's questioning look.

"I have never," announced Raffles, "seen anyone look more like a criminal. Now admit. Would you have faced Mackenzie with more confidence if you had *not* known about the silver?"

"Yes, of course I would." Bunny agreed.

"Would you have been happier?" demanded Raffles.

"Yes," said Bunny, his voice dropping.

"Am I right to choose what I shall tell you and what I shall not?" continued Raffles in a determined way.

"Yes, Raffles," Bunny sighed. "You're quite right."

"Then in future," Raffles promised, "I shall choose."

Bunny hung his head. He felt deservedly chastened and wished to make amends. He cleared his throat nervously.

"I nearly had a heart attack," he confessed shyly. "He came so near."

"He came nowhere near," Raffles contradicted him. "He is a Scottish ignoramus. I gave him a sporting chance. He failed to take it. He does not deserve to catch me."

"I'm sure not," Bunny said hastily. "But why not?"

"What month is it?"

"November," Bunny said, mystified.

Raffles drew himself up to his full height and squared his shoulders.

"Every true-born Englishman knows that the cricket season ends in September," he said proudly. "But the Scots have only heard of golf, which is played in all weathers and all the year round; and they foolishly imagine that cricket, which is also about hitting a ball, must be the same. . . . I didn't make fun of him, Bunny," he added in a more gentle tone, "but there's no fool like a clever fool."

While Bunny stared at him in admiration, Raffles calmly selected a handsome silver cup from his cricket bag and placed it fastidiously in the center of his mantelpiece.

In this way both Bunny and Inspector Mackenzie were taught a salutary lesson, although the latter, remaining in presumptive ignorance of England's national game, could not benefit therefrom. That Bunny did so was to be amply demonstrated before long, for now he could proudly regard himself as the innocent right-hand man of the very Prince of Professors!

Four

THE GOLD CUP

•••—◆—•••

IN WHICH HER MAJESTY QUEEN VICTORIA RECEIVES AN UNEXPECTED JUBILEE PRESENT, AND RAFFLES WIPES THE SLATE CLEAN

THE EARL OF Thornaby was, in the words of his charming daughter, chairman or president of practically everything. The fact that he had never played cricket in his life had not prevented him from being made president of the Marylebone Cricket Club, any more than the fact that he maintained an uncharacteristic silence in the House of Lords precluded him from regarding himself as a valuable member of that august chamber. Although he could not be regarded as a connoisseur of art, his enterprise had brought about a committee of anonymous patriots to purchase and present to the nation a rare and beautiful gold cup of medieval date, exquisitely enameled with scenes from the life and martyrdom of St. Agnes.

A. J. Raffles, on the other hand, was an undisputed connoisseur and found himself quite bedazzled by the cup when, as a member of Lord Thornaby's select viewing party, he was invited to the British Museum to inspect the fruits of the peer's considerable efforts.

Raffles had a passing acquaintance with the earl as a result of his brilliant association with the M.C.C., and anything that he found uncongenial in being taken up by the ex-president was more than compensated for by the company of Lady Alice, the earl's pretty and intelligent daughter. She, too, took a noticeable pleasure in Raffles's gallant attentions, and it was from her that he learned of a less widely publicized office which Lord Thornaby had taken upon himself. This was the chairmanship of the Criminologists' Club, a small body of students of contemporary crime who dined periodically at each others' houses in order to discuss the ingenuity and boldness of the latest and more celebrated criminal doings.

In the year 1897, a year destined to be writ large in the history books and universally celebrated as the Jubilee of Her Gracious Majesty's inspiring and amiable reign, the members of the Criminologists' Club had been much exercised by the consideration of certain daring crimes. Among these were included the theft of Lady Lochmaben's tiara and the baffling raid on the Sloane Street branch of the City and Suburban Bank. These, aligned with others which predated them, seemed to Lord Thornaby and some of his fellow students, to bear an individual and recognizable signature. The makings of a suspicion, all the more attractive because so preposterous, had begun to form in the noble earl's mind and would, shortly, crystallize into something approaching a certainty.

Raffles, his eyes ravished by the combined splendors of the St. Agnes Cup and of Lady Alice, was quite unaware of any threatening cloud on his horizon. His artistic sense had been enflamed by the cup which he later declared to Bunny was the most beautiful thing he had ever seen in his life. Bunny, whose powers of artis-

111

tic appreciation were not well developed, evinced little interest in the object of Raffles's enthusiasm until the latter announced his fixed intention to steal it.

"I want to look at it," he explained in his most reasonable tone, "without dragging all the way to the British Museum. I want to see it *there*," he concluded, smacking his hand down on his very own mantelpiece.

Truth to tell, there was something more than the natural lust of the connoisseur to possess a magnificent object in Raffles's determination. As he confided to Bunny, he was becoming disenchanted with precious stones which only brought them a paltry proportion of their actual value, and went on to bewail their dependence upon their obliging but parsimonious fence.

"What we want," he continued, warming to his subject, "is an Incorporated Society of Thieves, with some public-spirited and philanthropic old forger to run it for us on business lines. Otherwise, we shall be forced to steal only those things that can be sold openly and publicly for something like their real value."

"Such as what?" demanded Bunny, who viewed with some alarm these high-flown schemes of his friend.

"Gold," replied the schemer promptly.

"You couldn't sell that cup publicly," Bunny pointed out.

"I could melt it down into a nugget," said Raffles carelessly, "and make them pay up in hard cash over the counter of the Bank of England."

"How much is it worth?" inquired Bunny, partly to humor his friend and partly because he liked to know the value of things.

"Thornaby's committee paid eight thousand for it. Intrinsic value—a thousand? I'm only guessing."

"Not a great reward for the risk of stealing it from the British Museum," Bunny remarked dubiously and,

112

too late, realized that this was quite the wrong argument to advance.

"Ah, the risk!" said Raffles dreamily. "The risk is its own reward."

Oh dear, thought Bunny, who recognized that in these "artistic" moods Raffles invariably became as stubborn as he was ingenious.

"At any rate," Raffles said, discarding his introspective stance, "we might go and have a look at it, Bunny, don't you think?"

"When?" asked Bunny cautiously.

"Tomorrow, if you like."

"Only to look?"

"We must do so before we leap," Raffles said in a tone that suggested that he would never act without a full preliminary reconnoiter. "We must count the number of paces from the room to the outside street. We must spy out a good hiding place. We must investigate all the possibilities."

"Very well," Bunny agreed, feeling reassured. "Tomorrow it is."

Raffles nodded, glad to have it settled.

"And we must discuss what to wear," he said. "I fancy this is a costume piece, and we should embellish ourselves with wigs and strange disguises. Now, what would it amuse me to be?" He considered, absently picking up his cloak and throwing it around his broad shoulders. "I rather think an elderly invalid. And you, of course, will be my devoted attendant," he cried happily. "The Café Royal for dinner, do you think?"

Bunny, who had grown more and more alarmed at the elaborate nature of these plans, picked up his hat and cane and, with a notable lack of enthusiasm, assented.

"It's near, and it's as good as anywhere."

As a result of this conversation the following morning saw an elderly, bespectacled gentleman, much swathed about by scarves and with his hands thrust into the warm recesses of a muff, being wheeled in a bath chair across the forecourt of the British Museum. At the foot of those wide, imposing steps leading to the handsomely pillared portico, the gentleman, complaining in a high, quavery voice was assisted from the chair by his companion, a heavily moustached man wearing a flat cap. It can safely be vowed that even their respective mothers would not have recognized in these singular personages the identities of A. J. Raffles and Bunny Manders. Yet these they were, the one hugely enjoying the impersonation, the other admiring the efficacy of it but feeling somewhat apprehensive as well as misused.

Once the chair had been dragged up the steps and Raffles again ensconced therein, they set out down the long corridors of the British Museum. Raffles frequently complained of the distances, demanded directions and spurred Bunny on with feigned bad homor. At last they arrived at the room where, in a glass case, the St. Agnes Cup stood in all its glory, unattended save by a solitary but stalwart constable. To Bunny's great alarm, Raffles had no sooner finished extolling the virtues of the cup than he announced, in his assumed voice, that he would like to steal it. This unusual announcement immediately attracted the attention of the policeman.

"You'd better not try, sir," he said gravely.

"Going to run me in, are you?" cackled Raffles. "That would be a joke, my hat!"

"I didn't say as I was, sir," said the constable. "But that's queer talk for a gentleman like you, sir, in the British Museum."

"I simply said I should like to steal it," argued Raffles. "And so I should. It's so beautiful. So beautiful that I should like to have it as my own."

"I daresay there's many as feels like that, sir," said the policeman, softening.

"Exactly. And I say what I feel. And I must say," he continued, gazing at the cup, "that I doubt if a valuable thing like this is safe in a glass case."

"Safe enough so long as I'm here," retorted the constable, on his dignity.

"But is one man enough?" cried Raffles. "What do you think, James?"

"James," who was not accustomed to this name and who was in a state of some agitation as a result of Raffles's indiscreet remarks, gaped for a moment in silence. Then, with a start, Bunny said:

"Oh . . . yes, I should think so."

"You're a fool, James," retorted his master. Then, turning to the constable, who had rather enjoyed this exchange, he said: "You appear to be single-handed. Is that wise?"

"I'm not single-handed," the policeman contradicted him. "See that seat by the door? One of the attendants sits there all day long," he explained smugly.

With a great show of arthritic difficulty, Raffles twisted around to stare at the palpably empty seat.

"All day long? Then where is he now?" he demanded.

"Talking to another attendant outside," said the policeman patiently. "If you listen you'll hear them for yourself, in the corridor."

Raffles listened. He had already noted the attendants as he and Bunny had approached the room. Now they could be heard, but not seen.

"The public treasure ought to be guarded better

than this. I shall write a letter to the *Times* about it," Raffles promised testily.

"Lor' bless you, sir," said the policeman, smiling. "I'm all right. Don't you bother about me."

"I'm not bothering about you," came the quick retort. "I'm bothering about the cup. Why, you haven't even got a billy club!"

"Nor likely to want one, neither," said the constable, affronted. "In a few minutes this room will fill up; and there's safety in numbers, as they say."

"I shall write to the *Times* all the same. I won't have unnecessary risks run with the nation's property," insisted the old man, growing red in the face.

"I just have to blow my whistle, sir, and the attendants come running in at the double," the policeman said, anxious to humor this irascible old gentleman.

"Ah," he cried, waving a shaky finger at the policeman. "But supposing you can't blow your whistle?"

"And why should that be, sir?"

"Come over here. I want to whisper," replied Raffles.

"What?" said the constable, taken aback by this new eccentricity.

"Without my man hearing," Raffles said in the tone of a man sorely tried by the slow wits of those around him.

Bunny, who had been listening to this conversation with some amusement, moved obligingly a few steps away from the chair, which the policeman forthwith approached with an expression of good-humored indulgence. In response to Raffles's urgent beckoning, he stooped and approached his ear close to the old man's lips. At once two mighty blows fell on the back of his

116

neck. Silently, the policeman slumped sideways only to be neatly caught by an astonished Bunny.

"Good man!" whispered Raffles approvingly. "Put him down in the corner somewhere and run to the door and see if those attendants have heard anything."

Bunny obeyed as though in a dream. His mind was as stunned as the policeman's body which he dragged across the room and propped in a waiting chair. Then he peeped carefully around the door. The attendants had not moved and the low murmur of their voices continued uninterrupted. Bunny turned back, ready to convey this information to Raffles, but stopped in his tracks. Raffles was already lifting the lid of the glass case and, in a wink, the St. Agnes Cup had vanished into his copious muff. With a bound he returned to the bath chair, slumping at once into the posture of an infirm ancient.

"All right, James," he said loudly in his false voice. "I think we can go now."

"Yes, sir," Bunny said automatically, grasping the handles of the bath chair and wheeling it toward the corridor.

"I've no idea," hissed Raffles in his true voice, "how long he'll stay knocked out, so slow march. We may swing for him if you show indecent haste."

Swallowing his panic, Bunny applied himself to the task of wheeling the chair at normal speed, while every nerve in his body urged him to flee as fast as his shaking legs would carry him.

"Stop," ordered Raffles as they drew level with the attendants. "Can you tell me the way to the Prehistoric Salon?" he demanded.

"Yes, sir. Go along here and the first stairs you come to, up them and it's top of the stairs."

117

"And we can work around that way to the Egyptian part?"

"Indeed you can, sir."

"Thank you very much. On, James."

Half-fainting with fear, Bunny leaned his weight against the chair which rolled quickly forward.

"Slow, Bunny," came Raffles's warning voice. "We'll get rid of the bath chair in the vestibule, then you can run as fast as you like."

And so it was, a few minutes later, that an elderly man clutching a muff, closely followed by a younger, clamping his cloth cap to his head, could be seen sprinting across the forecourt of the British Museum, loudly hailing a cab.

"Charing Cross," cried Raffles, hurling himself into the cab, with a breathless Bunny at his heels.

For several minutes they rode in silence, save for their labored breathing. Bunny pressed an anxious hand to his thumping heart and resisted the desire to lean out of the window to look for signs of a chase. Suddenly Raffles jumped to his feet, threw open the trap door in the roof of the vehicle, and demanded to know where the driver was taking them.

"Charing Cross, sir," came the startled reply.

"You idiot! I said King's Cross," fibbed Raffles. "Round you spin and drive like blazes, or we miss our train."

"King's Cross. Right, sir," growled the aggrieved cabbie, instantly obeying Raffles's instructions.

At King's Cross, Raffles booked two seats on a train to York which was due to depart at any moment, making quite sure that the ticket clerk got a good look at him and would remember his blustering manner. Then, with Bunny trotting in bewilderment at his side, he made for the platform, only to veer off into the subway which conducted them to the Metropolitan Line. Two tickets for Baker Street were swiftly purchased and, upon arrival, Raffles made straight for the gentlemen's cloakroom where, unnoticed by anyone, he divested himself of his wig and spectacles. With relief, Bunny too removed his disguise, watching in fascination as, with a flick of the wrist, Raffles converted his bizarre muff into a small bag. The objects of disguise stuffed therein, on top of the beautiful enameled cup, Raffles and Bunny, restored as it were to themselves, sauntered forth for a pleasant stroll back to the Albany, pausing only to procure the evening newspapers.

The moment they reached the safety of Raffles's rooms, the great cricketer snatched the cup from the bag and placed it, beaming, on the mantelpiece. Bunny, who had remained silent ever since they left the British Museum, scanned the newspapers thoroughly and with a sinking heart. With a sigh of relief he announced that they carried no mention of the theft.

"No," said Raffles, without much interest. "They're fast, but they're not as fast as all that. Sullivan, Bunny?"

"Not until I have told you frankly and exactly what I think of you and your latest deed," said Bunny, trembling now with anger.

"Oh?" said Raffles, raising his eyebrows. "Was there something wrong with it?"

"The thing that is always wrong," cried Bunny.

"What? I thought it went so well," said Raffles with a puzzled air.

"You make one plan, and you tell me another!" accused Bunny.

"I didn't. Not today, Bunny. I swear."

"We were going there for a preliminary reconnoiter,

119

nothing more. To 'investigate the possibilities,'" he reminded his friend.

"That's right," agreed Raffles blandly.

"Then why on earth did you go and do what you did?" demanded Bunny with exasperation.

"Have you never felt the temptation of the moment?" asked Raffles. "It was perfectly irresistible, when Roberto meekly bent his head in front of me. It's not a thing I care to do, and I shan't be happy until the papers tell me the poor devil is alive. But a knockout shot was the only chance for us," he said.

"Why? You weren't trying to get away! He wasn't trying to run you in!" Bunny protested.

"I'd have deserved running in if I hadn't yielded to that temptation, Bunny. We might go there every day of our lives and never again be the only visitors in the room, with the attendant out chatting in the corridor at one and the same time," Raffles explained, recalling these circumstances with wonder and delight. "It was a gift from the gods," he concluded rapturously. "Not to have taken it would have been flying in the face of Providence."

Bunny considered for a moment, his righteous anger dwindling in the face of such enthusiasm. Gruffly, he decided to forgive Raffles.

"Forgive me rather for the sake of St. Agnes," Raffles begged. "Doesn't she look well up there?" He smiled ecstatically at the fine workmanship, the delicate beauty of the purloined cup.

"Yes, until the police come to collect her," said Bunny bitterly.

"Why on earth should they come here, to look for an elderly invalid in a bath chair? A bath chair that is identical with every other such chair in London, not to mention the provinces?" Raffles asked with every appearance of innocence.

"It'll be an enormous weight off my mind when you get the cup melted down and disposed of," Bunny said, refusing to be so easily persuaded of their immunity from suspicion.

"Melted down! Who said I was going to do that?" said Raffles with all the indignation of the connoisseur.

"You did," Bunny said firmly.

"I deny it," retorted Raffles with equal firmness.

"You said you'd melt it down into a nugget and . . ."

"I said that I *could* melt it down. Not that I *would*."

"A wretched quibble," Bunny said with scorn.

"Taking it was an offense against the laws of the land," admitted Raffles hotly. "But destroying it would be a crime against God and Art, and may I be spitted on the vane of St. Mary Abbot's if ever I commit it!"

At this, Bunny fell silent. Raffles, he knew, was a man of passion and few things aroused his passions so powerfully as Art. He knew therefore that it was worthless to argue any further with his friend, yet the conviction that he had allowed the love of beauty to mislead him remained and kept Bunny in a taciturn mood. In this mood he returned to his own quarters in Mount Street to dress for dinner and reluctantly agreed to collect Raffles later, with the final editions of the evening newspapers. These, as his friend had confidently predicted, carried full accounts of the deed. Raffles read the reports avidly, taking particular delight in the description of his accomplice as "a middle-aged man of blackguardly appearance and criminal type."

"Hits you off rather neatly, don't you think, Bunny?" he chortled.

"It means my disguise was good," replied Bunny dryly.

121

"Nothing can disguise the essential you . . ." Raffles said with studied casualness, returning to the paper where he was rather put out to read that Lord Thornaby had described the perpetrator of the theft as a common sneak thief. In Raffles's expert opinion, it had been a decidedly uncommon theft. He read on, noting that Lord Thornaby had pledged all possible assistance to Scotland Yard in their task of tracking down the criminal.

"He's a great man," Raffles opined, tossing the newspaper aside.

"And he has a deliciously pretty daughter," Bunny said mockingly.

"Yes, he has, by Jove!" Raffles asserted enthusiastically.

Bunny, who did not much care for the delectable Lady Alice on grounds no more personal than that she had occupied a very great deal of his friend's time of late, shrugged dismissively and stared at his highly polished evening shoes.

"Bunny," said Raffles suddenly, "I've an idea after your own heart. I know where I can place it after all."

"Do you mean the cup?" asked Bunny, looking up and not quite daring to hope that he did.

"I do."

"Then I congratulate you."

"Thanks."

"On the recovery of your senses," said Bunny tartly.

"Thanks galore."

"What is your idea, pray?"

"You've been confoundedly unsympathetic about this whole thing, Bunny," Raffles complained. "I don't think I shall tell you my scheme until I've carried it out."

"As usual. That will be quite time enough," said Bunny with a haughty air.

"It's no good getting short with me, Bunny. You have an important part to play in the scheme." Raffles informed him. "You have to go out first thing in the morning and buy me a big box of biscuits."

Bunny stared at his friend in amazement. Could it be that the excitement and the love of Art had turned the great man's brains?

"What kind?" Bunny asked meekly.

"Any sort of biscuits you like, only they must be Huntley and Palmer's and absolutely the biggest box they sell," said Raffles, snatching up his hat and advancing with a light step toward the front door.

"What do you want biscuits for?" inquired Bunny, hurrying to catch up.

"No questions, Bunny," forbade Raffles, opening the door. "You do your part, and I'll do mine."

Sighing, Bunny asked no more questions and did his very best, throughout dinner, to put the entire matter from his mind. By morning he believed himself to be blessedly detached from all curiosity as to Raffles's latest and probably harebrained scheme. He purchased, as bidden, the largest box of Huntley and Palmer biscuits available, and delivered it to Raffles's rooms. There, in stony silence, he watched as his friend tipped its entire contents onto the table and whistling a jaunty tune, carefully wrapped the cup in pages from last evening's newspapers before placing it in the box. More pages served as packing, and the whole was wrapped in stout and unremarkable brown paper. All this Bunny studied. Then, with parcel tucked under his arm, Raffles prepared to go out, inviting Bunny to remain in his rooms until he returned.

"Oh," he added, popping his head around the door,

as an afterthought. "Do help yourself to a biscuit, Bunny."

Sullenly Bunny did so, thinking that it would help to pass the time. Fortunately, for Bunny was not frightfully adept at cooling his heels, Raffles returned within the hour, his hat at a carefree angle and evidently in the very best of spirits.

"Congratulate me," he commanded. "I have placed the cup."

Bunny was mightily relieved, and fast in the wake of his relief came a new and pleasant thought.

"How much for? How much for?" he asked eagerly.

"Let me think," said Raffles, furrowing his brow. "I had a couple of cabs, and the postage was a tanner, with another twopence for registration. . . . Yes, it must have cost me . . . exactly five and eight."

"It cost you?" said Bunny puzzled. "But how much did you get for it, Raffles?"

"Nothing," replied the other amiably.

"Nothing!"

"Not a crimson cent."

To Bunny this was a blow, though not an entirely unexpected one.

"I'm not greatly surprised," he admitted. "I never really thought it had a market value. I told you so in the beginning," he added pointedly.

"Yes, you did," agreed Raffles, still affable.

"So what have you done with the thing?" Bunny asked, more out of politeness than real curiosity.

"Given it to the Queen as a Jubilee present," Raffles confessed, offhand.

"What? You haven't!" exclaimed Bunny, alarmed yet beginning to be delighted.

"Well, I sent it to her private secretary, Sir Arthur Bigge, to present to Her Majesty, if that will do for you. I thought they might take too much stock of me at the G.P.O. if I addressed it to the Sovereign herself," he confessed.

"But why on earth do such a thing at all?" groaned Bunny, imagining instant discovery, the patient tracing of the biscuit tin to Raffles and to himself.

"My dear Bunny," said Raffles, "we have been reigned over for sixty years by infinitely the finest monarch the world has ever seen. The world is taking the present opportunity of signifying the fact for all it is worth. Every nation is laying the best it has to offer at her royal feet. Every class in the community is doing its level best to bring her gifts—except ours: the criminal class. I have tried," he continued grandiosely, "to remove one reproach from our fraternity, one blot from our sullied reputation."

"Suppose they trace it to us?" said Bunny, mindless of Raffles's admirable thoughtfulness and loyalty.

"There's not much to catch hold of in a biscuit box by Huntley and Palmer, lined with yesterday's newspaper. And I didn't write a word on a sheet of paper which could possibly be traced. No, the G.P.O. was the one danger: there was one detective there I spotted and the sight of him has left me with a thirst. Whisky and Sullivans for two, Bunny, if you please."

Bunny hastened to pour the drinks, his worries allayed at last. And as he handed a glass to Raffles, he was overcome by the emotion of his friend's latest exploit. It was a fine thing, indeed, and one quite shining with honor. He seized Raffles's hand and pumped it warmly.

"Raffles, I must say, you always were a sportsman," he said with glistening eyes, "and you always will be."

Smiling, Raffles raised his glass.

"The Queen," he cried, "God bless her!"

"God bless her," Bunny echoed him, greatly moved, and together they solemnly and loyally drank to Her Majesty Queen Victoria.

The matter of the St. Agnes Cup did not, however, end there. It was inevitably, as Raffles was reminded by the evening newspaper, of grave concern to Lord Thornaby whose diligence and abilities, not to mention a proportion of his fortune, had helped to secure it for the nation. Now that nobleman, as we have seen, already entertained certain thoughts which, when he considered in detail the daring theft of "his" cup, hardened into a strong suspicion. In his view—one he shared with select members of the Criminologists' Club—the theft bore that very personal signature he had already noted in the affair of the Lochmaben tiara, to mention but one famously infamous crime. His guess—for it was no more, albeit an educated one—as to the identity of the bold man whose signature he had learned to recognize was not universally accepted by his fellow criminologists, but even the skeptical saw that it would be jolly to test the nerve of one who was known to be a sportsman of the very highest caliber. Even Lady Alice, who might be considered biased in her opinion of the suspect, was persuaded that a small dinner party at which A. J. Raffles was entertained by the Criminologists, could do no harm. Indeed, she loyally asserted that it would serve to vanquish forever the base suspicions entertained by her otherwise dear papa, and in return for her services as gracious and beautiful hostess, she extracted a promise from her father that she should be translated, for that one night, into a full member of the club and excused the onerous duty of having to withdraw when the port circulated. By this means Lady Alice determined to keep a sharp eye on the proceedings and to ensure that the Criminologists played fair. A date was agreed and invitations dispatched. Raffles received his with delight and promptly dropped a hint into the receptive ear of Lady Alice that his dear, good friend Bunny Manders was himself a student of crime. As a consequence of this, the merest hint of a hint, Bunny too received an invitation, though he read it with more alarm than pleasure and, pausing only to snatch up his hat, hurried at once to Raffles's chambers.

It was, of course, the reference to the Criminologists' Club which had put Bunny into such a bother. Patiently Raffles explained who they were and the nature of their purpose in meeting, but Bunny remained perplexed. Accepting a whisky, he asked:

"But why have they invited you?"

"They are studying the influence of crime on sport—whether professionalism and the money motive necessarily bring crime in their train. It's rather in my public line."

"In yours if you like, but not in mine," said Bunny. "No, Raffles, they've got their eye on us both, and they mean to put us under the microscope, or they never would have picked on *me*," he said with mounting agitation.

"I almost wish you were right, Bunny," said Raffles, smiling. "It'd be such fun. But it may console you to hear that it was I who gave them your name. I told them you were a far keener criminologist than myself."

"*I* am?" cried Bunny, flabbergasted.

"I said you were fascinated by crime. How splendid that they've taken my hint and invited you, too."

"They're on the track of that cup," insisted Bunny, who did not think it in the least splendid.

"They only have to inquire at Buckingham Palace," Raffles calmly reminded him. "The only question is whether the Queen has decided to give it back to the nation—whoever the nation may be—or has decided to keep it for herself. I sincerely hope the latter. It's too good for a nation; but it's fit for a great Queen."

"But wherever the cup is now," Bunny said impatiently, "they can still arrest us for pinching it."

"It'd be damned unsporting, but I agree, the police are not always as good sports as they might be," said Raffles regretfully.

"For once I'm not worried about the police," Bunny said mournfully. "But I'm confoundedly worried at the thought of these Criminologists."

"Solemn students, that's all, who meet to wallow in the latest crimes. We can wallow with them." Raffles was quick to reassure him.

"And Lord Thornaby is chairman of the cup committee *and* of the club," Bunny said, revealing the nub of his anxiety.

At this, Raffles grew rather pensive and withdrawn. It took him but a moment to realize that Thornaby House, a solid, four-storied mansion in Park Lane, was situated close to the corner of Mount Street. Bunny agreed that it should be possible to view the back of those premises from his bedroom window. Raffles immediately became most anxious to test this surmise, and they went at once to Bunny's rooms. There, with the aid of powerful field glasses, it proved possible to make a thorough inspection of the rear portion of the Thornaby mansion. To Bunny, it was a dull view, a mere row of windows that held no interest for him. But Raffles remained for several hours and returned on subsequent days to take up his vigil anew. His reasons for doing so he kept secret, and Bunny refused to inquire.

On the day of the Criminologists' Club dinner it was

arranged that Raffles should collect Bunny, en route for Park Lane, since the latter felt distinctly nervous about arriving without the moral support of his friend. His anxiety when, at five minutes to eight—the invitation was for a quarter to the hour—Raffles had not arrived, can be imagined. Bunny snatched up the telephone and asked to be connected with Raffles at the Albany. There was no reply. Thinking that he might encounter his friend at the door, and mindful that politeness demanded that he present himself without further delay, Bunny hurried the short distance to the Thornaby residence. He could not sight Raffles anywhere and was rather conspicuously loitering near the portico, when two men approached. Instinctively Bunny pressed back into the shadows, not wishing to meet two Criminologists alone. The men, one plump and sleek, the other possessing a shaggy head of unkempt hair, passed Bunny, quite unaware of his presence, and rang the doorbell. While they waited, their conversation carried easily to Bunny's astounded ears.

"Thornaby has a bet about it with Freddy Vereker," said the shaggy man, evidently continuing some earlier conversation. "Freddy can't come, I hear. Of course it won't be won or lost tonight. But the dear chap thinks he's been invited as a cricketer!"

"I don't believe he's the other thing," the second man said. "I believe it's all idle chatter."

"I think you'll find it more than that," the other warned as the door opened and swallowed them up.

Poor Bunny. He clung weakly to the pillar that had concealed him. A trap! He knew it was a trap! And Raffles wouldn't listen. There was nothing to do but to enter this dreadful house. He owed Raffles so much, no matter where he was. With a trembling finger, Bunny

129

rang the bell and was instantly admitted by the butler, who led him through a capacious hall to a well-appointed library. There, entertaining a small group of gentlemen, in whose midst Lady Alice glowed like a rare gem in an inferior setting, was none other than Raffles. A storm of emotions assailed Bunny—anger, relief, fear—so that on entering he appeared quite gauche.

"You promised to pick me up on your way," he managed to say reproachfully when Raffles greeted him.

"Oh, did I? Then I forgot," Raffles said as though it mattered not a jot.

Lady Alice, sensing a slight strain, moved gracefully to Bunny and said:

"Mr. Raffles had been explaining how he hoodwinks people. . . ."

"What?" cried Bunny, staring in alarm at his foolhardy friend.

". . . when he's bowling," Lady Alice finished gently, and handed the startled young man over to her father, who proceeded with the introductions.

It was an august and daunting company: Lord Selby, the High Court Judge, Sir Ernest Kingsmill, Q.E., and Mr. Parrington, the celebrated crime novelist. With a fluttering heart, Bunny recognized these latter two as the men he had overheard at the door.

"So you're the famous Mr. Manders," Parrington greeted him heartily, wringing his hand.

Bunny gaped nervously.

"Famous?" he queried. "What for?"

"For being the friend and associate of Mr. Raffles," he replied jovially.

Never had Bunny imagined a time or circumstance in which to be so identified would seem to him a decidedly mixed blessing, but so it seemed then. With a sinking feeling, he followed the others into the silk hung dining room and took his place at table. The repast fully justified the Earl of Thornaby's reputation for keeping one of the best and most tempting tables in Europe, but to Bunny each succulent dish tasted like ashes. This was not caused by any culinary disaster, but by the conversation. It sounded to his ears that every other word spoken was "burglar" or "burglary" and that both Kingsmill and Selby took an inordinate pleasure in describing the most heinous crimes and the blood-chilling punishments they had procured and meted out. Raffles, like Bunny, though for quite different reasons, did not contribute to the reminiscences and speculations which flowed back and forth across the table. He listened politely and ate with relish until Lord Thornaby invited his opinion on what he termed "the enterprising burglar."

"It must be the most amusing branch of the business," Raffles opined.

Bunny held his breath.

"Amusing," Raffles added with a quiet smile, "for the people who do it. Not for the people who get burgled."

"Amusing in what way?" inquired Lord Selby sternly.

"Well, I only imagine these things . . . but I imagine there are some people who get an excitement, a thrill out of pitting themselves against the best brains of the law. . . . In much the same way," he added laconically, "that I get my excitement out of pitting my skill as a bowler against the best batsmen in the land."

Bunny let out his breath.

There was a general murmur of interest when

Raffles had finished and Kingsmill, as though rehearsed, asked generally:

"Then who would you say is the reigning king of burglars?"

"I'd say the man who stole the Lochmaben tiara," said Thornaby firmly and at once.

"Oh really? I know him well," said Raffles.

Bunny tried to swallow, could not and held his breath again.

"What?" cried Thornaby, after a shocked silence. "You know the thief?"

"I wish I meant that," said Raffles, smiling innocently. "But no, I just meant I know Lord Lochmaben."

Bunny coughed noisily.

"It's rather a coincidence," said Thornaby through Bunny's splutters, "that you know Lord Lochmaben. I believe you also know the Milchester people, where Lady Melrose had her necklace stolen last year."

"Yes," agreed Raffles. "I was staying there at the time."

"We believe," said Thornaby ponderously, glancing at his fellow Criminologists, "it to be the same man. The crimes are both in the same style."

"I suppose there is a slight similarity," conceded Raffles, while Bunny frantically tried to recall the details of the Melrose robbery. "But surely it's not enough to found a theory on?"

"Well, let me quote you a third crime—the theft of the St. Agnes Cup from the British Museum."

"Good heavens!" exclaimed Raffles. "Has that been stolen?"

"It has," Thornaby informed him dryly.

"But we were looking at it only the other day. You and I and Lady Alice . . ."

132

"It was stolen the very next day," Lady Alice said quietly. Then, fixing her father with a reproving eye, she added: "That's why my father has jumped to his wrong conclusion."

"What conclusion?" asked Raffles, his face the very portrait of excited interest.

"Hardly a firm conclusion yet," said Thornaby huffily. "More in the nature of an inspired guess."

"May we hear it?" asked Raffles. "I'm sure we'd be most interested, all of us," he said, looking at Bunny who had grown slightly purple in the face.

"Well, Mr. Raffles, it starts from the kinship between the Lochmaben tiara theft, and the Melrose necklace and the St. Agnes Cup. You admit there is a kinship?"

Raffles considered very carefully.

"I agree there seems to be a sort of similar brilliance," he said at last. "I only wish I could meet the chap."

"I wish we could meet him, too," agreed Thornaby, fixing his eyes intently on Raffles.

"It might be easier than you think," Raffles said, smiling.

"You mean he might be in the house now?" Lord Thornaby suggested with deliberation.

"What a joke if he were!" laughed Parrington, much amused by the idea.

"Heaven forbid!" muttered Raffles, apparently alarmed.

"It would be quite in keeping with the character of this man," Kingsmill said. "To pay a call on the chairman of the Criminologists' Club and to choose an evening when he happened to be entertaining the members."

"Quite in keeping," agreed Raffles. "One sees a certain wit in all his doings."

"He might be robbing us now. What a horrible thought," cried Lady Alice in some alarm.

"Hardly possible," said Lord Selby dismissively.

"Yes," agreed Bunny, hoping to change the subject. "It is a bit farfetched."

"Father," pleaded Lady Alice, "send someone to make sure. I know I'm being silly but . . ."

"That's all right, my dear," said her doting father soothingly. "Legget," he called, motioning the butler forward, "just go upstairs to see if all the doors are open and the rooms in proper order."

Legget left at once to do his master's bidding. There was a marked change in the atmosphere at the table characterized by a certain bluff reassurance and a general dismissal of Lady Alice's foolish fears. Lord Thornaby was himself charged with having led them to this unsettling topic.

"Only by talking about styles of crime," he defended himself. "We think, Mr. Raffles, we Criminologists, that every crime has a signature appended. As identifiable as the work of a great artist."

"And according to our theory," Parrington took up the explanation excitedly, "there is only one man in England who could have committed certain crimes."

"Oh, who?" asked Raffles with interest.

"Well, our idea was . . ." began Lord Thornaby when he was interrupted by the returning butler.

"I beg your lordship's pardon, but I think your lordship must have forgot."

"Forgotten what?" demanded his lordship angrily.

"Locking your lordship's door," replied the butler. "I've seen for myself, my lord. Bedroom door, dressing-room door, both locked."

134

"By whom?" roared Thornaby, his face becoming puce with rage. With one look at his fellow Criminologists, he rose from the table and hurried toward the stairs. Eagerly, one by one, the guests began to follow him until there was a press of gentlemen scurrying anxiously up the wide staircase. Courteously, Raffles, who had remained seated, offered to escort his hostess to the upper floor.

When they arrived at the first-floor landing, having proceeded at a sedate pace, it was to hear the novelist Parrington announcing that the door had been jammed on the inside with a wedge and gimlet. Thoroughly enjoying his secondhand knowledge of criminal methods, the redoubtable Mr. Parrington volunteered, if a ladder could be procured, to enter the bedroom, burglarlike, via the window and to open the door. The offer was immediately accepted and Parrington trotted off, full of his own importance.

"Dashing fellow," said Raffles. "I'm thankful it's not me. I have no head for heights."

"Our friend Parrington takes more kindly to all this than I do, I can tell you," grumbled Lord Thornaby.

"It's grist to his mill," Raffles pointed out.

"Exactly! We shall have the whole thing in his next novel," Thornaby agreed.

"Once they catch the criminal," said Raffles. "Assuming there is one. We don't know yet that there has been any crime at all."

"Why else should anyone bother to lock the door?" demanded the irate earl.

"Were there any valuables in your bedroom?" inquired Raffles civilly.

"Yes. Cuff links, studs, things like that. And some cash."

"Cash, eh? Any burglar would be glad to have that," said Raffles with remorseless good humor.

"The man I'm thinking of," snapped Thornaby, "would be more interested in the jewelry."

"Correction," said Kingsmill. "The man you *were* thinking of. The burglar must have been at work while we were downstairs having dinner."

The indisputable truth of this statement had an instant effect on Lord Thornaby. His face showed anger and the bitter disappointment of a child thwarted of its heart's desire. He glared at Raffles, bidding a mental farewell to his inspired guess that had so nearly become a conclusion.

At that moment, Parrington could be heard inside the bedroom. Another moment and he threw open the door, proudly displaying the wedge and gimlet which, as he had predicted, had barred the door. The room, as the company saw at once, was in riotous disorder. Stud boxes were strewn about the floor; drawers hung open, their contents spilling out. On a corner chair, a clock reposed, partially wrapped in a monogrammed towel. Lord Thornaby stared at the wreckage helplessly and, in a weak voice, demanded that his valet be sent for to make a thorough check of his property. In an open cupboard Kingsmill espied a large trunk, its lid open and its body empty.

"What did you have in this?" he inquired of his dismayed host.

"My peer's robes and coronet," said the earl, advancing toward the ransacked trunk.

"What earthly use would a burglar have for your peer's robes and coronet?" mused Kingsmill. "He could hardly hope to attend the Jubilee in your place."

"The metal in the coronet has some intrinsic value,

136

perhaps?" suggested Raffles, wrinkling his nose at the disorder.

"Not enough to make it worth anyone's while recovering it," said Thornaby glumly.

"Then it must be," said Raffles gaily, "that the burglar is going to a fancy dress ball, and is at his wit's end for what to wear."

This remark was greeted with loud laughter, during which his lordship's valet arrived and was immediately set to check the contents of the room. Legget was dispatched to telephone the police, and the rest of the party returned to the dining room and their interrupted meal.

On hearing, as he shortly did, that only his peer's robes and coronet had been taken, Lord Thornaby swiftly recovered his good humor and insisted upon toasting the burglar whose signature they had been discussing, for nothing in the world would dissuade him from the conviction that that same audacious thief had paid him a characteristic visit.

"The audacity was his and his alone," he lectured the company. "I look no further than the fact of his honoring me on the very night when I try to entertain my brother Criminologists. That's no coincidence, but a deliberate irony, which would have occurred to no other criminal mind in England."

"You may be right," agreed Raffles, raising his glass.

"I'm quite certain of it. No other criminal in the world would have crowned so delicious a conception with so perfect an achievement."

And the evening's entertainment was completed by the arrival of one Inspector Woodward of Scotland Yard, who was able to inform the diners that the robbery had taken place between a quarter past eight and the half hour. Lord Thornaby's valet had been in the bedroom, as usual, until a quarter past, and the clock, about which the burglar had evidently had second thoughts, was stopped by rough handling at twenty minutes past. So it was concluded that the burglary had taken place just as the party was commencing upon the excellent saddle of lamb. Lord Thornaby dismissed the policeman jovially, expressing the wish that the criminal, one with such a remarkable sense of occasion, might never be caught.

"By the way, Raffles," he said as he and Bunny were taking their leave. "Are you a member of the Atheneum?"

"I do not have that honor," admitted Raffles.

"I don't know about that," said his lordship frankly, "but I wondered if you'd like to join? I'd be glad to put you up, and I have a number of friends on the committee," he finished with a roguish wink.

Raffles accepted, expressing his pleasure, and he and Bunny set out for the Albany and a nightcap. Once there, Bunny quickly recovered his spirits. He was much excited by Lord Thornaby's offer to Raffles, who was himself rather more taken by an invitation to ride with Lady Alice in Hyde Park.

"In fact," said Bunny expansively, "they did everything except apologize for their unworthy suspicions."

"Unworthy?" questioned Raffles, raising an ironic eyebrow.

"You certainly proved beyond a shadow of a doubt that it couldn't possibly have been you, and therefore that it couldn't have been you that stole the cup and so forth."

"Well, that was useful," agreed Raffles.

"It wiped the slate clean," Bunny enthused. "They'll eat out of your hand for the rest of their days."

"Good," said Raffles, going into his bedroom.

"Though at one time," reflected Bunny, "you were skating on terribly thin ice. I began to think you were putting your head in the lion's mouth for fun. And I was there to see the fun," he called.

"Bunny, I like you being there to see the fun," Raffles called back. "Wouldn't you say this is fun?"

He stepped from the bedroom draped in the robes of a peer of England and with a coronet set rakishly upon his head. With an athletic grace he twirled around while Bunny watched in astonishment.

"Thornaby's?" he managed to whisper when Raffles had ceased his victory pirouettes.

"Don't you think it would do well for a fancy dress ball?"

"But you couldn't have taken it!" said Bunny, sitting down quickly.

"I and no other."

"From Thornaby House?"

"From that very place."

"It's impossible." Bunny shook his head. "You were having dinner at the time. I was there! I saw you!"

"And the Criminologists' Club saw me. They know, like you, that it's impossible. But here are the robes and the coronet to prove the opposite."

"But how. . . ?" asked Bunny.

"Magic, my dear Bunny. Magic."

"No, seriously."

"Seriously, then . . ." Raffles assented, sitting down and taking a sip of his Scotch before beginning his explanation.

First he reminded Bunny of the thorough study he had made of the back windows of Thornaby House from Bunny's Mount Street flat. By so doing, he had familiarized himself with the domestic routine of the household and had identified his lordship's valet. A few discreet inquiries had revealed a certain romantic attachment between that young man and a house parlormaid in the service of a neighboring family. A telegram suggesting a secret rendezvous with the young woman was sufficient to lure the love-sick valet from his duties sharp at eight o'clock. This, of course, he would not confess to the police for fear of Lord Thornaby.

Access to the bedroom had been obtained by means of the window and with the aid of an ingenious cane which, as Raffles demonstrated to Bunny's delight, opened out in sections which fitted one inside the other. A hook could thus be fixed to the gutter to provide a stable anchorage for the yards of fine, knotted rope which, as he presently revealed, could be wound around the waist beneath a waistcoat without possibility of detection.

"But how long did the whole thing take you?" asked Bunny, quite lost in admiration.

"I suppose five minutes in all," was the casual reply.

"What? You mean to tell me you climbed up and down, in and out, broke into the cupboard and that big tin box, pinched the robes, wrapped up the clock, pulled out all the drawers, spilled the studs and all the rest of it, all in five minutes?" cried Bunny in disbelief.

"Of course I don't and of course I didn't," said Raffles. "I made two bites at the cherry, Bunny. I had a dress rehearsal in the dead of last night. Our noble friend was snoring throughout and I could take as long as I pleased. And, of course, I was very tidy, and left the place exactly as I found it, like a good boy. Except that I took the robes. Tonight I simply had to muddle the room a bit and make it look as if I'd taken the robes *tonight*. I was ringing the bell at the front door by five to eight," he concluded proudly.

Bunny gasped in astonishment. Now he understood why Raffles had not collected him and now that he did so, he did not mind a bit.

"By George!" he cried happily. "It's the biggest thing you ever did in your life, Raffles."

"Well," admitted Raffles modestly, "I've shown those dear Criminologists that I couldn't possibly have done it, so it's some other fellow who did it, whom they've been perfect asses to confuse with me."

"You've done a miracle, Raffles," Bunny said solemnly.

"Perhaps. But now do you mind if I ask you to go, Bunny? I am short of sleep and fed up with excitement." Raffles stretched sleepily, the robes slipping from his shoulders.

Bunny stood up at once and went to fetch his coat from the hall.

"Oh, Raffles," he said over his shoulder, "what are you going to do with the robes?"

"Ah, yes. Well, they're no use to me. What are you doing in the morning, Bunny, while I'm riding?"

"Buying a biscuit tin?" suggested Bunny, gleefully popping his head around the sitting-room door. "Huntley and Palmer's?"

"No, not a biscuit tin." Raffles smiled. "It wouldn't be half big enough."

"What then?" inquired Bunny, racking his brains.

"Well, my daily woman has been on at me for some time now to buy her a newfangled kind of carpet sweeper, with a pump-type cleaner. I think it's time I did her that kindness. They come in big, plain cardboard boxes, with no distinguishing marks, which, afterwards, you can leave in the cloakroom at Charing Cross Station," he suggested idly.

"And?" prompted Bunny.

"And send Lord Tornaby the ticket—in plenty of time for the Jubilee."

And so Lord Thornaby was able to attend the Jubilee celebrations which, it may be surmised, were lent a little piquancy by Her Majesty's receipt of an extremely beautiful if unorthodox gift. Her Majesty, sensible as always of the proprieties, could not personally retain the St. Agnes Cup, but she hit, in her wisdom, upon an admirable compromise. It was placed on loan in the British Museum, that it might be enjoyed, if not actually owned, by the nation.

Five

A TRAP TO CATCH A
CRACKSMAN

••••——◆——••••

**IN WHICH RAFFLES IS CAUGHT IN A
TRAP AND BUNNY PLAYS THE HERO'S
PART, ONLY TO BE BURGLED FOR
HIS PAINS**

THE THEFT OF the gold cup and of Lord Thornaby's robes had done much for morale and to avert tiresome suspicion, but they had netted precisely nothing to swell the coffers of A. J. Raffles and his friend. The cricket season in that Jubilee year proved exceptionally expensive for one who, thanks to his brilliance, received almost as much honor in sporting circles as Her Majesty rightly commanded everywhere. But honor for one of nonroyal blood is expensive and by the close of the season, Raffles was forced to acknowledge the necessity of embarking upon some new and lucrative adventure. He considered various wealthy targets but in each discerned some impediment. He lacked, he came to realize, that essential spur—a challenge.

He still had not formulated any plan on the evening of the International Sporting Club's annual dinner, at which he was to be one of the guests of honor. Bunny, whom he had cordially invited to accompany him, was in a recalcitrant mood. He would, he declared, prefer a music hall and dinner at Willis's. Raffles reminded his friend of the honor that was being done him and the need for economy. After all, the dinner would be free. But these arguments, for all they were wise and truthful, fell on deaf ears. The fact of the matter was, as Raffles quickly discovered, that Bunny still nursed a considerable resentment about the amount of time Raffles had lavished of late on Lady Alice Thornaby. He felt himself to be second choice, a choice of necessity since ladies were naturally not admitted to the International Sporting Club, and because he could be relied upon not to yawn through the speeches. Raffles listened to these complaints patiently, while adjusting his black tie.

"The real reason for taking you there tonight," he explained with candor, "is that you, my dear Bunny, are my partner in crime."

"Is it crime tonight?" asked Bunny, instantly alarmed.

"Not tonight," Raffles calmed him.

"Well, that's something."

"You are no more a natural-born criminal than I am, Bunny," Raffles continued. "You need to have your criminal tendencies refreshed from time to time. You need to have your feelings of greed and envy sharpened—whetted like a knife."

"Do I?" said Bunny blankly, for the thought had never occurred to him.

"You do," Raffles assured him. "And the International Sporting Club is the perfect place to do it. Everyone there is purple with wealth, dripping with masculine jewelry."

"And you hope to find a suitable victim among them?" Bunny suggested, brightening.

144

"I hope to make you as eager for loot as I am," Raffles replied, swinging his evening cloak about his shoulders and tucking his cane under his arm.

During the short cab ride to the International Sporting Club, Raffles expanded his theme. Necessity pressed upon them and here was a heaven-sent opportunity to reconnoiter the field. If, he concluded, opportunity should not only present itself but also constitute a challenge, then he would be perfectly happy. This exposition did much to cheer Bunny, who surveyed the company, which was every bit as rich and brilliant as Raffles had predicted, with new interest. The dinner, considering that it was free, was acceptable and the speeches, though boring, not of inordinate length.

After dinner the gentlemen circulated so that the maximum number might have an opportunity to meet the eminent guests of honor. Bunny trotted round after Raffles like a shadow, inwardly applauding and endorsing the many compliments that were heaped upon his handsome head. It was during one such exchange that Raffles saw, out of the corner of his eye, Sir Cyriac Morrison, an old acquaintance who was beckoning him. Raffles gracefully excused himself and went toward the gentleman.

"Hello, Swigger. Did you want me?" Raffles inquired.

"Raffles. I want to introduce you . . ." he said, waving a vague hand toward a giant of a man who lowered over him. "Barney Maguire, heavyweight champion of the United States. Barney, this is Mr. Raffles, the cricketer."

Raffles extended his hand and immediately felt the brute strength of the man. His keen eyes also noted the eighteen-carat gold bangle which adorned the pugilist's massive, hairy wrist.

"Great honor to bring two such great sportsmen together," Swigger Morrison said to no one in particular, swaying alarmingly.

"You play cricket, Mr. Raffles?" said Maguire in a deep, resonant voice.

"Yes, I do," confirmed Raffles, noting the priceless studs which adorned the American's barreled shirt front.

"With those long-handled mallets and hoops?" he queried.

"No, the mallets are only for when we can't hit the ball with the bat," joked Raffles, but Maguire's face remained impassive, so he added: "The usual game is much more like your baseball. Except there's much more skill in it."

"How d'you figure that?" boomed the boxer, obviously doubting it.

"Well, I'm a pitcher," Raffles explained. "I cannot only make the ball curve either way, but we usually make the ball hit the ground and turn either way, without altering our action when we throw it."

"You don't say." Maguire was clearly impressed. "How d'you do that?"

"There's a fellow now, plays for Middlesex with me, he's invented what we call a bosie, or googly," Raffles went on enthusiastically. "He holds the ball like this . . ." Raffles held out his hand and demonstrated the grip. Maguire leaned toward him. "I say," said Raffles, "that's a magnificent watch chain you've got."

"You like my watch chain?" said the American, plainly pleased and fingering the heavily jeweled article with pride. "You ain't seen nothing yet."

Clapping Raffles on the shoulder he immediately began to itemize the priceless possessions which his skill in the ring had brought him. But talking about them

146

would not suffice. Raffles and his young friend must see for themselves. Still describing the insignia of his wealth, in a voice which Bunny constantly feared would awaken the dead, Maguire conducted them to his rented home in Half Moon Street.

"Let's go through to my den," he cried as soon as they arrived. "I keep most of my loot in there."

Raffles could not suppress a smile.

"You call it 'loot?' " he inquired.

"Sure. What'd you call it?"

"Loot," said Raffles blithely.

"Same word, same thing, both sides of the Atlantic. And got the same way," Maguire asserted jovially.

"Oh, really?" said Raffles, still smiling.

"I don't know how much money you make out of playing cricket," said Maguire, leading them into his den, "but I'll lay it ain't half what I get out of boxing."

He crossed the room to where a small, sallow man was dozing in a leather wing-chair before the fire. He shook the man roughly by the shoulder.

"Nor one quarter," agreed Raffles. "Nor one hundredth."

"Jeez," said the boxer with a great show of sympathy. "I knew this was a poor country, but are you paid as bad as that?"

"I am an amateur, Mr. Maguire. I am paid nothing at all," said Raffles with dignity.

"Then what the hell d'you do it for?" demanded the astounded Maguire.

"Partly for love of the game . . ."

"You're crazy!" Maguire said and, turning to the man in the chair, added: "Hey Jethro, did you hear that? This guy," he said, pointing to Raffles, "is a big international sportsman, and he says he don't make anything out of it!"

"He's crazy," agreed Jethro soberly.

"Jethro's my secretary," Maguire explained. "He knows what I make."

"And it ain't peanuts," Jethro supplied.

"It sure ain't. Sit down, Mr. Raffles. Take a load off your feet. And your friend. What'll it be? Scotch?"

Raffles and Bunny accepted and found themselves chairs. While they did so, Maguire picked up a silver-labeled decanter from an octagonal table and carried it to a revolving spirit table. From this he took a second decanter, unlabeled, and replaced it with the first. Then he poured exceedingly generous measures of whisky for his guests, his secretary and himself.

"Greatest invention your country ever dreamed up," he announced, lifting his glass in an informal toast.

"Scotland?" queried Raffles mildly.

"That's somewhere in England, ain't it?" said the American, smacking his lips noisily.

"You're Irish yourself, I take it, Mr. Maguire?" said Raffles.

"Sure am," he agreed heartily. "My grandparents came to New York in the famine of eighteen-forty. I only wish they could see me now! I ain't done bad for a boy from the wrong side of the tracks." He paused and took another swig of "England's greatest invention." "I'm the greatest fighter in the world, that's all. That's why they give me all those things I was telling you about." He strode across the room and took down from its place on the wall a heavily bejeweled belt. "Look at this, Mr. Raffles. And your friend," he cried expansively. "Presented to me by the State of Nevada. It says it, right across the back. 'Presented to the greatest fighter in the world—Barney Maguire,'" he recited bombastically while Raffles examined the belt

148

before handing it to Bunny. "I guess that proves it," Maguire said with a note of challenge in his voice.

"I guess it does," agreed Raffles.

"The citizens of Sacramento gave me this," Maguire went on, somewhat mollified. "A gold brick, made out of their own gold dust."

"Valuable," commented Raffles, hefting the brick in his hand.

"It ain't so much the value, it's the thought behind it. Know what I mean?" said the pugilist sentimentally. "But when it comes to value in terms of hard cash, I guess this is my most valuable possession," he said, picking up a solid silver statuette and staring at it fondly. "And I guess I treasure it most in sentimental value, too," he added.

"May I see?" asked Raffles politely.

"I don't usually let anyone else handle it," Maguire said gruffly, but passing the object into Raffles's hands.

"I'd feel the same way if it were mine," Raffles assured him, inspecting the statuette carefully. "Why, it's you!" he exclaimed.

"Yep," agreed Maguire. "Silver statuette of me, done by a famous sculptor and presented to me by the Fisticuff Club of New York. That's the most famous sporting club in all New York."

"I say," said Raffles, in tones of deepest appreciation. "May I give it to Bunny to hold for a moment? I just want him to feel how much weight of silver there is in it. It'd be worth a small fortune, even melted down," he said to Bunny as he passed the statuette to him.

"Nobody ain't never going to melt that statue down," cried Maguire, wresting it from Bunny's startled grasp and restoring it to pride of place on his trophy shelf.

"But don't you keep it in a safe?" said Raffles with concern. "And these things?" He touched the gold brick and the belt. "They're worth so much money."

"I don't like 'em safes. I like looking at 'em," explained the boxer, restoring his other treasures to their rightful places.

"But they must be a terrible temptation to burglars," said Raffles. "Aren't you afraid?"

Maguire's face broke into a grin in which guile and pride mingled unpleasantly.

"I have a trap to catch the cleverest cracksman alive," he announced.

"Oh yes. What?" asked Raffles, greatly intrigued.

"That's my secret."

"Can you guess, Bunny?" Raffles asked, turning to his friend.

"I imagine . . ." Bunny began hesitantly, only to be drowned out by Maguire.

"Imagine what you like. I ain't telling. Neither you nor anybody else."

"Your secret would be perfectly safe with us," Bunny said gently. "We're gentlemen."

"Sure you're gentlemen," Maguire agreed, nodding his head sagely. "That's what makes you so dangerous."

"What do you mean?" demanded Bunny, affronted.

"You wouldn't do anything crooked yourselves, so you wouldn't suspect anyone else of being crooked. You wouldn't see any harm in saying, 'Did I tell you what Barney Maguire told me the other night?'" he mimicked lamentably. "And out it comes."

"You're quite right, Maguire," Raffles agreed quickly. "That's exactly the kind of thing we might say. Take my advice, don't dream of telling us."

Pleased with Raffles's understanding, Maguire plied

them with second generous measures of whisky, insisting quite rudely when Bunny attempted to decline. The latter gave way with what grace he could muster, while the long-silent Jethro proposed a toast.

"Barney Maguire!"

"And his success in his fight next week," Maguire added.

Raffles and Bunny quietly echoed the toast and drank.

"You're fighting next week?" Raffles said pleasantly.

"Fighting the British champion. Can't remember what his name is."

"You think it's all right to drink like this when you're in training?" asked Raffles out of professional curiosity.

"Listen," boomed the fighter. "To fight an Englishman I don't go into training."

Bunny drew in his breath sharply, but Raffles only commented:

"Oh, really?"

"Say, I like you, Raffles. Other Englishmen I've met would've been offended by that remark," said the American, beaming. "I want you to know you can come round here any time you like and I'll give you a drink."

"And my friend Bunny, too?" asked Raffles, with a bow of acceptance.

"And your friend Bunny, too," assented Maguire.

"Thank you," Raffles said, his voice trembling slightly.

A few moments later, much to Bunny's relief, Raffles made their excuses and bade the Americans "good night." Outside, Raffles strode along in silence and, when they reached the Albany entrance, dismissed Bunny with a curt "good night." Bunny had seldom seen the great Raffles angry and it was an awesome sight. He knew better than to protest and besides felt that his anger was more than justified. He was also certain that Raffles would want and have his revenge. Thus it came as little surprise to him when, a few days later, Raffles, on glimpsing Maguire's name in the newspaper, launched into the following tirade.

"I am going to get my revenge on that monstrous ape, on behalf of my countrymen. He had the nerve to say that other Englishmen would have been offended by his remark! Yes, they certainly would. And I was offended, too! I'll have his gold brick and his silver statuette for that—just see if I don't."

"Yes," said Bunny calmly, settling himself before Raffles's blazing hearth. "I thought that was the point at which you decided to have them."

"I was tempted already. That was the last straw," Raffles cried angrily, smiting his clenched fist into the palm of his left hand. "Bunny," he said, suddenly growing calmer, "knowing me as you do, would you say I was the cleverest burglar alive?"

"Without a doubt," agreed Bunny sincerely.

"Barney Maguire says he has a trap to catch the cleverest cracksman alive."

"What do you suppose it is?"

"I shall have to find out on Friday."

"Friday you're going to do it?"

"Thursday is his fight. Judging by the way he drinks whisky before a fight, afterwards he'll drink even more. He'll be off his guard."

"I hope he loses," said Bunny vehemently, "even though I've got a bet on him to win."

At this Raffles furrowed his brows disapprovingly.

"Isn't that rather unpatriotic, Bunny?"

"No, no. Not at all. I wouldn't dream of being unpatriotic. It's just that old Swigger Morrison was going on about how good our man is, and I said I thought Maguire looked the stronger of the two. Before I knew where I was, I'd got a bet on my hands."

"How much for?" inquired Raffles, satisfied of Bunny's motives.

"No money. Loser has to stand the winner a dinner at his club."

"When is it going to be?"

"Friday. Oh! That means I . . ."

"I've worked out what I'm going to do," Raffles said firmly, "and I'll be better off on my own."

"I can help you with that big brute," insisted Bunny. "I boxed at school, you know."

"My dear Bunny, one blow from Maguire and I'll be past all helping. I mean to defeat him not by strength but by cunning."

"How?" said Bunny, leaning forward eagerly.

"He's a boxer, I'm a slow bowler. Every man to his trade," was the enigmatic reply.

"You don't want to tell me how," said Bunny resignedly. "Look, I'll change the dinner," he offered.

"No. I insist," said Raffles and no amount of argument or pleading on Bunny's part would make him change his mind.

For once Bunny did not take his exclusion too badly. He realized that Maguire's manner and uncouth remarks had touched a deep spring of honor in Raffles, that most honorable of sportsmen, and that the challenge had become, at least in Raffles's view, a personal matter. He had to do it alone, amateur sportsman against professional braggart. Besides, who but Raffles could risk a trap to catch the cleverest criminal alive?

Therefore Bunny did not alter the arrangement he

had made with Swigger Morrison but, when Maguire won the fight with arrogant ease, quite cheerfully reported to Swigger's club for a dinner which promised to be one of the most liquid he would ever experience.

Meanwhile, that same Friday evening, Raffles took a cab to the King's Road, Chelsea, and, having alighted, made his discreet way through the dark alleys to his studio. Once there he inspected his wardrobe of disguises, selecting, after some thought, a suit of the most dilapidated and tattered appearance. When arrayed in this garment, he applied a liberal amount of soot from the chimney to his aristocratic features, transforming himself thereby into an unremarkable down-and-out, whose passage toward Half Moon Street attracted no attention whatsoever.

Like a shadow with a crowbar, he gained swift access to Maguire's house, propping the door shut with a convenient umbrella. The den, to which he went silently and at once, was lit only by the embers of a good fire. Noting that the thick brocade curtains were tightly drawn, Raffles put on the light and calmly transferred the jeweled belt, the gold brick and the silver statuette to a small bag he had brought with him. The entire operation had taken but a few minutes. Highly pleased with himself, Raffles glanced around the room, looking for other portable valuables, but there were none. Instead his eye lit upon the silver-labeled decanter of Scotch whisky. Just a taste, he thought, moving toward the octagonal table, to test his theory.

It was about that very time that Bunny, rather the worse for wear, was experiencing some difficulty in placing his key in the lock. It had been a splendid dinner and Swigger Morrison almost the best of company, but now Bunny was ready for bed. Apart from anything else, his sitting-room floor seemed to have developed the disconcerting habit of undulating and rising to meet him. He crossed it with caution, only to encounter the same phenomenon in his bedroom. He walked unsteadily to the bed and was about to throw himself gratefully upon it when the telephone began to ring. Obediently Bunny turned around and made the perilous crossing of the floors once more. Pleased with himself for having made it more or less upright, he picked up the telephone and held it to his ear.

"Hello?"

"That you, Bunny?" said a voice familiar but faint and, it seemed to Bunny's rather clouded brain, full of weariness.

"Yes. Are you Raffles?" he asked, holding the telephone away from him in a puzzled way.

"Bunny. I want you . . . quick," said the voice and now, as alarm began to thin the mists of alcohol, it was unmistakably Raffles speaking.

"Raffles! What has happened? What has happened?" he repeated more slowly and distinctly.

"Extraordinary thing," said the voice, leaden and dreamy at once.

"I'll come at once. Where are you?"

"Maguire's."

"Where's Maguire?" demanded Bunny, fearing the worst.

"Half Moon Street."

"I know where it is," said Bunny. "Where's he? Is he there?"

"Noooo," said the voice, growing fainter. "Not here."

"Raffles," shouted Bunny. "What's the matter?"

"Come quick." The voice seemed to drift down the wire.

"I'm coming. What's the matter?"

"Caught . . . I'm caught . . . in the trap. . . . Just as he said . . ."

The voice faded away into something resembling a groan. Then Bunny heard a crash as of a body falling heavily onto the floor.

"Raffles! Raffles!" he cried, his heart racing. But there was no reply, only the silence of disaster.

If a man may, as the poets have claimed, travel at the speed of light, then Bunny Manders did so that night. Never has a cab been sought and found with such haste; never driven through the sleeping streets of London at such fiery speed, nor deposited a more anxious passenger. Bunny flew to the door of Maguire's house before the cabby had pocketed the fare. Once he rang the bell and stood straining like a dog on a leash. Again he rang, packing back and forth, but no one came to open that suddenly sinister portal. Stooping low, Bunny pushed open the flap of the letter box and peered into the gloom of the hall. He felt the door give under his impatient fingers and pushed. An umbrella propped against it on the inside fell with a clatter to the floor, and the door swung wide. Bunny stepped boldly over the threshold and, holding his breath, made a steady advance toward a crack of light which shone under the door of Maguire's den. His ears straining, he drew close to the door when, behind him, issuing down the street, magnified by the silence of the night, he heard three voices raised in song.

"She's my lady love,
    She is my dove, my baby love,
    She's no gal for settin' down to dream,
    She's the only queen Laguna knows . . ."

Bunny froze in horror. Two of the voices were masculine and markedly American. He retreated from the door of the den, pressing himself back into the

156

shadows of the hall as Maguire, Jethro and a florid woman tumbled out of a carriage. Their cries of merriment were instantly silenced by sight of the open door. Jethro dashed forward and switched on the electric light, revealing Bunny cringing against the wall. With a growl, the mighty frame of Barney Maguire, the greatest fighter in the world, bore down upon Bunny.

"Mr. Maguire. Don't you remember me? I came round here with Raffles the other night. You must remember Raffles, even if you don't remember me," Bunny said on a single breath.

Maguire hesitated and slowly lowered his enormous fists. Jethro and the woman crowded close behind him, peering at Bunny.

"Raffles? That the guy who plays cricket?" said Maguire thickly.

"He's a famous cricketer," supplied the woman in an unsatisfactorily refined Cockney accent. "Everybody knows that."

"I'm his friend," cried Bunny. "I came here with him."

"What you doing here now?" demanded Maguire.

Bunny thought rapidly and grasped at the first straw his memory offered.

"You told us to look you up any time we liked. Any hour of the day or night," he said.

"That's so, Barney," Jethro confirmed, to Bunny's great relief.

Bunny held his breath as the boxer's angry expression faded, to be replaced by one of suspicious welcome. He put out his hand to Bunny.

"I took you for some darned crook," he explained. "If you hadn't spoken up slick like that, I'd have bust your face in."

"Lucky I did," said Bunny, wincing from the powerful, mashing grip of the pugilist.

"Where's your pal, Raffles?" asked Maguire, mercifully dropping Bunny's hand.

"I expected to find him here."

"Here?" said Maguire, surprised. Then he looked ominously over his shoulder at the open front door. "Did he break the door open or did you?"

"No. Neither," said Bunny at once, realizing that he should not have said that he had come in search of his friend. "I don't suppose he came here at all. Or if he did, he went away again," he improvised quickly.

"Jehoshaphat!" yelled Maguire, bounding past Bunny and surveying the den door. "I locked that door! And there's a light on now where there wasn't before! Ladies and gentlemen," he announced excitedly, "lay around where you are, while I see if we've caught us a burglar."

With a flourish, Maguire threw open the door with a crash and disappeared into the room. There his delighted eyes saw the unconscious body of a ruffian on the floor, the telephone dangling by its cord above him. He let out a great bellow of laughter and called for the others to come in.

"Come right in, Florrie, and see what happens to crooks who try to rob me. Come right in, sonny boy, and see how, for the second time in two days, America has come out on top."

Bunny stood back politely to allow the woman called Florrie to precede him into the den. Jethro, meanwhile, had gone to shut the front door, but soon hurried to see the spectacle of the trapped burglar.

"He does look an ugly specimen and dirty, too," said Florrie, peering at the supine figure and wrinkling her nose.

158

"I wouldn't soil my knuckles on his filthy face, but if I had my heavy boots on, I'd kick the soul out of his carcass," vowed the prizefighter, lowering over the figure.

"He's not worth spoiling your shoe leather on, dear," Florrie said soothingly.

"Who is he?" wondered Bunny, stooping down beside the figure and turning the unconscious head slightly the better to inspect the face. It took a moment for him to discern, beneath the grime, the familiar features of Raffles. His heart missed a beat and then another.

"Some crook from your East End, I suppose," said Maguire without interest. "Well, he's got what he deserved."

"D'you know him?" asked Jethro, peering over Bunny's shoulder.

"Good Lord, no!" said Bunny, rising hastily. "I just wanted to see if he was dead."

"He's alive all right," said Maguire. "He just fell into my trap."

"What trap?" asked Florrie.

"Shall I tell 'em, Jethro?" Maguire asked, enjoying himself hugely.

"It's for you to say," replied the secretary diplomatically.

"Ain't it the darndest thing you ever heard?" cried Maguire happily. "To think I've only got to invent a trap to catch a cook and along comes a crook and walks right into it. You, sonny boy," he said, turning to Bunny, "you remember that night when you were here with the other sport? You wanted to know about it."

"We had a wager between ourselves on what it was," Bunny replied.

"Well, at the time you wanted to know too much.

But I'm going to tell you now, or else bust!" he chortled.

"Well, go on then," urged Florrie, who was becoming rather impatient.

"See that whisky decanter on the table?" said Maguire, grinning.

"I've been looking at it for some time now," replied Florrie. "You don't know what a turn it gave me, seeing him on the floor like that, or you'd have asked me to have a little something."

"Whisky?" offered Maguire at once.

"Yes, please. I will take a little, now you mention it."

Maguire picked up a glass and, ignoring the decanter to which he had referred, took another from the spirit table and poured from it a large drink for Florrie.

"Thank you," simpered Florrie, taking the glass. "I take it for my health, you know. Aren't you going to have some?" she added.

"I sure am. To drink eternal confusion to my enemies. And a big glass for Jethro, who got me the poison from an Indian out West. That's all my trap is," he crowed. "The whisky is laced with poison."

With a scream both shrill and long, Florrie hurled the glass from her and subsided into the corner of the couch, her hand pressed to her heaving bosom.

"Not the whisky I gave you, my darling," Maguire said, laughing. "The one on the table there, that *he* drank out of."

"Oh," panted Florrie. "Well, you could have said so earlier. Giving me a shock like that!"

"That's my trap for crooks and cracksmen. The decanter on the table, in full view, and convenient to the hand. With that silver label round its neck to show *me* it's poisoned. Looks just the same as the other decanter, tastes just the same . . ." He handed Florrie a new drink. "But it's ticklish stuff that poison. Knocks a man out even better than one of my fists."

"What a filthy trick!" cried Bunny involuntarily.

"Yes, but I reckon I'm entitled to defend myself against crooks any way I please," replied Maguire menacingly.

Bunny was forced to agree with him, though it rankled. Maguire went on to expound his theory that no burglar could resist the temptation of helping himself to liquid refreshment while about his nefarious work. At the mention of this, Jethro picked up the bag lying beside the unconscious Raffles and placed it, open, on the table. Maguire stared into it and saw, with mounting rage, his precious trophies which he had so nearly lost. With a savage cry he delivered two thudding kicks to Raffles's ribs.

"Don't do that," protested Bunny, advancing toward him.

"Play light, Barney," agreed Jethro. "The man's drugged as well as down."

"He'll be lucky if he ever gets up, curse him," cried the incensed pugilist.

"I should judge it's about time to send for the police," declared Jethro.

"Not till I've done with him."

"What do you say?" Jethro turned to Bunny. "You're an Englishman, you invented the rules. The police, or let Barney smash him?"

In the next few moments Bunny understood, as clearly as any man living, the dilemma encapsulated in the ancient saw. He was, figuratively, between the Devil and the deep blue sea.

"Er . . . the police, I think," he said reluctantly, and

161

added, "Now!" as Maguire again approached his friend with malicious intent.

"Hey, what happened to the phone?" said Jethro, suddenly noticing the dangling ear piece. "I guess our friend was trying to make a call when he was knocked out by the drink." He replaced the fallen receiver.

Bunny faced yet another dilemma, but was distracted, momentarily, by Florrie who tugged at his sleeve.

"Would you mind just giving me another glass of Scotch, dear?"

Bunny did so gladly, mindful of her injunction to pour it from the good decanter. Meanwhile, he listened to an ominous exchange between Jethro and Maguire.

"I wonder who he was calling?"

"Who the blazes should he call?" growled Maguire.

"They'll tell us at the Central Exchange. They keep a record of all calls. We'll find out easy enough," said Jethro knowledgeably.

"I wonder . . ." said Bunny, not at all sure whether he should say it or not. "I wonder if he rang me up?"

"You, sonny boy? Why should he do that?" asked Maguire, his eyes narrowing suspiciously.

"I just wondered. . . . Because someone did ring me up. I thought it was Raffles. I told you."

"I don't see what he's got to do with the crook," said Jethro.

"Neither do I," Bunny agreed quickly.

"What the hell," cried Maguire, draining his glass of Scotch and helping himself to another.

"Were you cut off suddenly?" inquired Jethro.

"Yes. So suddenly that I never really gathered who it was who rang me up. That's why I wondered," Bunny said with a little more confidence.

Maguire thrust the decanter toward Bunny, who had not yet taken a drink.

"No, thank you. Not any for me," he said.

"What's that? Won't have a drink in my house?" said the boxer menacingly.

"I've been dining out," Bunny explained. "With Swigger Morrison. I've had my share, really I have."

"Look, sonny," Maguire said, "I like you a lot. But I shan't like you if you're not a good boy. You'll drink with me."

"While you're here," put in Jethro, "you do what Mr. Maguire says."

"Very well. Very well. One finger, if I must," Bunny said quickly as Maguire splashed a great many fingers into his glass.

Maguire sat down by the fire and Jethro pulled a chair up to the octagonal table. Bunny politely perched on the edge of a similar table, facing him, holding his unwanted whisky nervously.

"If it was that crook who called you," Jethro said doggedly, "why should you have thought it was your friend Raffles?"

This was the question Bunny had been fearing. As he tried to think of a convincing explanation, he glanced at Florrie and at Maguire. To his surprise, the former seemed to have fallen fast asleep, while Maguire's head was nodding, drooping onto his chest.

"Well," he began, looking at Jethro, "I was half asleep and rather drunk. Raffles was the first person who occurred to me. You see, we both have telephones. I don't know anybody else who has one. And I expected to hear from Raffles because we'd made a bet," he added, recalling what he had said earlier.

"What kind of a bet?" asked Jethro, whose eyelids seemed to be in danger of closing fast and of their own volition. He took another draft of his drink and shook his head.

"About the very thing we've just had explained to us," said Bunny. "I was sure it was a man trap Maguire meant. Raffles thought it must be something else." He was now almost certain that Maguire had fallen asleep. "We had a tremendous argument about it. Raffles said it wasn't a man trap. I said it was," he went on relentlessly, quite sure now that Maguire was unconscious. "I put my money on the man trap. Raffles put his on the other thing. And Raffles was right," he added brightly as Jethro blinked, pulled a face and tried to hold his head up. "It wasn't a man trap. I thought it must be." Jethro slumped forward, his forehead hitting the polished top of the octagonal table with a tremendous crash. "But it was every bit as good. And the whole bunch of you are caught in it, except me," he concluded joyfully, standing up and checking, one by one, that all three were indeed unconscious.

Once satisfied that the drugged whisky had taken effect, Bunny turned anxiously to Raffles. How to revive him? He shook him, called his name in an urgent tone, but received no response. There was nothing for it but to essay more brutal methods, even though they were uncongenial to him. He rolled Raffles over onto his back and dealt him several sharp blows on the face.

"I'm sorry about this, Raffles," he panted, "but you've got to wake up. Sorry, but believe me, you'll be grateful to me afterwards. I'm going to twist your wrist. That's good. Now the other one." A low, muffled cry escaped Raffles's lips. "Good," said Bunny, looking quickly around for some other means of reviving his friend. His eyes lit almost at once on a full bottle of soda water. He snatched it up and, standing well back, directed the full force of the bubbling stream on

Raffles's face. A series of groans issued from Raffles. He blinked, shivered, shook his head and, at last begged:

"Stop!"

"Raffles," exclaimed Bunny happily.

"Hello, Bunny," he replied with a ghost of his normal smile.

Bunny bent down beside him.

"You came," said Raffles weakly.

"Yes."

"I knew you would."

"Of course I came."

"Have they turned up yet?" asked Raffles, suddenly recalling the predicament he was in. "They will any minute."

"No they won't," Bunny assured him. "Look."

He helped Raffles to his feet and watched with pleasure the expression of relief that showed on the great man's face as he surveyed the heavily sleeping trio.

"How much did they have, Bunny?"

"Two glasses, each a good three fingers."

"Then we don't need to whisper and we won't need to walk on our toes," he cried.

"Servants?" asked Bunny.

"The servants come by day and go home at night."

"Good."

"Oof!" said Raffles, taking a few steps and instantly clasping a hand to his ribs. "I dreamt somebody was kicking me in the ribs."

"You can guess which one of them it was," said Bunny bitterly. "The beast is jolly well served."

"I should think he's safe till the forenoon," Raffles agreed. "How much of the stuff do you suppose I drank, and it knocked me cold for an hour?"

"A tablespoonful?" suggested Bunny.

"A teaspoonful at most! I guessed what it was but I couldn't resist making sure. The minute I was sure I swapped over the decanters, and put the silver label on the other one. I knew I'd been poisoned by a subtle drug. I didn't stand a chance of getting away from here before I collapsed."

"So you rang me up," supplied Bunny. "Thank heavens you did."

"It was my last brilliant inspiration—a sort of flash in the brain-pan—before the end came. I remember very little about it. I was more asleep than awake."

"You told me where you were and that you were caught. You fell to the floor before you came to the end," Bunny remembered with a shiver.

"You didn't hear that through the telephone?" said Raffles in surprise.

"Yes, as if I'd been in the room with you. Except that I thought it was Maguire who had sneaked in and knocked you out."

"You thought that," said Raffles solemnly, "and yet you came like a shot to do battle with the heavyweight champion of . . . of the world now, I suppose?"

"You'd do the same for me," said Bunny, blushing.

"I suppose I would," agreed Raffles. "But as fast as all that and as bold as brass? Jack the Giant Killer wasn't in it with you, Bunny."

"It was really a sort of Dutch courage," Bunny owned, shuffling his feet. "I was bold because I was a bit tipsy."

"In vino veritas, Bunny. It just helps your natural courage to come out," Raffles assured him.

"Are you all right, really?" asked Bunny, keen to change the subject.

"I've got a thundering headache, if that's what you

mean. But it's of no consequence at all. I'm happy as a clam not to be handed over to the police."

"Or beaten up by Maguire," Bunny added ruefully.

"Thank the Lord I avoided that," agreed Raffles wholeheartedly. "Though it might have made me even more unrecognizable. He didn't recognize me, did he, Bunny?" he asked, the possibility suddenly occurring to him.

"Not for a moment."

"Then I'm safe and free and I have my revenge on him," Raffles cried gaily, picking up the bag of valuables from the table. "I'll take the greatest pleasure in melting down his silver statuette, done by a famous sculptor," he sneered.

"And we'll have dinner on the gold brick presented by the citizens of Sacramento," whooped Bunny.

"A big dinner," Raffles promised.

"Hooray!"

"So big the jeweled belt won't fit us."

"Ready?" said Bunny, rubbing his hands together in anticipation. "Let's go!"

"What?"

"All we have to do is walk out the door!"

"No, Bunny," Raffles said with a solemn, regretful shake of his head. "I'm afraid you have to stay here. It's all right for me to go, but if you clear out too you're incriminated straightaway as my accomplice. And they know you. And once they had you they'd have a compass with the needle pointing straight at me."

"Yes," Bunny agreed miserably.

"Is there any plausible way," Raffles pondered, "you could let me escape, without being my accomplice? Of course! I've got it," he said, slapping his forehead.

"You drank some of the stuff, too. Not nearly as much as they did, but you fell asleep, too."

"Splendid," cried Bunny. "They were pressing it on me at the end. Jethro was the last one awake. He was staring at me when I had the glass raised to my lips."

"And of course you drank. And you fell asleep like them. Naturally, with such a small dose, you were the first to come to yourself. I had flown, so had the loot! You find yourself in this situation. The only one awake. What do you do?" Raffles demanded.

Bunny thought, wrinkling his brows in an effort of concentration.

"Try to rouse them?"

"You try," assented Raffles, "and you don't succeed. What do you do now?"

"Er . . ."

"What is the one and only innocent thing for you to do in the circumstances?"

"Send for the police?" suggested Bunny, his unwillingness to do any such thing quite apparent.

"Yes," confirmed Raffles.

"Must I?"

"Bunny, you've been so brave till now. It's no great effort. There's a telephone installed for the purpose. Try not to look blue about it, Bunny. They're quite the nicest fellows in the world, that is, if you haven't done anything criminal, and you haven't." Raffles tried to cheer him.

"I feel as if I had," Bunny said miserably. "And I shall have to lie to them. I hate lying."

"Yes. You're so obviously honest you're a marvelous liar," Raffles congratulated him.

"I wish you wouldn't say that," grumbled Bunny.

"And it's really the most convincing story one could conceive. Nothing that needs to be explained away.

168

Not a loophole in it anywhere. Except perhaps one," he added.

"You mean," said Bunny, "they'll find out you rang me up."

"No. Why should they suppose I rang anybody up? I see I managed to replace the receiver all right."

"Raffles," said Bunny in a quavering voice. "You didn't replace the receiver. You just dropped it."

"Hell!" expostulated the burglar, dropping the bag.

"Jethro put it back and he wondered how you—the burglar—had been calling. And I'm afraid I gave something away," he concluded with a rush.

"Gave something away? What? Out with it!" demanded Raffles very sternly.

"You see, Jethro knew they would have a record of the call at the telephone exchange, so I thought it best to take the bull by the horns and admit that I had been called by somebody." Bunny stared disconsolately at his feet. "To be absolutely honest, I even went so far as to say I thought it was Raffles who had rung me."

"You didn't, Bunny," Raffles said in a shocked whisper.

"I only said I thought it was you," he defended himself. "I could see they weren't going to recognize you. There was no idea of your being the burglar. And I told them a yarn about having a bet with you about what the trap was. And I'd already told them that I half expected to find you here. It all fitted together. And it made the part about the telephone fit in rather well, too."

There was a long pause. Bunny did not dare to raise his eyes to Raffles. He wished devoutly that the floor would open and quite swallow him up.

"I should think it did, Bunny. I couldn't have done better myself," Raffles said at last.

"Really?" Bunny asked, risking a shy glance at his friend's admiring face.

"You will forgive me saying that you have never in your life done half so well. You've played the hero's part," he cried.

"You really think so?" breathed Bunny, his spirits rising.

"You know me, Bunny. I wouldn't say it if I didn't think it. The only thing is, we've still got one problem to solve. And there's precious little time for thought as well as action," Raffles said, beginning to pace up and down with a preoccupied air.

Bunny glanced at his watch and realized that it would be daylight in two hours at the very most.

"There's only one thing for it, Bunny. We must divide the labor. You deal with the police—wait an hour at least before you ring them—and leave the rest to me."

"You're going to think of a reason," asked Bunny hopefully, "for the sort of burglar they think you were, ringing up the sort of man they know I am?"

"I haven't thought of anything yet," admitted Raffles. "But I daresay I shall."

"How shall I know what it is?" said Bunny dolefully.

"My dear Bunny," Raffles reminded him, "it isn't for you to give the explanation. It would be highly suspicious if you did."

Bunny had to admit that he supposed it was so.

"Trust me to hit on something, that's all," Raffles urged him.

Silently Bunny took his friend's hand. He did and would trust him.

"Goodbye, Bunny," Raffles said, picking up his bag and making for the door, "And good luck."

"Goodbye, Raffles," said Bunny quietly.

170

He felt quite solitary in the room, despite his three comatose companions. He walked around for a time, then sat down, but he soon began to feel very drowsy and did not trust himself to carry out the plan successfully if he allowed himself to sleep. He got up and took another turn around the room. The trouble with that was that if one of the others should awake sooner than expected, it would look suspicious. Bunny sat down again and wrestled with the overpowering desire to sleep by glancing frequently at his watch—never had the long minutes passed so slowly—and trying to remember exactly what he had to say to the police. But at last a crack of bleak gray light showed between the heavy curtains and Bunny felt it safe to move. Stretching from his long vigil, he stood up and made a good show of attempting to arouse his companions. They slept soundly on. Feeling very nervous indeed, he went to the telephone and asked to be connected with Scotland Yard.

For all his doubts about confronting the police, Bunny had to admit that, when summoned, they reacted with efficiency and speed. In no time at all an unnecessarily large—in Bunny's biased opinion—contingent of them had arrived, led by the small, brisk figure of one Sergeant Thompson. In minutes they were joined by a doctor who set to forthwith examine the still sleeping Maguire and his friends. Bunny stumbled through his story as best he could and was then kept waiting while Thompson conducted a long and enigmatic conversation with the supervisor of the Central Telephone Exchange. Meanwhile, several burly constables came and went, busy with tape measures and notebooks.

"Well, that's good," said Thompson when he had

completed his call. "They've confirmed that it was you that was telephoned from here."

Bunny found the man's beaming smile rather disconcerting. He determined to be brave, however.

"That's what I told you," he remarked.

"Yes, sir, and they confirmed that you were telling the truth," the policeman said, still smiling.

"Do you need their confirmation?" asked Bunny, feeling a little piqued.

"Well, people don't always tell the truth to us, sir," Thompson informed him, his smile intact.

"The word of a gentleman . . ." Bunny suggested.

"Yes," said the policeman dryly, his smile switching off like an electric light. "We don't find it completely reliable, sir. Not always."

"How dare you say that!" said Bunny, deeply offended and half rising from his seat.

"Oh, they always lie from the most high-minded of motives, sir," the policeman assured him cheerfully. "Like protecting another person—a lady or a friend. They make you feel that telling the truth is a rotten thing to do."

"It's obvious," said Bunny, resuming his seat and lifting his chin, "you've no idea what a gentleman is. . . ."

"I'm sure, sir," Thompson agreed. "But I doubt if you've got much idea what a policeman is."

"What's that got to do with it?"

"Just trying to explain, sir," said the policeman coolly, "why I confirmed your story with the exchange."

"Because I might be protecting somebody?" Bunny was quite pleased with his tone which, at least to his ears, suggested the utter preposterousness of such an idea.

"That's right, sir," said Thompson, unmoved.

"Ridiculous."

"Now, sir, could you tell me about this telephone conversation?"

"I've told you already," Bunny protested.

"Would you mind going over it again, a bit more carefully, sir? Sort of step by step?" the policeman requested, indicating that his fund of polite patience was inexhaustible.

"If I must," agreed Bunny reluctantly.

Sergeant Thompson expressed his gratitude and Bunny related once more how he had returned from dinner with Sir Cyriac Morrison and how the telephone had rung with the unsurprising result that he had answered it.

"What did you say, sir?" interrupted the policeman. "If you remember."

"Yes I do," said Bunny firmly. "I said 'Hello.' "

" 'Hello.' "

"That's right. Just 'Hello.' "

"And what did he say?"

"He said, 'Is that you, Bu . . .' " Bunny bit his lip, considered correcting himself and decided to cross his fingers in the hope that Thompson had not heard the involuntary syllable.

" 'Is that you Bu,' " repeated the sergeant thoughtfully. "What did he mean by that, sir?"

Bunny drew a deep breath and tried to cross his toes as well.

"I was going to say, he said, 'Is that you, Bunny?' But then I realized he couldn't have said that; he didn't know my name, my nickname, was Bunny."

He stared at the policeman's impassive face.

"Supposing you just tell me what you remember, sir,

173

without correcting it in the light of what you realized later. He said, 'Is that you, Bunny?' "

"No," Bunny said firmly. "He said, 'Is that you?' And I added 'Bunny' in my imagination," he persisted. "Because I thought it was my old friend Raffles calling me. But I wasn't sure. So I said, 'Are you Raffles?' "

"Why did you think it was your old friend Raffles?"

"He's the sort of person who would quite likely telephone me in the middle of the night," said Bunny promptly.

"He's a very old friend, is he?" inquired Thompson lightly.

"Yes, he is."

"Your best friend, would you call him?"

"Yes. My best friend."

"You see him every day, perhaps?"

"More or less every day."

"And he telephones you a lot?"

"Yes. Why?"

"And you can't recognize what is and what isn't his voice on the phone?" said Thompson in a louder and far from casual voice.

"That's just it," Bunny answered at once. "I thought it would be Raffles, but it didn't sound like him. And, of course, it wasn't," he added confidently. "It must have been the chap who burgled this place."

"May we get back to just plain remembering, sir?" asked the policeman politely.

"If you like," Bunny assented.

"You asked him if he was Raffles. And he said. . . ?"

" 'I want you quick. Come here.' "

"And you said?"

" 'What's happened? Where are you?' Something like that."

174

"You didn't pursue the question of whether he was Raffles or not?"

Bunny shook his head.

"That's what I'd have done, if I'd been you."

"Would you?" asked Bunny, as though it were a matter of complete indifference to him what the sergeant would have done.

"Unless you'd already settled the question to your own satisfaction," Thompson prompted him.

"Inspector . . ." began Bunny.

"Sergeant," the policeman corrected him dryly.

"Sergeant, you have never dined with Swigger Morrison. I took that telephone call with a bottle of champagne, two bottles of burgundy, most of a bottle of port and a half a dozen brandies inside me. I was incapable of working out whose voice it was, and I was pretty well past caring," Bunny explained.

"Would you say you were drunk, sir?" inquired the policeman.

"I was drunk," Bunny sighed.

"But you remember the conversation pretty well, sir. And you rushed round here pretty quick."

"I had got the impression that my friend was in trouble," Bunny repeated with a great show of patience. "I wanted to help him."

"Your friend Raffles?"

"Raffles," Bunny agreed.

"Is he a gentleman?" the officer asked casually.

"Of course!"

"Your kind of gentleman?"

"A better one than me," Bunny vowed.

"He's not a burglar, sir?"

"What do you mean?" demanded Bunny, alarmed and offended. "Of course he's not!"

"I was just wondering," the policeman said, "how

175

you could confuse a gentleman's voice with a burglar's. However drunk you were."

"I don't know how. But I did," Bunny said tiredly.

"At what stage exactly did you stop thinking it was Raffles and realize it was the burglar?" pursued the policeman.

"Afterwards."

"Afterwards?"

"Yes. Can I go now?"

At that moment the doctor called to Sergeant Thompson who excused himself and went with the medico to hold a whispered conversation. After a few moments, the sergeant returned to Bunny, who instantly repeated his request.

"Not just yet, if you don't mind, sir," the policeman replied stiffly.

"I do mind," protested Bunny. "I'm exhausted. You don't realize," he complained. "I haven't had a bit of sleep."

"What's that, sir?" asked Thompson sharply.

"I haven't had any sleep all night," Bunny repeated, close to exasperation with the man's obtuseness.

"Would you mind repeating that, sir?" Thompson said in a suspicious tone.

"Certainly. Why?" Bunny said and then, like a chill hand gripping his heart, he realized what he had said. "Oh!" he muttered, confused. There had to be a way out of this. If only he weren't so damnably tired. "I mean," he said, "apart from unconsciousness. I don't count that as sleep. Mere insensibility. Didn't do me any good. Like sleep does. I want to get some *real* sleep."

The policeman stared at him for a long time. Bunny, by sheer force of will, managed to meet his stare.

"Just one or two more questions, if you don't mind, sir," he said at last.

"Oh, all right," Bunny assented with little grace.

"Do you know any burglars, sir? Any of your friends? Acquaintances? I mean, you don't dabble in the underworld like some gentlemen do?"

"What do you take me for? No," said Bunny, who was really rather put out that the sergeant should suspect him of being a man of that sort.

"Just a question, sir."

"A very impertinent one."

"I was trying to find a logical reason for what must just be an accidental coincidence," explained Thompson heavily. "You said that when you first met Mr. Maguire he kept boasting about his trophies." Slowly, Thompson leafed through his notebook until he found the desired page. "Particularly you mentioned a jeweled belt, a gold brick and a silver statuette. And Mr. Maguire brought you here and showed you these things. You and another gentleman."

"Me and my friend Raffles, yes," Bunny said impatiently. This recitation of unremarkable events was becoming tedious.

"Well, those are exactly the things that have been taken."

"What?" said Bunny, suddenly grasping the policeman's slow but inexorable drift.

He started visibly as the telephone rang. A constable answered it.

"There must be some other explanation. . . ." he began, but Thompson cut him short, being called to the telephone by the constable. Bunny sat miserably, trying to think what that other explanation might be. So engrossed was he in this puzzle that he did not at first notice Thompson again standing in front of him.

Fearfully Bunny raised his eyes to the impassive face of authority.

"I haven't any more questions for you. At the moment," he said.

"Thank heavens!" exclaimed Bunny with relief, "Can I go?"

"You're going to your flat?"

"Yes."

"In Mount Street?"

"Yes. Why?"

"It's just around the corner. I'll come along with you," said the sergeant in a tone that invited no opposition.

"Oh . . . er . . . well, actually, I thought of calling at the Albany first," Bunny said hastily. "To call on my old friend Raffles. And tell him what's happened. He'll be quite interested."

"Well," said Thompson with one of his cheerless smiles, "I'd be interested to meet your old friend Raffles. I'll come along with you, if you don't mind," he added, politely standing back so that Bunny could lead the way.

Of course, Bunny had no choice and, as they walked in solemn silence over to the Albany, he could think of no way out of a new dilemma that had occurred to him, except to trust once more to Raffles's powers of invention.

The cricketer, resplendent in a handsome silk dressing gown, greeted them jovially and with an immediate invitation to have breakfast with him. Sergeant Thompson declined and asked to be allowed to make a telephone call, to inform Scotland Yard of his whereabouts. Raffles agreed and led Bunny into the comparative privacy of his sitting room.

"Is it all right?" he asked, *sotto voce*.

"I haven't yet thought of a reason for the telephone call and he's going on about the three things that Maguire boasted about to us being the three things that have been taken," Bunny gabbled.

"Hm," said Raffles contemplatively. "Good point."

"He seems to think it's a bit fishy."

"So would I if I were him," Raffles agreed. "Why did you bring him here?"

"He was going to go back with me to my flat!" Bunny's voice cracked with nervous alarm.

"Well?"

"Well, I daren't let him in there! I've got half the silver you've pinched. Family silver, but it's certainly not my family," he added desperately.

"Under lock and key, Bunny. With a special Bramah lock fitted to the bottom drawer of your wardrobe." Raffles, who had insisted upon these sensible precautions, now reminded him.

"Yes, I know, but all the same . . ."

"You're afraid you'd blush?"

"I'm not made of brass."

"So, we must try to keep the sergeant from visiting your flat?"

"Please," Bunny pleaded as the sergeant came into the room.

After ascertaining that Bunny had thus had time to recount his nocturnal adventures to his friend, the policeman urged that they should proceed forthwith to Mount Street. Bunny looked immediately to Raffles for help but the latter, to Bunny's chagrin and surprise, announced his intention to accompany them, if they would be so good as to wait one moment while he finished dressing.

Immaculate in morning gray, Raffles cheerfully led a dithering and rather grumpy Bunny and the continually affable sergeant to Mount Street. Once there, Bunny was about to ring for the lift when that machine descended and the porter greeted Bunny with a cry of relief.

"Thank heaven's you've come sir!"

"Oh, why?" asked Bunny, surprised by this unexpected welcome.

"You've been entered in the night, sir," said the porter in a doom-laden tone.

"What?"

"You've been broken into, sir. The thieves have taken everything they could lay their hands on."

Raffles laid a supporting hand on his friend's shoulder while Thompson demanded to know if the police had been sent for. On learning that they had and that they were even now *in situ,* the sergeant hurried a quaking Bunny and a cool Raffles into the lift.

The door to Bunny's flat has been forced with a jimmy. The occupant, casting a bare glance at it, and ignoring the policeman whom Thompson greeted, hurried through into his bedroom. So much, he thought miserably, for a stout Bramah lock. The damaged drawer of his wardrobe was open and horribly empty.

"Something valuable, sir?" asked Thompson sympathetically, coming up behind him.

"Yes, indeed. Family heirlooms. Silver and so forth," Bunny managed to answer.

"Perhaps you'd be so kind as to make a list later on," suggested the policeman.

"I . . . I . . . don't know . . . that I can remember," Bunny stammered.

"I'll help you, Bunny," Raffles offered. "I think I've seen everything you've got at one time or another."

"Is there anything else gone?" asked the sergeant.

Bunny made a cursory and heavyhearted inspection

of his rooms and gave it as his opinion that the rest of his property was intact.

"Probably they knew in advance what they wanted and went straight for it," Thompson said sagely.

"The explanation of the telephone call?" suggested Raffles. "At Maguire's. Bunny told me all about it."

"Yes. Yes, very likely. Yes, that would explain everything, in fact," the sergeant agreed. "I saw it before we came here," he admitted. "I should tell you," he said, addressing Bunny, "I've known that you were burgled before we left Maguire's place. That telephone call I received. But you wanted to go to Mr. Raffles, and I hadn't the heart to stop you."

"But what would explain everything?" Bunny asked.

"Well, why should a burglar call an innocent gentleman away from home?"

"Well, why?" said Bunny, with great agitation.

"In order to burgle you, too, of course," said the sergeant with an air of triumph.

"Oh!" said Bunny, who understood at last. "But why on earth me?"

"Well, I see it this way, sir," commenced Thompson, obviously enjoying himself. "You told me you met Mr. Maguire at the International Sporting Club, with Mr. Raffles. Now, I don't know if Mr. Raffles would agree, but there's some very queer fish at the International Sporting Club. Very queer fish indeed," he repeated darkly.

"Yes, that's true," confirmed Raffles without a moment's hesitation.

"Not to mention the waiters and servants around the place."

"By Jove, I hadn't thought of them," cried Raffles excitedly.

"And you told me," Thompson pursued undeterred,

"you walked back with Mr. Maguire through the streets of London. And he bragged about how much money he made from fighting, and the trophies he'd got. Loudly? So that people could hear?"

"I think we have to admit, Bunny, that Maguire has a very loud voice," conceded Raffles.

"And no doubt, sir, you probably boasted about your own possessions," suggested the policeman gently.

"I . . . er . . . I . . ." Bunny did not quite know what he should say.

"Oh, Bunny," Raffles rebuked him. "I remember you doing it."

"Of course. So what happens? You are overheard; you are followed; you are worked into the same scheme, and you are robbed on the same night!"

"Congratulations," Raffles cried. "Brilliant. Of course it's clear now."

"You think so?" inquired Bunny.

"Clear as purest crystal," Raffles assured him.

All that remained was for Sergeant Thompson to complete his notes and assure Bunny that Scotland Yard would use its beast endeavors to find and punish the criminal, reminding him that their task would be greatly facilitated if he would supply, at his convenience, a detailed inventory of the missing silver.

A few days later, Bunny called in on Raffles at the Albany and gladly accepted a glass of whisky. He had reached a decision and meant to impart it to Raffles, but first he sought a little reassurance.

"So Maguire's burglar was the same man who robbed me," he stated.

"Perfectly true: he was," agreed Raffles.

"And took my family silver?"

"Any time you want it back, you can have it," promised Raffles.

182

"You really think they swallowed the story?"

"It went down as smoothly as an oyster."

This was just what Bunny wanted to hear.

"Then give me another cigarette, my dear fellow, and let me push on to Scotland Yard."

"Scotland Yard!" exclaimed Raffles in mock horror.

"To give a false description of what was taken from that drawer in my wardrobe," Bunny announced confidently.

"A false description! Bunny, you have no more to learn from me. Time was," reminisced Raffles, "when I wouldn't have let you go there alone to retrieve a lost umbrella, let alone a lost cause."

Greatly pleased and wreathed in smiles, Bunny set down his glass and bade his friend farewell. Smiling and shaking his head fondly, Raffles watched the redoubtable Bunny skip down the stairs, whistling gaily.

In this way the honor of England's sportsmen was avenged and the resources of the amateur shown to be superior to that of the vulgar professional. Raffles's personal satisfaction was, of course, greatly boosted by his having discovered and escaped the trap to catch the cleverest criminal alive and in this hour of glory he could afford to indulge Bunny's new-found confidence. Indeed, he took almost as much pleasure therein as he later did in converting the ostentatious fruits of Maguire's professionalism into much-needed English bank notes.

Six

A BAD NIGHT

•••• ◆ ••••

IN WHICH RAFFLES PLAYS THE INNINGS OF HIS LIFE AND MEETS A WOMAN AFTER HIS OWN HEART

THE FOLLOWING SUMMER found Raffles in uncharacteristic mood. His loyal friend and champion, Bunny Manders, inclined to the view that this was the natural result of the idiocy displayed by the England selectors who had dropped A. J. Raffles Esq. from the England team for the First Test Match against the Australians. The English defeat by an inning served to underline the perversity of this decision, and it was with unbounded joy therefore that he read in the newspapers of Raffles's reinstatement to the team for the second test at Old Trafford. This news, on which he hurried to congratulate Raffles, did little, however, to lift the latter's spirits.

The truth of the matter was that Raffles's enforced idleness had given him time for introspection and for concern about other matters. It was one of those periods, common to the lives of all men, even of great cricketers and burglars, when everything seems to conspire to enforce a personal reassessment. Such reassessment, as all men must own, is never accomplished without a measure of pain. For example, Raffles had been much taken by the publication in the *Times* of a new poem by Mr. Kipling, a writer whom he justly admired. Two lines from the poem had particularly struck home and were, indeed, indelibly impressed upon his memory.

> Then ye returned to your trinkets; then ye
> contented your souls
> With the flannelled fools at the wicket or the
> muddied oafs at the goals.

It seemed to Raffles that the insight of the poet cast his public career in a new light. Was he then no more than a "flannelled fool," a mere player of games? It seemed to him in his troubled mood that he could make no higher claim, and such a claim was, of course, demeaning to a man of his intelligence and dignity. His mood stemmed, as we have seen, from his rejection by his country, but it was fed and complicated by disturbing news coming out of the colonies, notably out of South Africa where the Germans and the Dutch seemed set, unimaginable though it sounded to patriotic ears, to challenge the supreme authority of Her Majesty Queen Victoria and therefore of all Englishmen.

His mind had been morosely running on these rumors when circumstances demanded that he make, in his private capacity, a visit to his fence. This man had frequently confided in Raffles as an esteemed customer and a gentleman, and the latter had long known of a two-way traffic between the fence and certain insurance companies. These companies often found it cheaper to purchase back from the fence various items of jewelry and plate than to pay the full compensation to the burgled owner. Since the price offered invariably exceeded the value of such items when broken up or

185

melted down, both sides were content with the unorthodox trade. And during these transactions valuable information was often acquired by the fence. So it was that, during the aforementioned visit, Raffles learned that one Mynheer Van Der Berg, an expatriate Dutchman, whose own affairs were of a somewhat dubious nature, had recently approached the Burglary Insurance Company of Cheapside to make a special arrangement concerning the wedding presents that his eldest daughter expected to receive upon the occasion of her nuptials to a wealthy English businessman. Mynheer Van Der Berg, with the arrogant confidence which, in Raffles's view, characterized the high-handed manner of all foreigners, had forbidden the presence of insurance company officials to guard the anticipated expensive gifts, maintaining that he and his family were sufficient deterrent for any burglar.

This information, casually imparted by his fence, rankled in Raffles's mind and brought him to the conclusion that since he was frustrated of doing his patriotic duty on the cricket field, he might do it by striking a blow against a wealthy interloper whose race had the temerity to challenge the inalienable rights of Empire. On reaching this conclusion, he began to feel better, to feel like a man who was doing something positive. That his plan to purloin a few valuable trinkets from among the nuptial array would further increase his funds was a pleasant bonus.

It was for this reason that his reaction to the news of his selection for the Old Trafford Test was noticeably less than jubilant. Had the series been against "the jarring Germans or the dull-as-ditchwater Dutch," as Raffles put it, then he would have perceived a worthy challenge such as would have quickened his blood, but the Australians, by comparison, were kith and kin.

Still, he determined to play, if only to prove that he was a cleverer "flannelled fool" than his opponents. In that there might be some satisfaction. And even more would be gained by relieving the shady Rotterdam financier and his family of some part of their burden of wealth. All this he confided to Bunny, as was his wont. Bunny expressed some surprise at the vehemence of Raffles's opinions, which smacked of the political. Raffles shrugged off the charge and Bunny was prevented from pursuing it by the sudden occurrence of a thought.

"What date is the Second Test?" he inquired as Raffles poured him a cup of matutinal coffee.

"Sixteenth, seventeenth and eighteenth," came the ready reply.

"And what date is the Van Der Berg wedding?" asked Bunny with studied innocence.

"Thursday the sixteenth," replied Raffles. "Oh, my God!"

"You do realize," continued Bunny, taking the coffee cup from Raffles's startled fingers, "you can't be in Manchester playing cricket and in East Molesey stealing the wedding presents at the same time?"

"You're absolutely right, I can't," agreed Raffles. "I wonder if we can get Van Der Berg to change the date of the wedding?" he suggested with scant hope.

"He's sent the invitations out already." Bunny had read as much in the newspaper.

"It's damned unfair," cried Raffles. "I was relying on him to support us through the summer. Now he's gone and messed the whole thing up. Well, bang goes East Molesey," he said, dropping dejectedly into a chair.

"Not necessarily," said Bunny.

"But if I can't go, and you said it yourself, I can't. . . ."

"Someone else can go instead."

"Who, for heaven's sake?"

"Me," said Bunny with modest confidence which, as Raffles was quick to perceive, concealed a stubborn determination.

He also recognized at once that his unavoidable absence rendered him powerless to prevent Bunny taking the theft upon himself. With caution designed not to offend Bunny who was, he knew, extremely sensitive on the subject of his competence as a burglar, Raffles did his best to dissuade the young man. His temperament was not suited to the task, being hotheaded and impulsive, while such missions required the steel-cold nerves of a slow bowler. But no matter how many objections and obstacles Raffles contrived to raise, Bunny swept them all aside. The cricketer therefore sensibly concluded that there was nothing for it but to give Bunny the benefit of his experience and expertise, and to trust to luck.

In order to instruct his friend, Raffles applied himself to discovering as much as possible about the circumstances likely to occur on the night of the deed. The household, once the guests and the newlyweds had departed, would contain only the immediate family and two domestic servants. Mrs. Van Der Berg suffered from a heart condition, while her husband, Raffles learned, could be relied upon to consume sufficient alcohol at the festivities to ensure a sound sleep. The servants were elderly and the remaining daughter a mere girl. His heart lightened. He informed Bunny that, given the opposition, he confidently expected him to triumph.

So it was that, a day or so later, a keen eye might

have espied the distinguished figure of A. J. Raffles, accompanied by his friend, concealed behind a leafy tree in a field which conveniently overlooked the elegant riverside villa of the Van Der Bergs. And what a charming scene delighted their gaze beyond the white-painted fence! Seated at a garden table, a handsome young woman of about twenty-five years applied pen to paper. In this pursuit she was interrupted by a younger and much prettier member of her sex. A veritable Dresden-doll of a girl, in fact, who, unbeknown to the distant admirers, began to quiz her sister on matters of the heart. Netje—for such was the ungainly name of this exquisite creature—demanded to know of her sister, Tesje, if she and her future husband were in complete accord about the honeymoon.

"Of course," replied Tesje, glancing up from her letter of thanks to the donor of a fine present. "It says in the Bible, 'Man and wife are one flesh.' "

"Brr!" said Netje with a theatrical shudder. "That always makes me think of a butcher's shop and carving knives."

"You are not romantic," replied her sister.

"Well, I don't think it's very romantic to marry a businessman."

"I love him," was the calm reply.

"He is rich," pointed out Netje pertly.

"Only because his father is rich. The same as ours."

"I suppose that will do as an excuse. But I should like him better if he were not so rich, and he played cricket, for instance," sighed Netje.

"Cricket? Why cricket?" asked Tesje, looking at her sister with puzzled fondness.

"Oh, no reason. I don't know. They look so beautiful, in white, on the green field. . . ."

189

"Peter plays rugby," said Tesje firmly. "That is very English of him."

"No, no, rugby is wet and muddy and dangerous," argued Netje. "But cricket is sunny and peaceful and lovely, lovely . . ." she sighed, closing her eyes on some imaginary field of white-figured green.

It can be imagined what such heartfelt sentiments would have done for the morale of one "flannelled fool" had he been able to hear them. As it was, he admired the charms of Netje from a silent distance, remarking to Bunny that she was older than he had imagined.

"I reckon the best way to get in," offered Raffles, with a care for the real purpose of their clandestine visit, "would be that door on this side of the house."

Bunny noted the door, which led into a conservatory.

"Doesn't it seem a shame," he said, "taking presents from girls like that?"

"Until you think that what they throw aside after a couple of days, because they're tired of it, would keep us in funds for a whole year," said Raffles. "Don't pity the rich, even when they're good-looking. Just remember you're a burglar," he advised.

At this moment their attention was caught by the arrival in the garden of a stout matron, evidently the mother of these two flowers. She came, as her daughters promptly discovered, in search of help to check the wedding guest list against the acceptances received. Tesje pleaded the urgency and volume of her correspondence, while Netje flatly refused.

"I'm sorry, Mother," she added, "but I've got to do my practicing."

"It won't take more than a minute," pleaded Mrs. Van Der Berg.

"But I've got to do it before Father comes home. You know he doesn't like it."

"Then why do you do it if he doesn't like it?" cried the mama of this independent creature.

"Because it may be necessary," she asserted, rising from her seat and flouncing into the house.

Her mother, quite at a loss, sighed and sat in the vacated chair.

"I wish," she said with true feeling, "we could get Netje married, too, to a good man like Peter."

"Like Peter won't do," smiled Tesje. "You must find her a cricketer."

"A cricketer? Why?" asked Mrs. Van Der Berg with a confused air, but her elder daughter only smiled and shrugged.

The lady's puzzlement was apparent to the distant watchers in the field, but its cause was a matter of surmise and Raffles, therefore, concentrated on advising his friend about the burglary. One-thirty A.M., he guessed, would be a good time. By then even the most ardent guests should have departed and the family be suitably exhausted or inebriated. Bunny was cautioned to watch for the extinguishing of the bedroom lights and not to be deterred by that commonly supposed bar to burglars—a single burning light in a downstairs room. Even so, Raffles advised, it was only sensible to take a preparatory peep through the windows before entering. And in the unlikely event of his being challenged, Raffles hinted that, were he in Bunny's shoes, he would claim to be officer of the Burglary Insurance Company sent, despite Mynheer Van Der Berg's wishes, as an extra precaution. Bunny accepted these instructions with due humility and, their mission accomplished, the two friends strolled away across the field in the general direction of the railway station.

As they did so, Miss Netje Van Der Berg was preparing for her practice. In the gloomy, heavily curtained library, she set up a thickly padded screen. In front of this she placed a metallic circle which was operated by a small clockwork motor. Attached to the circle which, once the motor was set in motion, began to revolve, were six clay representations of ducks. Taking careful aim with a revolver from the opposite end of the large room, the delicate young woman fired six times in rapid succession. Each shot quite demolished a clay duck, as she had known it would. Smiling, she surveyed her singular handiwork while, in the shattered peace of the summer garden, her parent and sister exchanged despairing looks at this aural evidence of Netje's practicing.

A few days later Bunny accompanied his friend to Euston Station from whence Raffles was to embark for Manchester and the Second Test. Raffles, who detested protracted farewells, bade Bunny "goodbye" at the ticket office.

"Goodbye then, Raffles, and good luck tomorrow," said Bunny, shaking his hand heartily.

"Weather's dashed dry," commented Raffles. "I'll need the luck."

"I'm relying on you to skittle out the Aussies." Bunny grinned.

"And I'm relying on you to make mincemeat of the Dutchies." Raffles beamed.

"Never fear, I will," said Bunny confidently.

"Only one thing—promise me not to take a revolver," said Raffles with sudden seriousness.

"Why not?" said Bunny, surprised.

"What you take I'm afraid you're the chap to use."

"You mean you don't trust me?" said Bunny, quick to take offense.

"Here are my keys," said Raffles, handing them to him. "There's an old life preserver somewhere in the bureau—take that if you like. But not the revolver. Promise me?"

"Let the rope be round my own neck for once," pleaded Bunny.

"That's just where I don't want it to be," Raffles replied.

Bunny gave his reluctant promise and, relieved, Raffles thanked him.

"But whatever I do, Raffles, I shan't give *you* away," Bunny said with great sincerity. "And you'll find I do better than you think and am worth trusting more than you seem to want to."

"Keep your voice down, Bunny," beseeched Raffles, glancing around. "People may hear."

"Let them hear!" cried Bunny, now thoroughly warmed to his text. "You've been wrong about me right from the start. You've just wanted to use me as a pawn, that's all! Well, you can't do that this time. Tomorrow night you won't be on the stage or anywhere near it. And the understudy will be playing the lead! And you'll find out how well he does it!" Bunny concluded in a triumphant tone.

"I hope you're right, Bunny," Raffles said coldly. "I must catch my train or I shan't get a seat in the restaurant car. Goodbye."

So saying, the cricketer turned on his heel and left Bunny, who felt instantly penitent.

"I'm sorry, Raffles. I didn't mean it . . ." he said after the receding figure.

Left to his own devices, however, Bunny soon grew angry again. Why should he be sorry? What he had said, albeit in the heat of the moment, was nothing but the unvarnished truth. Perhaps he had been a little hotheaded but even so. . . . In fact, Bunny knew that he was in the wrong, but he refused to admit it. He was determined to show Raffles his true worth and nothing would now stop him. Yet, as a concession, he took only the ancient life preserver from Raffles's bureau drawer.

And late the following night, wearing a coat with many capacious pockets and a smart brown derby, Bunny took a train to East Molesey Station and walked by a circuitous route to that spot close to the Van Der Berg villa where he and Raffles had lately stood. The building was in darkness and the balmy summer night was blissfully silent save for those noises which can safely be attributed to Mother Nature about her nocturnal business. Bunny approached the garden gate and entered through it into the garden with a stealth worthy of the great Raffles himself. Checking his watch, he saw that the hour lacked some minutes of one-thirty and so settled himself in the garden seat at which he had observed the Misses Van Der Berg and lit himself a soothing Sullivan. This he smoked with great and evident pleasure, gazing at the distant stars. By the time the cigarette was finished, the appointed hour had arrived. Noiselessly Bunny crept to the conservatory door, the handle of which turned easily and silently under his grip. He stepped over the threshold, his eyes veiled by an impenetrable dark. He paused, willing his eyes to adjust to the gloom when, with a rasping sound that caused his heart to somersault, a match was struck and swiftly applied to a candle.

"Come in," said a charming voice, the owner of which was instantly revealed as the younger Miss Van Der Berg who leveled, with an entirely professional precision, the deadly barrel of a revolver at Bunny's leaping heart. "What can we do for you?" she calmly

194

inquired. "Perhaps I shoot you? I am a very good shot."

Bunny did not doubt it for one moment, odd though the claim struck him, issuing from such charming lips.

"Who are you?" those same lips inquired. "A burglar?"

"No. I'm a detective officer," said Bunny, recalling Raffles's advice.

"From the police?" asked the young markswoman, arching her pretty eyebrows in the most provocative manner.

"From the Burglary Insurance Company."

"The Burglary Insurance Company agreed that they would not send anyone," the well-informed young lady told him.

"They agreed with you. But they sent me just the same," Bunny improvised.

"Is that so?"

"Better safe than sorry," he said, with a conciliatory smile.

"What?" The young woman frowned ominously.

"It's an English proverb," Bunny offered.

"I don't know it."

"But you speak English very well, Miss Van Der Berg," said Bunny gallantly.

"How do you know my name?" she asked, realigning the weapon with Bunny's heart.

"They told me at the office before I came down here." This seemed to satisfy her, so Bunny elaborated his bluff. "Well, I'm sorry you saw me. It's a mere matter of routine and not intended to annoy anybody. I propose to keep a watch on the place all night. But I admit," he said, introducing an apologetic note, "that it wasn't necessary to trespass as I have done. I was going round the house testing the doors to make sure they were fastened all right. That door wasn't so I opened it and came in." Bunny threw a longing glance at the door. "And now I'll go out again," he said, stepping backward, "with my apologies for disturbing you."

"Stay where you are."

Bunny halted at once, his eyes fixed on the menacing revolver which remained pointed at his chest.

"You don't look like a detective," the young woman said.

"I'm glad to hear you say that," replied Bunny jovially.

"Why?"

"There'd be no point in my being in plain clothes if you could recognize what I was."

"There's something in that," conceded his captor. "But you look like an amateur, not a professional."

"How should I have been dressed?" queried Bunny. "Inverness cape and deerstalker? We're not all Sherlock Holmes, you know." Bunny essayed a laugh, but Miss Van Der Berg did not join in, so he stopped.

Instead, she demanded a cigarette, which Bunny, though disapproving, hastened to offer her. With a wave of her revolver she motioned him back as he moved toward her, holding out his silver cigarette case.

"Take one out and throw it to me," she ordered.

Bunny did so, inwardly applauding the deftness with which she caught the Sullivan and lit it from the candle, all without the revolver wavering, or her soft and beautiful eyes leaving her chosen target.

"Don't you trust me?" he asked, a trifle offended by her elaborate caution.

"I think we will go in the library," she said. "Here it is too near the garden. This way."

She pointed brusquely with the revolver. Bunny,

much hampered by the dark, groped ahead, attempting to obey her instructions. They passed through a room in which the candlelight following him struck dazzling gleams from the display of wedding presents set out on several long tables. Netje, seeing his curiosity, confirmed that these were indeed the nuptial gifts which, she pointedly added, *she* was guarding. From this treasure trove she directed him to the library where, under her instructions, with shaking fingers Bunny lit a lamp.

"Now," he said, facing her across the lamp, "can we get things cleared up?"

"Certainly," agreed the young woman, blowing out the candle. "You will explain to me how you can be a detective employed by an insurance company when your accent is unmistakably public school, when you carry a silver cigarette case, from which you smoke Sullivan's cigarettes, your hat is made by Lock's of St. James's and your boots are by Lobb's?" she demanded sternly.

"How do you know?" said Bunny in astonishment. "I mean about Lobb's?"

"Do you deny it?"

"Of course I don't. I've always gone to them."

"Explain." The command was reinforced by an impatient gesture with the revolver.

"Quite simple," said Bunny. "They're the best at making boots."

"Explain how you are a detective," she insisted, her voice threatening.

"Oh . . . well . . . well, I fell on hard times. And I thought it'd be rather exciting, catching burglars and so on. I didn't want to be a policeman. Rather dull that, ugly uniform and all that sort of thing. Then I saw this place, the Burglary Insurance Company, and I thought that sounded rather more like it. So I went in and volunteered. Asked them if they wanted anyone to do some detecting. And to my astonishment they said yes, they did! They sent me down here. So here I am, boots and all. Sullivans and all. Not much money in it, but it's good fun."

Bunny treated her to a dazzling smile. He felt very proud of himself. That was something like a tale!

"Tell me," pursued the relentless Miss Van Der Berg, "is it not usual for detectives to have a badge or card from the company that employs them, to prove their identity?"

"Yes, quite usual, I believe," Bunny agreed cheerfully.

"Have you such a badge?"

"Er . . . no."

"Or such a card?"

"No."

"Or such a letter, perhaps?"

"Afraid not," said Bunny.

"Or anything of any kind to prove your identity?"

"Nothing," Bunny was forced to admit.

"Then I cannot believe your story," she said dismissively, raising the revolver a fraction and squinting down its barrel.

"They didn't have time to make me a badge or print me a card," said Bunny very quickly. "They only hired me this evening, and I came down straight away. And I wasn't expecting you to hold me up with that . . . that revolver, or I'd have insisted on something," he said with considerable conviction.

A strange almost excited look crossed the young woman's beautiful face. She lowered the revolver a little and asked:

"You were in Cheapside this evening?"

198

"Cheapside? Why?" asked Bunny, momentarily lost.

"The offices of the insurance company are there," the girl said impatiently.

"Oh, yes, Cheapside. Yes, of course." Bunny laughed.

"So you bought an evening paper?"

"Right," agreed Bunny, mystified. "In fact I bought them all."

With a sigh that was almost ecstatic, Netje allowed the revolver to droop and asked:

"How was the Second Test?"

"You mean you don't know?" said Bunny, truly shocked.

"No. We don't get the London evening papers. We have to wait till the morning to see the scores."

"Poor thing," said Bunny with feeling.

"Yes," agreed Netje, who felt the delay cruelly.

"I'm sorry to say I left the papers in the train," apologized Bunny. "But I can remember . . ."

"Please . . ." beseeched his charming captor, her eyes shining.

"Well, it was marvelous. Well, it wasn't exactly marvelous, not for England, but it was marvelous for me," said Bunny excitedly.

"Why?" asked Netje, not at all understanding.

"Being such a friend of his," explained Bunny.

"Whose?"

"Raffles."

"Ah," said the young woman meltingly. "Raffles. Yes, he *is* marvelous!"

"Right," agreed Bunny proudly.

"What did he do?"

"Well, England won the toss and batted first, of course. It was a dry day and a hard wicket and the Australian bowlers were right on top of their form.

They skittled the England openers and had five wickets down for sixty-three!"

"Oh!" cried Netje in a tone of tremulous horror.

"Then Raffles came in fifth wicket down," Bunny hurried on, "and at close of play he was still there, with seventy-eight not out, and England were two hundred and ten for seven!"

"You're right," cried the girl, with a rapt expression. "That *is* marvelous."

"Isn't it?"

"And you say he's a friend of yours?"

Hearing this from those delightful lips gave Bunny pause. He had said it, but it might not have been wise to say it.

"Did I?" he asked, trying to sound offhand.

"Yes," insisted Netje. "A great friend, I thought you said."

"It's not important," said Bunny with a shrug.

"Oh, but it is! I thought perhaps you were a criminal, but if you are a friend of Raffles, you cannot be a criminal," she exclaimed happily, lowering the revolver to her side.

"Well, yes, actually I do know him rather well," Bunny admitted, his face positively radiating relief.

"I adore him," said the young woman dreamily.

"Yes, I'm pretty fond of him myself," Bunny agreed.

"Seventy-eight not out! And they picked him for his bowling."

"Not the first time it's happened," Bunny reminded her. "Of course, he's an all-rounder really."

"Oh I do hope he will get a century tomorrow!"

"Strange," mused Bunny, "a foreign girl like you being interested in cricket."

"Oh, I have been here for years," she explained. "And in Holland, too, we play cricket."

"Oh, do you? I didn't know," said Bunny, interested.

"Not so well as in England," she admitted gracefully.

"No. I imagine not," said Bunny. "By the way, is it a Dutch habit for young ladies to sit up all night guarding their sister's wedding presents?"

"Oh no, it is not so at all," Netje hastened to reassure him.

"Then why do you do it?" asked Bunny.

"It is simply that I cannot sleep. Ever since I was a child, it is always the same. If there is any excitement, I cannot sleep. I know this. So I stay awake. And then perhaps two days later I sleep for twenty-four hours."

"But tonight," said Bunny with a sinking heart, "you won't sleep at all?"

"Not a wink."

"Don't you think—of course you know better than I do, but it seems to me it would be a good idea—if you went up to bed and lay down—I mean, don't get undressed if you don't want to—but if you *tried* very hard to go to sleep . . ."

"Oh no, it is not possible," she said, dismissing the suggestion as preposterous.

"You're sure?" ventured Bunny.

"Quite sure."

"Well, in that case there's no hope, is there?" he said glumly.

"No, none."

"So what are we going to do?"

"Stay here. Till morning."

"And *me?*" said Bunny, his voice squeaking with alarm.

Before Netje could reply, they both heard a noise from the next room. It was a sort of bump or thud, soft but nonetheless sinister. A moment later it was re-

201

peated. Bunny and the young woman exchanged anxious glances.

"Someone there," she whispered.

"Yes."

"A burglar?"

The noise was heard again.

"I'll go and see," offered Bunny.

"Careful."

Pulling out the life preserver, Bunny quietly opened the door. The lamp in the library behind him gave sufficient light for him to make out a ruffianly human shape stooping over the wedding gifts. Without hesitation, Bunny leaped forward and brought the life preserver down with a resounding crack on the interloper's head. The body fell heavily to the floor. Bunny knelt beside it to examine the physiognomy of him whom he had felled. With an indescribable feeling of alarm he saw a trickle of blood on the head as, simultaneously, he descried beneath the familiar disguise of chimney soot the features of A. J. Raffles.

"Have you knocked him out?" asked Netje from the doorway.

"Yes," confessed Bunny, appalled at what he had done.

"Well done," Netje congratulated him.

"He's bleeding," said Bunny desperately.

"Serve him right. Is he dead?"

"No," cried Bunny, shocked by her tone. "And I don't know how long he'll be as much as stunned."

"Hit him on the head again," suggested the bloodthirsty young Amazon.

"No, that won't be necessary," Bunny said with authority.

"But we'll need someone to go for the police."

"You," she said at once.

"And leave you alone with him? At his mercy? I couldn't."

"I have my revolver."

"But I couldn't dream of it! A woman . . ."

"I would shoot him if he tried to get away," Netje assured him.

"No, you mustn't do that," cried Bunny, who had no doubt that she would.

"Why not? I think in law you can shoot a man who is a burglar?"

"Well . . . look . . . A fine detective I'd look, leaving you here with a great hulking ruffian like that. No, I should never hear the last of it."

"But with my revolver . . ." argued the young lady.

"No, no. Against all my principles. Against everything I've been brought up to believe. Weaker sex and so on. Must be protected. No, you must go to the police."

"We don't need to, I've just thought."

With sinking spirits, Bunny learned of the recent installation of a telephone by means of which the police could be summoned. But then Miss Van Der Berg changed her mind. The telephone was on the upper floor. Its use would necessitate the making of noise which would disturb her dear mama. And she would be so alarmed to learn of the burglar. Any shock to that good lady's system could prove dangerous in view of her medical condition. Bunny's spirits rose.

"But if it saves us the trouble of going?" he protested in the face of this daughterly devotion.

"No. It's no trouble. I will go."

"Thank you," said Bunny with relief. "Is it far?"

"No. Quite near. I shall be back in a quarter of an hour. I will leave you my revolver. My advise is to shoot him. It is safer. But no, that would also wake Mother. No. Don't shoot him."

"All right," promised Bunny. "I won't."

"See you in fifteen minutes," called the redoubtable young woman, hurrying off into the night.

The moment she was out of earshot, Bunny crouched again beside his friend.

"Raffles," he called.

Raffles opened his eyes, much to Bunny's relief.

"*Et tu,* Bunny. My own familiar friend."

"Then you weren't even stunned! Thank God for that!"

"Of course I was stunned," grumbled Raffles, struggling to a sitting position and touching his head. "And no thanks to you that I wasn't brained."

"I thought you were in Manchester," said Bunny in his own defense.

"So you whanged me over the head!"

"I had to prove that I was a detective."

"And I was going to let you run me in, and walk me off under arrest in the direction of the station," sighed Raffles. "The railway station, of course."

"We can still do it," Bunny exclaimed excitedly.

"You're not going to wait for Miss Van Der Berg?"

"No."

"A shame," regretted Raffles, "when you've succeeded so well in persuading her you're from the Burglary Insurance Company. She won't believe it very much longer."

"I can't help that," said Bunny, anxious to be off.

"Well, there's a three-twelve we can catch," Raffles said, consulting his timepiece, "with time for me to change back into the clothes I left under a bridge on the way here. Come along, Bunny."

"Right."

A bare half hour later the two friends were safely en route for Waterloo, Raffles having cleaned his face and donned a voluminous cloak and an opera hat. Naturally Bunny was eager to know why Raffles was not in Manchester. Apart from thinking that his friend might have a double who played cricket for him, there was no feasible explanation so far as Bunny could see. Raffles soon made all clear. Bunny had failed to notice in his excited perusal of the newspaper reports of the Second Test, that a cloudburst had closed play at five o'clock and that it had been sufficiently heavy to rule out any possibility of there being a resumption of play that day. Having changed and taken a cab, Raffles was suddenly seized with a desire to see Bunny at his self-imposed task, and to be on hand should anything go wrong. Without further thought he had instructed the cab driver to take him to the station rather than to his hotel. His whole idea had been to keep in the background. Had Miss Van Der Berg not disrupted this plan, Bunny would never have learned of his presence. And now the cricketer intended to return to Manchester and to present himself in the morning to complete what he owned was proving to be the innings of his life.

"Well," said Bunny gratefully, "you saved me, Raffles. That's one thing you've done tonight."

"I've done two things, actually," said the other laconically.

"What's the other one?"

"Three, if you count my batting in the test."

"What do you mean?" urged Bunny.

"Bunny, while you were in that house, posing rather brilliantly as the insurance company detective, how many of the presents did you steal?" asked Raffles, fixing him with a slightly reproving eye.

"I . . . I'm afraid I . . . I forgot all about that," admitted Bunny. "What with that girl and her revolver . . . And my pretending I was a detective and on her side . . ."

"And I'm sure I'd have done the same if I'd been in your place," Raffles comforted him.

"Nice of you to say so," said Bunny, pleased.

"But I was not in your place. So I didn't do the same. I suppose," he went on regretfully, beginning to feel in the pockets of his cape, "a lot of jewelry has gone on honeymoon with the happy pair, but these emerald cuff links are rather nice." He placed the open box on the seat beside him. "And I really don't know what the bride was doing to leave this diamond comb behind. And here is the kind of old silver skewer I've been wanting for years—they make the most charming paper knives in the world," he explained, examining the object. "And this gold cigarette case will be just the thing for your Sullivans."

As Raffles continued to produce and itemize priceless objects, Bunny gazed in silent admiration and amazement. Was there no end, he wondered, to Raffles's ingenuity and brilliance?

Most certainly not on the cricket field for the next two days, largely thanks to Raffles, saw the complete and utter rout of the Australians. Inevitably this triumph deserved to be celebrated and a short while later, after Raffles had paid a visit to his fence with some of the Van Der Berg booty, he and Bunny did so with tea and crumpets at the Albany. Raffles was pleased with the amount the items had fetched which, together with the mementos they had kept of that bad night—the emerald cuff links, the gold cigarette case; not to mention the silver skewer—added up to a considerable sum. But, as they were congratulating themselves,

Raffles wondered if the case might really be considered as closed.

"What do you mean?" asked Bunny who certainly thought that it was.

"I was thinking of that girl and her gun," admitted Raffles.

"Ah yes," agreed Bunny. "A very determined girl."

"I heard everything you said, you know," Raffles added casually.

"Nothing to be ashamed of, I hope?"

"No, no. But you'll admit that the character you played then is now obviously a criminal?"

"Yes, I suppose so. It doesn't matter. They can't trace me," said Bunny confidently, pouring tea.

"Now in that conversation I overheard, you said one thing that might perhaps help them to trace you," Raffles continued.

"What?" cried Bunny, setting down the teapot quickly. "For heaven's sake, Raffles, what?"

"You said you were a friend of mine," said Raffles dryly.

Bunny owned the truth of it.

"It helped me at the time," he protested. "She was suspicious of me till then. But no friend of yours could be a criminal."

"What a splendid thought," Raffles smiled. "But now you're proved to be a criminal and we must expect a visit from the police."

Bunny's stricken face turned ashen when, at that precise moment, there was a long and demanding ring at the doorbell.

"The police, I should think," said Raffles calmly.

"Are you a magician?" asked Bunny, quaking.

"I simply timed it rather well. I had a note from Sergeant Holly of Scotland Yard. Could he call on me at four o'clock this afternoon? He is punctual to the dot," explained Raffles, going to open the door.

He returned a few moments later with Sergeant Holly, whom he introduced to a stuttering and nervous Bunny.

"Would you like some tea?" Raffles inquired of the sergeant.

"I'll have a cup of tea, thank you, sir."

"No crumpets?" asked Raffles, pouring a third cup.

"No, thank you, sir. Crumpets make it too cozy."

"It isn't going to be cozy?" said Raffles, raising his eyebrows in polite surprise.

"That rather depends on you, sir," was the stiff reply.

"On me?" Raffles contrived to be even more surprised.

"On whether you're willing to give me information about those who claim to be your friends."

"I don't understand," professed Raffles. "Who claims to be my friend?"

With a heavy sigh, the sergeant set down his cup and produced a notebook, through which he leafed.

"On the night of the first day of the Second Test Match, sir, there was a burlgary committed in East Molesey, Surrey."

"Far enough away," remarked Raffles.

"But the burglar, sir, in conversation, claimed to be a close friend of yours."

"Of mine?"

"Of yours," confirmed the sergeant doggedly. "Of the eminent cricketer who was then performing at the Second Test in Manchester."

Raffles looked in silence for a moment at each of his guests in turn, then, facing the policeman, he inquired with icy politeness:

"Do you suppose I have friends who are burglars?"

"Isn't it the other way round, sir?" suggested the sergeant with equal politeness. "Do you happen to have any burglars who are friends?"

"What?" asked Raffles, genuinely confused.

"Forgive me, sir," said the policeman, "but I have if not lived at least worked a good deal among the upper classes. Which is why they put me on this job. Now, it's my experience with the upper classes that they tend to be a good deal more free and easy in their relationships and acquaintanceships than, for instance, the middle class would be. They wouldn't be so bothered about keeping up an appearance of respectability," concluded the sergeant tendentiously.

Raffles considered this statement with great care and then admitted that there was something in what the policeman said.

"Though I must say," added the sergeant, pleased with Raffles's acceptance of his point, "that this chap appears to have been upper class himself. Public school, anyway."

"These days," Raffles said slowly and with regret, "to have been to a public school is no guarantee of belonging to the upper class."

"Indeed, I know, sir," the sergeant readily agreed.

"That apart, you were asking if I had any friends who were burglars, or burglars who were friends—whichever it was. I don't know. What do you think, Bunny?"

"Eh?" said Bunny, startled.

"Come on, man you heard the question," said Raffles tersely. "Have we got any burglar friends?"

"Ah . . ." said Bunny, wiping butter from his chin.

"Exactly!" said Raffles. "Ah. He doesn't know either," he informed the policeman.

"I thought perhaps he was going to say something more, sir," said the policeman, looking at Bunny.

"Were you, Bunny?"

"No," he said, shaking his head quickly.

The sergeant sighed and drew a sealed envelope from his pocket.

"Then perhaps I should give you this letter from Miss Van Der Berg, sir."

"From whom?" asked Raffles, taking the letter and turning it over in his fingers.

"Miss Van Der Berg of the family that was burgled," explained the policeman.

"Ah. Would you excuse me?"

"Of course, sir."

Raffles opened the envelope with the aid of an old-fashioned silver skewer and read the contents of the single sheet.

"A very pretty letter," he remarked, refolding it.

"She's a very pretty young lady," supplied the sergeant with a smile.

"Oh, is she?"

"Will you be going down to visit her, sir?"

"I beg your pardon?"

"I do happen to know what's in the letter, sir," explained Sergeant Holly. "The young lady read it over to me. Can I give her any message?"

"No," said Raffles. "I shall write to her myself."

"Well, if I can't be any help to you, sir, and you can't be of any help to me, I'd best be getting along," said the sergeant, rising and putting away his notebook.

"Always delighted to see the police," said Raffles, standing.

"Very civil of you, sir."

"Give my love to Inspector Mackenzie."

At this the sergeant looked most put out. He swallowed and mumbled that he would. Raffles asked Bunny to show the policeman out, which he did, returning to the sitting room with a sigh of relief.

"You have too powerful a conscience, Bunny," Raffles advised him, interpreting his friend's state of mind with his usual accuracy.

"Perhaps," conceded Bunny.

"Now *I* have very little conscience and certainly not enough to interfere with my pleasure," expounded Raffles. "I shall go down to East Molesey and see the beautiful Miss Van Der Berg. I take it you don't want to come with me?"

"And be recognized as a thief?" cried Bunny.

"That would indeed be hard when you stole nothing," Raffles agreed. "But you received some of the stolen goods. I'm afraid you'll have to give back the gold cigarette case."

"Why?" asked Bunny, producing it nevertheless.

"It has, for Miss Van Der Berg, a sentimental value. As Miss Van Der Berg has a sentimental value for me," he added, taking the case from Bunny.

"You don't know her!"

"You forget I listened to a long conversation. She said, and she seemed to mean it, that she adored me," Raffles reminded him.

"Raffles the cricketer, not Raffles the thief," Bunny pointed out grumpily.

"The man who goes down to East Molesey will be Raffles the cricketer. Only a small percentage of him will be Raffles the thief."

"Raffles," said Bunny with alarm. "You're not going to try anything?"

Raffles drew himself up to his full height and assumed his most dignified manner.

"I am going there," he said quietly, "as a 'flannelled fool.' In England, there is no risk in that!"

But that there was a risk of some kind Raffles was certain. From the letter and the manner of its delivery it was only prudent to assume that Miss Van Der Berg and Sergeant Holly were in cahoots. This suspicion would have been in some respects strengthened and in others weakened had it been possible for Raffles to be present at an interview between these two which took place in the drawing room of the Van Der Berg villa shortly before Raffles arrived.

Had he been the proverbial fly on the damasked wall of that elegant room, which still contained the depleted display of wedding gifts, he would have discovered that the charming Netje was loath to admit even the possibility of his complicity in the theft. Yet some moral scruple in her Dutch nature forced her to appear to cooperate with the police. They, in the stolid person of Sergeant Holly, believed that Raffles's presence in the house on that fateful night was technically possible. Certainly his Manchester hotel room had not been occupied during the crucial hours. Above all he would have been delighted to learn that Sergeant Holly entertained a private suspicion concerning him. In short, this was that Raffles was a kleptomaniac, a term the officer carefully defined, with encyclopaedic quotations, to the disbelieving woman. To verify this theory—for that Raffles was the only known gentleman burglar in London was, Holly averred, a fact—he enlisted Netje's aid in setting a little trap for Raffles, but that the young woman was to apprise him of herself in due course.

As the great cricketer approached the villa, dressed in his most elegant afternoon suit, Netje at once and vehemently denied any possibility of his being the man she had held for so long at revolver point. Brushing aside the doubts of the detective, she hurried forward to greet her visitor. Raffles stooped over her pale hand, his eyes flashing admiration for what he saw.

"You wrote to me and asked me to come," he said.

"Yes," breathed the girl.

"I have come."

"Thank you," she said, and, recovering herself, introduced Sergeant Holly whom, she correctly assumed, he knew.

The two men greeted each other.

"Sergeant Holly," said Netje with dignity, "he is *not* the man."

At once the sergeant withdrew, his business with Raffles's delectable hostess apparently concluded.

"I apologize," said Raffles gently, "for not being the man. What man?"

"My burglar. A friend of yours," she replied levelly. "Or so he told me. And his voice had the ring of truth when he talked about you and about cricket. Not about anything else," she added more coolly.

"Did he seem an honest sort of fellow?" Raffles asked. "Given that he was a burglar."

"He seemed a very innocent man, given that he was a burglar."

Raffles could not suppress a smile at this so apt and observant an assessment of his dear friend Bunny, but he hastened to assure Netje that he had no innocent friends who were burglars.

"I am sorry to hear it," she said sadly. "As I said in my letter, I hoped that you might help me to get the gold cigarette case back."

"Alas," said Raffles, echoing her tone.

"It was my present to the bridegroom," she explained. "I am very fond of my sister and her husband.

213

I had chosen the case with great care. I hoped you had come to bring the case back."

"What can I say but alas?" apologized Raffles.

"Why did you come, Mr. Raffles?" she asked, with just a hint of becoming coquetry.

"Your letter was irresistibly persuasive," Raffles confessed. "And Sergeant Holly told me you were charming."

"So you came to see for yourself?" She smiled.

Raffles nodded his confirmation, holding her limpid eyes with his own.

"I didn't think," mused the young lady, "I was particularly charming to Sergeant Holly."

"But you confided in him," Raffles reminded her.

"Not at all." She denied it roundly.

"You read him your letter to me."

"No," she said emphatically. "I told him I had asked you to come here, that was all."

"I apologize," Raffles said again. "I was almost jealous of Sergeant Holly."

"I will confide in you," she said, lifting her exquisite face trustingly to his.

"I shall try to deserve it," Raffles promised, looking deep into her eyes.

Netje tore her gaze from his. Looking into his eyes she evidently could not speak.

"Sergeant Holly believes that you were my burglar," she confessed. "I tell him you're not: he accepts this, but I can see he does not believe it. However, Sergeant Holly has a second string to his bow. He thinks you are a kleptomaniac: If you are left alone with the presents, you will immediately steal some of them. So I am to leave you alone with the presents."

"And as soon as I steal one," suggested Raffles, "Sergeant Holly will rush in and arrest me?"

"Yes. He is longing to arrest you."

"I'm sure he is. Well, we must give him the chance. You must leave me alone with the presents."

"Of course," she agreed, giving him a tender, trusting smile.

"One condition," pleaded Raffles. "You will not show any sign of surprise at anything that happens."

Netje nodded and gave him her hand.

"Not at anything," she vowed. She moved toward the door, then hesitated. "One question, in case I have no opportunity afterwards?"

"Yes?" said Raffles.

"Why didn't you score a century in the Test Match? You so nearly got there. Ninety-nine!"

"Well, I thought to myself, 'After that rain, this is a pitch to be bowling on, not batting. What are you doing here, you "flannelled fool?"' And the very next ball, of course . . ." He spread his hands in a gesture of defeat.

"Out," confirmed Netje sadly.

"Can I have one question?" pleaded Raffles.

"Any."

"What's your name?"

"Netje."

"Netje," he repeated softly. "It's so that I can think about you."

She nodded gravely.

"And you, of course, are A. J. Raffles. I know from the newspapers."

"Arthur," Raffles supplied.

"No. A. J. I shall think of you as A. J."

"Thank you."

"And now I shall leave you alone," she said firmly, and seemed to Raffles's entranced eyes to melt from the room, a dear and silent spirit.

All this had been observed, though with some discretion, by Sergeant Holly. Now, seeing Miss Van Der Berg leave the room, he drew closer to the window and watched with mounting excitement as Raffles approached and inspected closely the array of gifts. To the sergeants' annoyance, Raffles contrived to keep his back perpetually turned to the window, but what little he could see of the cricketer's arm movements left him in not the slightest doubt. Suppressing a smile of triumph as unbecoming to the dignity of his office, Sergeant Holly burst into the room and demanded that Raffles, who looked the very epitome of guilt, should turn out his pockets. This he refused to do, whereupon the sergeant insisted upon searching him. Raffles submitted, assuming a bantering Cockney-esque accent while the sergeant found, in pocket after pocket, nought but the legitimate property of A. J. Raffles.

"What's the matter, Sergeant?" demanded Netje who suddenly interrupted this scene.

"I saw this man through the window stealing your things," he blustered, red-faced and angry. "He's got them somewhere in his pockets."

Netje cast a scrutinizing look at the tables.

"How could he have? They are all here on the table," she cried, drawing closer and checking the items off mentally. Suddenly she paused and calmly picked up a small gold cigarette case. "Yes," she said softly. "They are all here. I'm afraid Mr. Raffles was playing a game with you."

"I let you make a fool of yourself, Sergeant," Raffles agreed. "And you grabbed the chance with both hands."

The sergeant stared in apoplectic fury from Raffles to his charming hostess.

216

"Mr. Raffles is not a kleptomaniac," the latter informed him. "He is a cricketer."

"And, Sergeant," added Raffles gleefully, "I bowled you out middle stump."

With that, the sergeant turned on his heel and stalked away from the smiling pair.

"Not a good sport," said Raffles with a shake of his head.

"Did you expect him to be?" asked Netje.

"No. Thank you for concealing your surprise."

"What surprise?" she asked coolly, extending the cigarette case toward him. "Cigarette?"

"Thank you." Raffles took a Sullivan.

Netje helped herself from the case and accepted a light from Raffles. Through a cloud of smoke, she said:

"Of course, if Sergeant Holly had asked were their voices similar, I would have had to say yes. The same accent, the same way of saying 'Right'—the same school, perhaps?" she inquired with malicious innocence.

"Ah . . ." said Raffles, and offered her his arm.

Together, fully understanding one another, they went in to tea.

The following week Raffles was surprised to receive, by special delivery, a registered packet. Inside, he found a set of emerald shirt studs and a card.

" 'To go with the cuff links which you already have,' " he read.

Bunny peered over his shoulder.

"A girl in a million," whispered Raffles tenderly.

"But dangerous," Bunny added.

Raffles had to admit it. Looking at the studs, he said:

"Goodbye, East Molesey. Goodbye, love. But we'll keep the studs and cuff links."

And so Raffles was able to reconcile his public and his private patriotic duties. By doing so he learned a precious lesson: that even a foreign heart can be moved by the poetry of the willow bat, the stumps and bails, and even a "flannelled fool" can, for a moment, taste enchantment.

Seven

THE SPOILS OF
SACRILEGE

••••——◆◈◆——••••

IN WHICH RAFFLES AND BUNNY
BECOME A COUPLE OF FOXES AND
SPEND A NIGHT ON THE TILES

BUNNY WAS TO be discovered one afternoon, prudently enveloped in a strong apron, oiling Raffles's bat. As he did so, he delivered a monologue.

"I don't in the least mind oiling your bat for you! I don't mind whitening your boots for you, when you want to be fashionable. I don't mind running errands for you as if I was your fag at Uppingham all over again! I said I don't mind! And I don't! Not in the least!" On this avowal Bunny paused. He had spoken the last claims in a loud voice, directed at Raffles's bedroom. Now he waited for some response. There was none. He continued. "But what I do mind is that you won't let me do anything more useful. When we go burgling, it's you who decides everything. And who does everything! I'm just the plumber's mate! I hand you your tools, and go back for anything you've forgotten—except you're so clever you never forget anything!

I don't have to go back." Again the young man paused, glaring toward the bedroom.

Raffles, to his consternation, now entered the room from the hall and politely inquired as to where Bunny was going back.

"Didn't you hear what I was saying?" said Bunny, more surprised than angry.

"I thought you were talking to yourself," explained Raffles. "And I thought it wasn't polite to listen."

"I was talking to you," Bunny firmly informed him.

"Oh, I'm sorry. Was it interesting?"

"I was saying, you have no reason to split everything you make down the middle, and give me half!"

"It's so simple," Raffles said cheerfully. "I was never any good at arithmetic."

"Simply because it's simple . . . It's not a good-enough reason in the first place. . . ." Bunny began to protest.

"Ah," Raffles interrupted. "In the first place it was to save you from dishonor, Bunny. I thought that seemed a good-enough reason."

"Yes," agreed Bunny in a softened manner, touched as always to be reminded of that original act of kindness which he had never and could never forget. "And I'm eternally grateful to you."

"Then what are you moaning about?" asked Raffles, picking up and inspecting his bat.

"You've gone on doing it since!" Bunny cried.

"Friend and partner—what else could I do?"

"But half! The same as yourself!" To Bunny the injustice of this arrangement required no further elucidation.

Raffles set down the bat and said:

"You eat as much as I do. You drink as much as I do. You smoke as many Sullivans as I do. You . . ."

"But I don't do as much of the work as you do!" Bunny interrupted with the air of one who is hitting the nail resoundingly on the head.

"Ah," said Raffles again, recognizing familiar conversational ground. "The work . . . Burgling?"

"Yes," confirmed Bunny.

"You want to do more of the burgling?"

"Yes," Bunny repeated, with undiminished firmness.

"It's a very skilled job cracking cribs," Raffles said modestly. "I happen to be good at it, from a kind of natural cunning—as I happen to be good at spinning a cricket ball."

"I don't insist on cracking cribs," said Bunny, "but if I'm to get half of the proceeds, I do insist on earning it, one way or another."

"By the exercise of your natural talents?"

"Yes, if I have any."

"You have at least one great talent, Bunny," Raffles assured him. "For looking innocent. The whole of Scotland Yard could stare at you closely and every one of them would be deeply ashamed of himself for having even suspected you. And because you are innocent, I, your friend, am innocent too."

Bunny digested this familiar argument, but was in no mood to be persuaded by it.

"I'm sorry, but my innocent looks do not entitle me to half the proceeds," he insisted.

"Are you," inquired Raffles pessimistically, "going to make an argument of it?"

"Yes," vowed Bunny.

And so he did. Over sherry at the dear Old Bohemian where they had gone for dinner, Bunny complained that Raffles never took his advice on the planning and execution of their adventures. During dinner itself, Raffles discovered that the disproportion between Bunny's efforts and his rewards was making him feel guilty. This, Raffles admitted, was not to be tolerated, but how might the situation be remedied?

"I mean," he said, "if I think of enough places to break into and things to steal, and I'm the expert at actually cracking the cribs in question, and I'm the one who knows the fences who'll give us money for whatever we steal. . . . Well, what's left for you to specialize in?"

It was a good and pertinent question. It occupied Bunny throughout the brandy and the pleasant stroll to the turkish baths in Northumberland Avenue afterward. It was not, in fact, until the two friends were rather hotly ensconced in the steam room of that estimable establishment that he made an answer to the question.

"I could draw plans," he announced with confidence.

"What?" asked Raffles, whose mind had been elsewhere.

"I said I could draw plans. I used to be good at drawing."

"I'm sure you were," agreed Raffles. "Plans of what?"

"Plans of houses you were going to enter."

At this Raffles looked alarmed. It was not the matter of plans that caused his disquiet, but their public situation.

"It's all right," Bunny assured him casually. "There's nobody else here. I looked."

"In this steam . . ." said Raffles dubiously, peering at an impenetrable fog.

"You like working things out on plans," Bunny reminded him.

"Which houses do you know well enough to draw plans of?" asked Raffles, sensing that nothing else

222

would deter his friend. "I mean plans showing details like the window fastenings? And the bolts on the doors?" he added.

"I . . . er . . . well . . . er . . ." None sprang to mind. Bunny heaved a sigh. "None, I suppose. Except my own flat," he conceded unhappily.

"When you want me to break into your place, Bunny, just say the word," Raffles said, giving himself up to the relaxing and beneficial effects of the steam, and thinking that he had now successfully put an end to Bunny's ambitions as a draftsman.

This, however, was not the case. Bunny did think of a house, and a very suitable one at that. Pinfield Park, some forty miles from the metropolis and conveniently close to the Brighton line, had been Bunny's boyhood home. There, indulgent parents had allowed their boy the run of the mansion. Every nook and cranny were engraved upon his mind and for the next few days Bunny, although keeping to his Mount Street flat, constantly revisited that house in memory, translating his tender childhood recollections onto paper. The result was as fine a set of detailed plans as any architect or burglar could require and, surveying his handiwork, Bunny felt truly useful at last. He could scarcely wait to show them to Raffles. His walk became a skip, his run a dance that would have delighted Terpsichore herself as he hurried to the Albany and Raffles. With a flourish he unrolled the plans and proudly explained them. Raffles gave them a glance, no more, and mildly inquired why he should be interested in these admirable details of Pinfield Park.

"To commit a burglary there, of course," cried Bunny, frustrated and disappointed by this cool response.

223

"And why should I do that?" asked Raffles in the same tone.

"Because you're a burglar!" Bunny shouted.

"A burglar but not a thief, Bunny," Raffles spoke quietly, with a dignified hint of reproof in his voice. "At least not a thief who steals anything and everything out of habit, whenever the opportunity presents itself. That is a vice and a crime and deserves to be punished. I, on the other hand, steal only to remain virtuous, to pay my bills like a respectable member of society. I admit, there are times when I am tempted by a particular object, a necklace, a tiara, or by the difficulty of a particular task, the risk, the challenge. Then perhaps I go a-robbing, but I don't really think that entitles you to call me a burglar, as if I were Bill Sykes and wore a striped jersey and carried a bag over my shoulder marked 'Swag.' "

Bunny hung his head, partly in shame but, it must be admitted, mostly out of disappointment. At Raffles's command, he rolled up the plans.

"It's the most marvelous opportunity," he grumbled sadly.

"But not a challenge," Raffles insisted.

"And we're not hard up?" asked Bunny, clutching at straws.

"Not at the moment."

"And there's no particular object to tempt you?"

"None that I know of. Might there be one?" Raffles's eyes contained, as he asked this question, a glimmer of that gleam which always lit his countenance when a challenge or temptation presented itself.

"They're stinking rich," said Bunny. "The Osbornes. The people who bought the house."

"What kind of rich?" asked Raffles, still interested.

"Made their money in South American railways.

Run hundreds of horses. Hunt all winter, then the point-to-point at the end of the season, then polo all summer long. Never off the back of one horse or another. And I think they wear pink for dinner every blessed night of their lives."

"Not your style," said Raffles.

"Nor yours," agreed Bunny. "You don't know one end of a horse from another."

"And even if I did, I wouldn't know which end to aim at."

"If the Osbornes heard you say that, they'd have you hanged for treason." Bunny laughed.

"I know the kind. What are they like apart from that?"

"He's a huge, beefy, red-faced fellow. Eats like a horse and drinks like one, too. His wife doesn't eat like a horse, but she looks like one."

"You miss the point," Raffles said impatiently. "What does the wife wear?"

"Oh, clothes. Like a normal person," said Bunny obtusely.

"No, you ninny. What does she wear round her neck?"

"Oh, necklaces and so on."

Bunny was being deliberately evasive, having glimpsed a way to rouse Raffles's enthusiasm for the task he held so dear. He turned to the mantelpiece and idly inspected the impressive row of invitation cards. He picked up one, a duplicate of which rested on his own mantelpiece, and inquired if Raffles was planning to accept. His friend confirmed that he was, adding:

"Don't evade the question, Bunny. What sort of necklaces?"

"Oh, diamonds and that sort of thing," Bunny replied, as though such stones were of no particular interest.

"And that sort of thing!" echoed Raffles, shocked at this entirely unprofessional interest in their staple means of making a living.

"Yes, *you* know," continued Bunny in the same careless fashion. "Big as pigeons' eggs. I mean, with her husband so rich, she can afford it."

In fact, Bunny had lost none of his regard for diamonds. On the contrary, he saw in them the means to persuade Raffles to put his plans to good use. Accordingly, Bunny employed all his innocent charm to cajole their mutual hostess into inviting Mrs. Osborne to the dinner to which Raffles had said he meant to go. This accomplished, he crossed his fingers—which was all he could do to encourage Mrs. Osborne to wear her fabled diamonds on that occasion. She did so and, though perhaps not quite so large as pigeons' eggs, the stones were of sufficient weight and circumference to put that steely gleam in Raffles's eyes. So much Bunny was able to observe from the opposite end of the table. Time and again Raffles's gaze strayed from the face of the charming lady on his right to the dazzling array of jewels that adorned Mrs. Osborne. Bunny, highly pleased with himself, awaited the psychological moment before offhandedly remarking to Raffles that the lady was in fact the mistress of Pinfield Park.

"You deliberately got her invited, so that I could see that necklace and be tempted by it," Raffles accused him as soon as they had reached the Albany.

"I thought it was rather a good idea." Bunny smiled.

"Did you?"

"Well, I mean, it does get rather monotonous, you being the clever one," he said.

"So you thought you'd try it?"

226

"Yes."

"And you are very pleased with the result?"

"Well," admitted Bunny, "it did what I wanted."

"Tempted me."

"Yes."

"Satan!" cried Raffles, who was secretly rather pleased with Bunny's display of initiative.

"It's not that I *want* you to be a burglar, Raffles," Bunny hastened to explain. "It's just that if you *are* a burglar, then I want to help you. Really help you. I want to do my share."

"And so you shall," promised Raffles.

"You mean that?" Bunny's face was the very portrait of joy.

"I'll take charge of getting down to the place, but when we're in sight of the house, you take command."

Bunny could scarcely believe his ears.

"You'll bring your tools, of course?" he asked.

"But I shall use them only under your control and direction," Raffles asserted.

"By Jove!" cried Bunny, who was as thrilled as it was possible for him to be.

"A big responsibility, Bunny," Raffles warned.

"Yes, my word!"

"We have to decide what night it's going to be. We don't want to go on a night when Mrs. Osborne is wearing the necklace in London."

But Bunny had already made inquiries and now, with jubilant pride, he set about informing Raffles of his discoveries. On the following Friday week the Osbornes were giving their annual dinner for the members of the hunt. It was certain to be, according to Bunny's information, a lively night and therefore a good one for burglars.

"Still," mused Raffles, "if it's a dinner party, the

hostess won't leave her jewels upstairs. She'll wear them, my boy."

"Not all of them, Raffles. She might wear her rope of pearls and, of course, a ring or two, or three. I gather Mrs. Osborne is generally the only woman there. Now no woman is going to put on all her jewels for a roomful of drunken fox hunters."

"True enough, Bunny," Raffles agreed, making a mental note of Bunny's rapidly developing powers of observation and deduction.

He proposed a toast to the venture and the pair settled down to finalize the details. Since Bunny was no stranger to the area, Raffles, who occupied his usual position as commander until the house was reached, insisted that he travel to a railway station some distance beyond Pinfield and rendezvous with Raffles at a suitably late hour. Reluctantly, Bunny agreed to this proposal and resigned himself to a two-mile trudge through the byways of Sussex before his moment of glory began.

And so it was. The rendezvous accomplished on a fine, moonlit night, the pair walked together to a point at the edge of Pinfield Park which gave them a fine view of the house. It stood imposingly amid the parkland, four anachronistic towers rising from its corners and shining with celebratory lights. The two friends gazed at their target for some minutes.

"Well, Bunny," Raffles said at last. "From this moment on. . . ."

"Raffles," began Bunny, his tone positively thick with second thoughts, "do you think . . ."

"It is not my business to think, Bunny. You are in charge and I am in your hands," Raffles said firmly.

For a moment Bunny wished, quite devoutly, that it was not so, but he put a brave face on it.

"They're having dinner," he said, pointing out the blazing dining room.

"Let's have a look at them," said Raffles, taking a step forward. Instantly he stopped and turned apologetically to Bunny. "I beg your pardon. *You* must say what we shall do."

"Well . . . let's have a look at them, shall we?" suggested Bunny.

"Good. I hoped you'd say that." Raffles smiled. "Lead on."

Moments later, the young commander and his willing accomplice were surveying the company at dinner through the convenient slats of a venetian blind. It was indeed a riotous gathering of pink-coated men in the midst of which sat Mrs. Osborne, resplendent, as Bunny had predicted, in her rope of pearls and a quantity of rings. Swiftly and quietly, Bunny pointed out the florid-faced bulk of Mr. Osborne, the son of the house and other members of the party. Raffles was quick to congratulate his friend on the prediction concerning Mrs. Osborne's ornaments, and drew the inevitable conclusion that her diamonds must be upstairs.

"Shall we go and see?" he added.

"If you like," said Bunny.

"I beg your pardon. I meant, do you command that we shall go and see?"

"Yes."

"I obey, oh, master!" Raffles grinned impishly.

Bunny led the way to the back of the house and quietly indicated the door he had already marked on his plan as being the best means of access for burglars. It led, as he reminded Raffles, to the back stairs from whence it would take but a moment to reach the bedrooms.

"Am I to use my tools?" inquired Raffles, approaching the door.

"Yes," said Bunny resolutely.

Raffles reached out and turned the handle of the door. It opened noiselessly.

"First rule of burgling," he whispered. "Don't break in unless you have to."

Bunny was eager to proceed. He pressed close behind Raffles, who paused, however.

"May I not command but suggest," he suggested, "that we put our masks on at this point?"

"Yes, right," agreed Bunny impatiently.

"Since your face is known in the neighborhood, and mine is not entirely unknown to readers of the newspapers. . . ."

"Yes. All right. I'm putting it on," said Bunny sharply.

Suitably masked, Bunny led the way into the house and up the back stairs. These divided at a landing. A second flight went up into one of the four towers. The landing itself gave access to a long corridor which led to the main bedrooms. Bunny hurried down this corridor which was divided into two by a felt-covered door. This he shouldered with familiarity, knowing it to be of the swing-hinged variety. He recoiled in surprise, clutching his shoulder. He gave the door a sharp push. It did not swing.

"Damn the thing!" Bunny exclaimed.

"May I look?" asked Raffles politely.

"Do." Bunny stepped back haughtily.

Raffles applied his eye to a crack between the stubborn door and its solid jamb.

"Locked on the other side," he announced.

"Blast!"

"Any way round it?"

"No."

"What do we do?"

"Er . . ."

"Shall I have a go with my tools?"

"Yes, would you?" said Bunny with relief.

Raffles produced his slim, compact box of tools and selected therefrom a long daggerlike instrument with a serrated edge. Tearing a portion of material from the paneling, he swiftly began to saw a hole in the wood, close to the lock, explaining as he did so that though slower than a jimmy, this method had the advantage of being considerably less noisy.

"Sorry about this, Raffles," said Bunny stiffly.

"The great thing about the burglar's life is, you keep coming up against the unexpected," commented Raffles, busily cutting away.

At that moment, on the other side of the door, Mrs. Osborne's personal maid emerged from her employers's bedroom and saw the protruding point of a cutting tool appearing through the door. At once she realized the import of what she saw and, on tiptoe, hurried to the main staircase.

No sooner had she disappeared than Raffles was able to knock free the rough circle of wood he had cut from the door. He slipped his hand through the hole and turned the key. Once again Bunny took command, conducting Raffles to the master bedroom. Once there, he turned up the gas and announced that he left it to Raffles to unearth the jewels. The latter immediately approached another door which led into a small dressing room. This contained yet a third door, giving access to the corridor, which was securely bolted. Experience told Raffles that this was the repository of the jewels and his keen, professional eyes quickly spied a handsome antique chest, which bore a stout modern

231

lock. To this he applied his jimmy. The lock yielded with a sharp crack.

"Eureka!" he whispered. "Go and see if I've roused anybody, Bunny," he said as he lifted the lid.

Bunny did as he was bid. All seemed well, but he took the precaution of stepping out into the corridor to make absolutely sure. At the head of the main staircase a large, ornate mirror was fixed to the wall and what Bunny saw therein caused his heart to stand still. The male members of the hunt, resplendent in their pink coats and grasping riding crops with unmistakable determination, were creeping in stockinged feet up the stairs. Bunny turned on his heel and fled back to Raffles. The latter immediately handed Bunny two jewel cases which, out of long habit, he obediently pocketed while blurting out his terrible news.

"Did they see you?" hissed Raffles, rising at once and concealing two more cases in his pockets.

"No."

"Come on then."

He was already running and Bunny hastened to follow him. In the corridor they dashed for the door just as the hunt appeared at the top of the stairs. At once this formidable pack of gentlemen gave cry.

"Gone away! Gone away!"

"Yoick, yoick!"

"Yonder they go!"

Raffles and Bunny hurtled through the door which swung to behind them.

"Hold on," called Raffles, "I'll lock it."

The delay, though destined to be brief, might prove to their advantage. He pushed his hand through the hole he had cut and turned the key, but before he could withdraw his hand it was seized by Mr. Osborne himself with a yell of bloodcurdling triumph.

"What's up?" said Bunny, hopping from one foot to the other.

"My hand's held. They've got me tight. It's no good. I'm done," Raffles whispered.

"Got your revolver?" asked Bunny.

"In my pocket."

"Blaze away through the door."

"No."

"Or let me."

"No. You might hit someone."

"What you going to do?"

"I'm done," Raffles repeated. "You get out while you can. Never mind me."

"I'm not going without you," said Bunny with resolution.

At this, despite the pain in his hand which was being cruelly twisted by the baying huntsmen, Raffles managed a ghost of a smile.

"Good pal," he said. "Feel in my pocket."

"Revolver?" said Bunny, his hopes reviving.

"No. Oil bottle. With my tools. Just a chance. Run the oil down my arm, to the wrist."

Bunny located the bottle and, forcing himself to be calm, began to trickle the oil as Raffles had instructed. Raffles began to twist and wriggle. The commotion beyond the door increased, indicating that the oil was having the desired effect. At last, with a grimace of pain, Raffles twisted his hand free and pulled it through the hole. Immediately the clamor on the other side of the door became more ferocious. A hunting horn added its raucous brays to the din. Bunny and Raffles ran as fast as they could along the corridor but, on reaching the landing, found their route blocked. Some members of the hunt, anticipating Raffles's escape, had made a detour and were already climbing up the back stairs. At the same time, the remainder of the pack, led by the formidable figure of Mr. Osborne, burst through the felt door.

"Up here," shouted Bunny, making a dash for the second flight of stairs.

Raffles panted at his heels and the two friends emerged breathless in an attic room. Bunny did not pause but made straight for an ancient wooden ladder which led to a trap door. Up he went, as agile as a monkey, forcing the trap door open. He threw himself into the room above, swiftly followed by Raffles. With great presence of mind, Bunny recovered himself and slammed the trap door shut, just as the bald pate of Mr. Osborne appeared. With a cry, the stout gentleman fell back onto his followers. Bunny planted his feet firmly on the trap door. From below came the cries:

"Gone to earth! Gone to earth!"

"Where's the terrier?"

"Dig 'em out!"

Raffles struggled to his feet and, seeing a chair, pulled it forward onto the trap door. He sat down at once and, with a rueful expression, looked at his painful and damaged hand.

"Near thing," said Bunny quietly.

"Too close for comfort," agreed Raffles. He pulled off his mask and returned again to the contemplation of his hand. "Don't think I'll be doing any slow bowling for a week or two," he said.

"Don't say they've damaged your spinning finger?" cried Bunny in alarm, stripping off his own mask and bending in the gloom for a sight of the injury.

"Not permanently. But, yes, they have."

"The brutes!"

"It was when I wrenched my hand away," Raffles

234

explained. "Lucky I did, though. There's no cricket team in Wormwood Scrubs."

Bunny shuddered at the mention of that penal institution.

"Strike a light, Bunny, will you?" asked Raffles.

Bunny did so and held the match aloft. By its flickering, imperfect light he spied the stubs of two candles in dusty holders on a table a few feet away. He groped his way toward the table and soon had both candles burning. By their light Raffles saw that they were in an oddly shaped, neglected room at the very top of one of the four towers which adorned Pinfield Park. Three of the windows looked on to the empty sky. The fourth gave a view of the tiled roof of the building.

"I must have left those candles here a dozen years ago," said Bunny in an odd voice. "Osborne never comes up here, I suppose. And his son's too old. But this was my *sanctum sanctorum* when I was a boy."

"Was it?" said Raffles gently.

"I smoked my first pipe here. I wrote my first verse here."

"Who to?" asked Raffles with an indulgent smile.

"The rector's daughter. She was called Phillida."

"Did she flout you?"

"Yes," Bunny said sadly.

From below, Raffles's sharp ears heard the withdrawal of the hunt.

"They've given up hope of getting in from underneath," he said, interrupting Bunny's reverie. "So they're going to try some other way. What other ways are there?"

"Er . . ."

Bunny gazed about him blankly, his mind still clouded by memories of his vanished childhood.

"Come on, Bunny," said Raffles testily. "The whole reason for our coming here was you know the place backwards."

"Yes, I do. I was just working it out."

"Sorry, Bunny," said Raffles. "I don't mean to be sharp with you, but I'm blessed if I can see how we can get out of here."

"The roof," said Bunny quietly.

"What good is the roof to me?" snapped Raffles.

"No, I mean the only other way they can get at you. Up through one of the skylights and across the roof."

"Ah," said Raffles, getting up and walking to the window from which could be seen the moonlit roof of Pinfield Park. The gray slates gleamed eerily in the cold light. The stone chimneys rose into the sky, offering no help.

"Bunny," said Raffles quietly.

"Yes?"

"What are we going to do?"

Bunny said nothing. Raffles watched his face on which were etched lines of sadness and defeat.

"I ask," said Raffles after a long silence, "because you're in charge. We agreed. I simply do what you tell me to. So I'm waiting to be told."

Bunny looked at his feet. He rocked on his heels. He said nothing.

"Frankly," said Raffles, his voice betraying a slight edge, "I'm getting tired of waiting."

"Yes," said Bunny.

"What are we going to do? You must decide."

"Would you mind taking command, Raffles?" said Bunny in a low, emotional voice.

"Now?"

"Now and always."

"Do you mean that?" asked Raffles.

"I was a fool ever to think I could do it," confessed Bunny miserably. "The whole thing's my fault. I was a blithering idiot to lead you up here."

"Nonsense, Bunny," Raffles said. "There was no other way to run."

"But that damned door in the corridor. I didn't know about that."

"Of course you didn't. How could you have known?"

"Getting your hand caught in that hole . . ."

"That was my fault, not yours."

"I'll never forgive myself if you've damaged your spinning finger."

"I'll bowl left-handed. And I've done that before now."

"It's no good, Raffles. You can try and make me feel all right, but whatever you say, I know very well I'm simply not cut out to be in charge of things. I'm cut out to be a helper, that's all."

"A most loyal helper." Raffles smiled at him. "Who else would have stayed with me when I was trapped?"

"I couldn't have run. It wasn't possible," Bunny said with a firm shake of his head.

"That's what I mean. It wasn't possible—for you. It would have been possible for lots of other people."

"Oh . . ." said Bunny, understanding but not feeling any better.

"So I take command again?" asked Raffles.

"Please."

"And out motto is 'Victory or Wormwood Scrubs'?"

"Hear hear," said Bunny unhappily.

Just then he spotted a dim figure climbing through one of the skylights. It stood for a moment, a shadow silhouetted against the night sky. Bunny drew Raffles's attention to it. Instantly Raffles drew his revolver from his pocket, smashed the window and fired a shot toward the figure.

"You didn't hit him?" cried Bunny, craning over Raffles's shoulder.

"Of course I didn't. I damaged the bricks a yard to the right of him. Near enough to give him a bit of a fright, that's all."

"Good man," said Bunny with relief.

But Raffles knew that no one but Bunny would believe that he had not fired to kill. Should they be apprehended, and just at that moment this seemed to be extremely likely, the shot would add ten years to the sentence he would receive. All this passed through his mind as he scanned the roof for some possible means of escape.

"Is that a working flagstaff out there?" he asked, pointing to the distant pole.

"It always used to be."

"Then there'll be halyards," said Raffles, hope stirring in him.

"They were as thin as clothes lines," said Bunny.

"And they're sure to be rotten. And we would be seen cutting them down." Raffles thus dismissed his hope. "No, Bunny, that won't do." He stared again at the gray and dismal roof. "Wait a minute," he said. "Is there a lightning conductor?"

"There was," said Bunny, leaning out of the broken window toward the nearest chimney. "Yes. There still is. On that chimney stack."

"How thick?" asked Raffles.

"As I remember it, it was thicker than a lead pencil. Why?"

"Lightning conductors have wires that run to earth," said Raffles sagely. "Which is where we want to be."

. "What?" said Bunny, his mouth becoming dry with alarm.

"They sometimes bear you," Raffles informed him. "The difficulty is to keep a grip. But I've been up and down them before tonight. And anyway it's our only chance."

With grim determination, Raffles took from his pocket a pair of white kid gloves. He pulled them on and stuffed his handkerchief into the palm of the right.

"You're going to go down the wire?" asked Bunny, his voice trembling.

"And you're going to come after me," Raffles said. "If I get down all right."

"But if you don't?" cried Bunny in a panic. "Supposing it comes away from the chimney?"

"Then I shall get to earth even faster. And you'll have to stay here and face the music without me."

"Suppose it breaks!" persisted Bunny.

"Suppose it doesn't," replied Raffles. "Don't say, 'Be careful,' say 'Good luck.' "

With all his heart Bunny said: "Good luck."

"Give me a couple of minutes, then you come."

So saying Raffles opened the window and climbed out onto the roof. For a moment he paused, a wide grin on his face.

"Victory or Wormwood Scrubs!" he whispered to Bunny, adding to himself as he climbed across the slippery tiles toward the chimney, "Or, of course, heaven or hell."

Bunny stood at the window holding his breath. He saw Raffles reach the chimney stack and locate the wire. He seized it purposefully, adjusted his grip and letting the wire take most of his weight, began to walk slowly backward toward the edge of the roof. Before he reached that perilous point, however, Bunny had hidden his face in his hands. It seemed an age that he stood there, his ears straining for the scream, the sickening thud that would announce the end of his dearest, his most valued friend. No sound came. At last he lowered his hands and stared out of the window. The wire lay limp and intact on the roof. Raffles had made it! The joy this certainty brought him was almost immediately dampened by the realization that now it was his turn. Bunny looked around him. He did not want to risk the wire. He had such fond memories of this room. In the flickering candlelight he could almost see himself as he had been. A young, untainted, innocent boy. What a long and tortuous way he had traveled since then! What dishonor had been his lot! What a burden of guilt he bore! Bunny moved to the window and there, contemplating the journey he was about to make, he had another, a much clearer vision. He was lying at the foot of the walls of Pinfield Park. He was most surely dead, and spilling from his pockets was the incriminating evidence of his shame. No, he would not do it. He turned back into the room and took from his pockets the two jewel cases Raffles had thrust into his hands. He opened them sadly. The candlelight struck pure, innocent fire from the gems of Mrs. Osborne's necklace and her matching tiara. A cleansing, purifying fire, Bunny thought, placing these objects on the table. He would go to his death, he would be identified as Mr. Manders who had once been young and happy in this very house, but he would not be branded, even in death, a thief. To take these ornaments, he thought, fumbling the empty boxes back into his pockets, would be tantamount to an act of sacrilege and that, at least, was not in Bunny's style.

With a strange calmness now, Bunny pulled on his gloves and padded the palm of his right hand with his handkerchief. Briefly, he said farewell to the room, to his youth, and climbed out onto the tiles. He reached the chimney stack, took up the wire and tugged it experimentally. It held. He positioned his hands carefully and, closing his eyes, began to walk backward to his fate.

Below, in one of the well-tended flower beds, Raffles stared anxiously upward. He had traveled a very long and dangerous way. Now where was Bunny? He did not care to think of the drop had the wire not held. He only hoped it would hold as fast for Bunny. A slight sound caught his attention. Bunny, reduced to an indistinct black shape appeared at the edge of the roof, came over and began the last part of the descent, his feet braced against the sheer wall of Pinfield Park. He continued steadily downward until he reached a spot some twenty feet above the ground. From above him there was a rending sound, the clatter of mortar on the tiles. With a thundering heart, Raffles just had time to flatten himself against the wall as the lightning conductor flew past him, followed seconds later by Bunny. The latter landed with a dull sound in the soft part of the flowerbed. Masonry and mortar showered around him.

"You all right?" asked Raffles.

"Knocked all the wind out of me," panted Bunny, sitting up and not quite believing that he had survived.

"Legs all right?"

Bunny felt them tentatively. They seemed all right. He stood up. He was a bit wobbly, but upright.

"All right to run?" whispered Raffles.

"Yes."

"Come on. On the grass."

Raffles set off at a brisk trot, round behind the house and away over the parkland. Bunny did his best to

241

keep up and to keep low. Suddenly he collided with Raffles who had come to a sudden stop on the bank of a small boating lake.

"Where are we now?" asked Raffles.

"The lake," panted Bunny.

"Obviously."

"My father had it dug when we first came here," supplied Bunny. "I learned to row on it. Wonder if they still have . . . No. Mr. Osborne may be a sporting man, but I doubt if he's a boating man."

Raffles looked around him in the gloom.

"There's a boat," he said, making toward the partially concealed boat which was drawn up close under some reeds.

"For the ladies, perhaps," said Bunny irrelevantly.

"For us," Raffles corrected him, stepping in to the frail and swaying craft and picking up the pole from the bottom. "Come on. I'll try to remember how we used to do it on the Backs," he said.

Bunny clambered in, noting as he did so that Raffles was intending to pole from the front of the boat. He pointed this out as Raffles plunged the pole deep into the dark water.

"Good heavens, Bunny," he said with an offended air, "you don't suppose I was at Oxford? Where they do everything from the wrong end!"

Bunny could think of no answer to this. The boat slid smoothly out toward the center of the lake, Bunny peering into the dark to locate the boathouse he remembered so clearly on the opposite bank.

Meanwhile, the Osborne hunt, not a bit deterred by Raffles's warning shot had retreated, regrouped and now prepared themselves for a final offensive on the tower room. Armed with unsportsmanlike shotguns, Mr. Osborne led his baying pack up the ladder, threatening to blast the burglars to pieces at the least show of opposition. The trap door yielded, the huntsman and his followers climbed into the room. The candles flickered in the breeze from the smashed and open window, striking fire from Mrs. Osborne's most prized jewels which made a sort of still life on the table.

Now, for all it may seem otherwise, Mr. Osborne was a genuine sportsman. The recovery of the diamonds satisfied him, and his friends and family agreed with him that the "foxes" had given them a jolly good run for their money. It was decided, therefore, to dispatch only one man to inform the police of the incident—this being their duty as good country gentlemen—but to call off any further pursuit. A toast was proposed to the wily foxes, and Mrs. Osborne was persuaded to don her treasures that all might see the spoils.

It was the sound of that lone horse galloping away from the house that reached Raffles's ears as he and Bunny arrived at the comparative safety of the neglected boathouse. Raffles surmised that whay they had heard was only the front runner of the pack, sent to summon the police. He confidently predicted a full hue and cry at any moment. Bunny insisted that he did not wish to be hunted any more and Raffles assured him that he should not be. The pack would be off across country, scouring all roads that led to railway stations. It would not occur to them to seek their quarry in their very own park. But Bunny wanted to be off anyway.

"The very closeness is our safety," Raffles argued.

"I wish I thought so," said Bunny morosely.

"Even if you don't," Raffles ticked him off, "remember that I am in command and you do what I tell you."

"Yes, all right, Raffles. I remember," Bunny said. "But how long are we going to stay here?"

"Until the uproar dies down," replied Raffles.

Bunny kept silence. Tiny waves lapped from the lake against the sides of the boat. Apart from that and the quiet sounds of their own breathing, the silence was complete.

"Raffles?" said Bunny.

"Yes?"

"There isn't any uproar."

"No," agreed Raffles. "Strange."

"Very," Bunny assented.

"Just one man gone for the police and the hunt aren't turning out at all," Raffles mused. "I'm going to see what's happening," he said with determination.

With warnings to be careful, not to be seen, Bunny watched Raffles glide once more across the stygian lake. He felt useless and he felt depressed. He also felt very tired. He sat down, leaning his back against the wooden wall of the boathouse and prepared himself for a long wait.

In no time at all Raffles reached the bank and sped softly across the park to the still gaily illumined house. He drew close to the dining-room window and peeked again through the venetian blind. All was jollity and carousing within. The flushed, pink-coated men drank toast after toast, with loud bays of laughter and impromptu calls on the hunting horn. Raffles simply could not understand it. He frowned and shifted his point of vantage. Then he understood. Peering now between Mr. Osborne and a similarly well-fleshed comrade, he saw the unmistakable flash and gleam of diamonds. The two men obligingly drew apart. Mrs. Osborne beamed almost as brightly as her tiara and her necklace.

Raffles did not need to observe any longer. He retraced his steps, deep in thought, and, for the third time, made the crossing of the lake. Bunny heard his approach and leaped forward eagerly to steady the incoming vessel and to make her fast.

"I simply don't understand," said Raffles, stepping out of the punt. "They're as jolly as ever. They don't seem to be doing anything about us. Can you think of an explanation, Bunny?"

"No," said Bunny, his face wearing a less than usually innocent expression.

Raffles pondered in silence. The sound of carriage wheels on gravel carried to them across the still lake.

"Well," said Raffles, "there go their wheels on the drive, bearing the departing guests. There must be some explanation of why they gave up." He continued to wrack his brains.

"The influence of liquor, I should think," said Bunny.

"You think it made them kindly disposed toward us?" wondered Raffles.

"I think it made them do nothing more than want to go to bed."

"I suppose you're right," Raffles conceded after a moment. "Well, I'm going back."

"What for?" demanded Bunny with a start.

Raffles heaved a sigh.

"To get back to London we have to go to the railway station. We must suppose that there will be a policeman at the railway station, looking for two gentlemen in evening dress and toppers, with or without black masks. If he sees two such gentlemen, he will undoubtedly arrest them—and they'll deserve it for being so stupid!"

Bunny avoided his friend's eyes. Once again Raffles

stepped into the boat and signaled to Bunny to shove off. This he did, watching Raffles silhouetted against the lightening sky. The water looked gray now and wisps of mist, like tatters of chiffon, swirled around his friend and leader, his mentor in all things, and soon swallowed him up. Miserably, Bunny made himself as comfortable as possible on an old bench and in a short space of time was sound asleep. But it was a sleep without rest, a sleep haunted by images. Himself as a boy falling from the high, high roof of Pinfield Park, jewels scattering from his pockets. The inescapable figure of a dark and angry man drifting out of the mists of a black and bubbling lake. The man reached toward him. He sought, Bunny knew, explanations which he trembled to give.

Bunny woke with a start to find Raffles standing over him, his arms filled with clothing. These he dropped onto the floor and straightened up. He was transformed by breeches and a black hacking jacket, both several sizes too large for him. On his head a smart bowler and the whole bizarre rig covered by a gargantuan riding mackintosh.

"Steady, Bunny." Raffles laughed as Bunny started up. "Don't you recognize me now I've gone all horsey? Here, I've got some things for you."

"You've been in the house again," cried Bunny.

"I had to. We'd never have got away as we were."

While Bunny struggled into a similar outfit, also too large but somewhat padded out by his own clothes underneath, Raffles outlined his latest exploit, concluding with a graphic imitation of Mrs. Osborne's stentorian snoring.

"Ouch!" said Bunny as he pulled off his evening shoe.

"What's the matter?"

"I did something to my ankle when I fell, and it's gone a bit swollen," he explained, gently probing the injured limb.

"We'll make a virtue of your unsteady gait," Raffles said, putting stones into Bunny's patent leather shoes. "Write it into your character." He dropped the weighted shoes into the lake and watched them sink happily.

Careful of his ankle, Bunny put on a pair of stout brown brogues and stood up, leaning heavily upon his friend. Thus it was that two decidedly unsteady gentlemen of an equally decidedly horsey character reached Pinfield Halt in time for the milk train to London. Their lively speech and uncertain gait attracted the amused attention of a constable who was patrolling there. He was, however, used to such sights in the environs of the Osborne residence and did no more than to advise the gentlemen to go steady. He even helped them into the London train where, with relief, they exchanged tired smiles.

"Now," said Raffles, "as soon as we get off this train . . ."

"At Victoria," Bunny interrupted happily.

"No." Raffles shook his head solemnly. "We get off this train at Clapham Junction. And then we take a cab . . ."

"To the Albany, I hope," said Bunny. "I'm longing for a glass of your Scotch."

"We shall take a cab to Chelsea," Raffles informed him. "A second to Whitehall and a third to the Albany. I'm like you, Bunny. I never feel safe until I'm home again, but I like to confuse my trail in getting there."

Bunny's face fell, but Raffles promised him a generous drink as soon as they arrived. And that they did before nine o'clock. Having furnished Bunny with the promised beverage, Raffles withdrew to his bedroom and removed his riding clothes. He returned to the sitting room, fastening the belt of an elegant silk dressing gown, and helped himself to stimulating refreshment.

"I'll drink a toast to the expedition," he cried, raising his glass. "I've never been on one that ran so close to the edge of disaster or that ended in such a glorious triumph."

"I hope you're right about the triumph," Bunny said levelly. "It's enough for me that we're safe."

"Well, let's see. I've got two jewel cases," Raffles remarked, taking them from the pockets of the discarded mackintosh. "I gave you two, didn't I?"

"Yes," said Bunny, squirming slightly in his chair.

"Unfortunately, there's nothing in mine. I looked while I was waiting for the Osbornes to go to sleep." He tossed the empty cases onto a settee. "But you must have something in yours." He rubbed his hands together in eager anticipation.

"I'm very much afraid," said Bunny, who was, "that I'm in the same unlucky state as you." He produced the two jewel cases from his pockets. "These are empty, too."

"What?" cried Raffles, snatching one. "But they can't be!"

"I'm afraid they are."

Raffles opened the case he held and tossed it aside.

"By Jove! What a sell," he said. "Absolute swizz."

"Yes," agreed Bunny.

"Not a triumph at all, but a frost," complained Raffles.

"That's right," sighed Bunny.

"We put in all that effort for exactly nothing. Or

more precisely," he bitterly corrected himself, "for four empty jewel cases."

"That's so," sighed Bunny.

Raffles paused, picked up the case he had taken from Bunny and examined it.

"But this one must have held that magnificent necklace," he said. "And this one was obviously made to hold a tiara," he continued, inspecting the second case which Bunny had placed on the table.

Bunny agreed that very likely those priceless objects had indeed rested in those worthless receptacles.

"And she wasn't wearing either of them," Raffles went on relentlessly. "We saw that through the window. So where could they have been?"

Bunny forced himself to meet Raffles's puzzled gaze.

"Raffles," he said, steeling himself. "I'll be frank with you. I meant you never to know, but it's easier than going on telling lies. The items were in the cases all right. I left them behind me in the tower room."

"Why, Bunny?" Raffles asked in the most quiet and neutral of voices.

As best he could, Bunny related to Raffles the awful vision he had experienced in the tower room and his attendant feelings of shame and dishonor. Raffles listened in attentive silence.

"It was unbearable. It was sacrilege," Bunny said with emotion. "You may say that I ought to have thought of all this before, but I didn't. I only thought of it then, and that's all that there is to it."

"You were always a bad liar, Bunny," Raffles commented.

"Hopeless," agreed the young man despairingly.

"Will you think *me* one when I tell you that I can understand what you felt, and what you did? As a matter of fact, I have understood for several hours now," he confessed.

"What I felt, Raffles?" Bunny asked, not quite understanding.

"And what you did." Raffles confirmed with a nod. "I guessed it in the boathouse. You were in such a mood of just wanting to get away from the place, whatever the cost, and Osborne and his friends were so slow to come after us—they who'd been so keen on the chase—it seemed as though they'd found something that took the edge off their keenness. And then I went back to the house and took another look through the venetian blinds. And what do you think I saw?" he asked, plunging his hands into his dressing-gown pockets.

"I've no idea," said Bunny with complete truth.

"The whole lot of them, prematurely gloating over the recovery of these two pretty things."

With a simple flourish, Raffles drew from his pockets the diamond tiara and its complementary necklace. The morning sun struck an arpeggio of light from their many-faceted surfaces. Bunny gaped.

"I went back into their bedroom, Bunny," Raffles reminded him, putting the jewels on the table. "They'd left all their jewelry simply lying on the dressing table, for anyone to take. It seemed a shame not to. After all, we had risked life, limb and liberty. And I had none of your sentimental scruples," he added gently. "Why should I go empty away?"

"You stole them a second time!" gasped Bunny.

"I took back what had once, however briefly, been mine," Raffles asserted.

"I admit there is a logic in it and a kind of poetic justice," said Bunny.

"If you want to hear the full story of my second visit

to the Osbornes' bedroom, drive home for a change of clothes and meet me at the turkish baths in twenty minutes," said Raffles with sudden vivacity. "I feel more than a little grubby after my night on the tiles. And we can have breakfast in the cooling gallery."

"Done," said Bunny instantly, his heavy spirits suddenly lightening. He took a step toward the door but a thought, an important thought, made him pause. "Just one thing, Raffles. I have been no use to you tonight, and worse than no use. I shall be delighted to have breakfast with you, to celebrate your exploit, but I shall absolutely and definitely not take any share of tonight's proceeds. I didn't earn any."

Bunny had spoken with great dignity and Raffles was duly impressed.

"I agree with you, Bunny. And I had already considered this very question. I came to the conclusion that your share of the loot should be only the small stuff I picked up at the same time." With a broad grin of irrepressible happiness, Raffles delved again into his pockets. "The rope of pearls, the rings . . ." These and other small, costly items he tumbled onto the table. Bunny stared at them with renewed astonishment, and before he could protest, Raffles said: "A fair price for the pleasure of your company, Bunny."

Bunny, of course, accepted. What else could he do? He had learned a lesson that night more precious even than the life he had feared to lose. He had learned that his own qualities, although definitely not those of a leader, were yet valued and understood by one naturally equipped to lead. Through Raffles, to whom he had turned in desperation, Bunny had regained his honor and was concerned to retain it, even in death. But more, he had learned to value justly his own innate innocence, as Raffles had always done. He left the Al-

251

bany that morning with a new sense of self-respect, and he faced the future, whatever adventures it might bring, with a stout heart, knowing that Raffles would always bring him through.

ALL TIME BESTSELLERS
FROM POPULAR LIBRARY

☐	AFTERNOON MEN—Powell	04268-0	1.95
☐	MARINA TOWER—Beardsley	04198-6	1.95
☐	SKIN DEEP—Hufford	04258-3	1.95
☐	MY HEART TURNS BACK—Patton	04241-9	2.25
☐	EARTHLY POSSESSIONS—Tyler	04214-1	1.95
☐	THE BERLIN CONNECTION—Simmel	08607-6	1.95
☐	THE BEST PEOPLE—Van Slyke	08456-1	1.95
☐	A BRIDGE TOO FAR—Ryan	08373-5	2.50
☐	THE CAESAR CODE—Simmel	08413-8	1.95
☐	DO BLACK PATENT LEATHER SHOES REALLY REFLECT UP?—Powers	08490-1	1.75
☐	THE FURY—Farris	08620-3	2.25
☐	THE HEART LISTENS—Van Slyke	08520-7	1.95
☐	TO KILL A MOCKINGBIRD—Lee	08376-X	1.75
☐	THE LAST BATTLE—Ryan	08381-6	2.25
☐	THE LAST CATHOLIC IN AMERICA—Powers	08523-2	1.50
☐	THE LONGEST DAY—Ryan	08380-8	1.95
☐	LOVE'S WILD DESIRE—Blake	08616-5	1.95
☐	THE MIXED BLESSING—Van Slyke	08491-X	1.95

Buy them at your local bookstore or use this handy coupon for ordering:

HISTORY • BIOGRAPHY
• POPULAR CULTURE

Outstanding Non-Fiction Titles

Anne Tyler

"To read a novel by Ann Tyler is to fall in love"
—People Magazine

☐ A SLIPPING-DOWN LIFE	08596-7	1.95
☐ SEARCHING FOR CALEB	08565-7	1.95
☐ THE TIN CAN TREE	08617-3	1.95

Buy them at your local bookstore or use this handy coupon for ordering: